MISS MAYHEM

ALSO BY RACHEL HAWKINS

Rebel Belle

MISS MAYHEM

Rachel Hawkins

G. P. Putnam's Sons

An Imprint of Penguin Group (USA)

G. P. PUTNAM'S SONS
Published by the Penguin Group
Penguin Group (USA) LLC
375 Hudson Street
New York, NY 10014

USA | Canada | UK | Ireland | Australia
New Zealand | India | South Africa | China
penguin.com
A Penguin Random House Company

Library of Congress Cataloging-in-Publication Data
Hawkins, Rachel, 1979–
Miss Mayhem / Rachel Hawkins.
pages cm
Sequel to: Rebel belle.
Summary: "In the sequel to REBEL BELLE, Harper Price and her new boyfriend and oracle David Stark face new challenges as the powerful Ephors seek to claim David for their own"—Provided by publisher. [1. Magic—Fiction. 2. Supernatural—Fiction. 3. Oracles—Fiction. 4. Debutantes—Fiction. 5. High schools—Fiction. 6. Schools—Fiction.] I. Title.
PZ7.H313525Mis 2015   [Fic]—dc23   2014031151

Printed in the United States of America.
ISBN 978-0-399-25694-3
1 3 5 7 9 10 8 6 4 2

Design by Annie Ericsson.
Text set in Dante MT Std.
Interior images courtesy of iStockphoto.

For girls and their BFFs, their besties,
their sisters, their soul mates.
For girls creating mayhem, saving the world,
doing their best, figuring it out.
This one is for y'all.

MISS MAYHEM

Chapter 1

"This is going to be a total disaster. You know that, right?"

There are times when having a boyfriend who can tell the future is great. And then there are times like this.

Rolling my eyes, I flipped down the visor to check my makeup in the little mirror.

"Is that your Oracle self talking, or your concerned boyfie self?"

David laughed at that, twisting in the driver's seat to look at me. His sandy blond hair was its usual wreck, his blue eyes bright behind his glasses. "Seriously, you have got to stop calling me that."

The visor smacked back into place with a snap as I smiled at him. "But you *are* an Oracle," I said with mock innocence, and now it was his turn to roll his eyes.

"You know which term I was objecting to."

The windows in David's car were down, letting in the breeze as well as the faint smell of beer and the pounding bass coming from inside the Sigma Kappa Nu fraternity house across the street. It was getting late, and there were a million places I would rather have been, but I had a job to do tonight.

Still, I could mix a little business with pleasure. Leaning over the seat, I tipped my face up so he could kiss me. "It'll only take a sec," I promised once we parted. "And besides, this is what we're supposed to be doing."

David's lips were a thin line, and there was a little wrinkle between his brows. "If you're sure," he said, and I paused, hand on the latch.

"What do you mean?"

David pushed his glasses up the bridge of his nose. "This whole changing-the-future thing. Sometimes I wonder . . . like, what if you can't change the future, Pres? What if you're only delaying it a little while?"

My hand fell away from the door as I thought about that, but before I could answer, a loud *bang* from the front of the car had us both jumping.

Two dark-haired guys in polo shirts and pastel shorts chortled as they walked past, their faces washed out in the glow of the headlights. "Nice car, asshat!" one of them shouted before they did some kind of fist-bumping move that made me want to bump my fist, too.

Right into their faces.

At my side, David heaved a huge sigh. "Well, if we're supposed to be fighting evil, I'm not sure guys like that qualify." He turned to look at me, one corner of his mouth lifting and making a dimple appear in his cheek. "Although I am a little more excited about watching you pound them into a pulp now."

I settled back into my seat, fussing with my hair. "Hopefully there won't be any need for that. I'm going to get in there, get the twins, and get out. And you won't be watching anything, since you need to stay in the car."

David scowled. "Pres—"

"No." I turned back to him, the streetlight overhead outlining him in orange. "There's no way those guys will let you in. Because you're . . ."

Wearing an argyle sweater and lime-green shoes, I thought to myself. "A guy."

He was going to argue again, I could tell. That V between his eyes was getting deeper and his knee was jiggling, so I hurried. "You've already done the Oracle thing, so let me do the Paladin thing, and then we can get the heck out of here as quickly as possible, okay?"

Not even David Stark could argue with that, so he gave a terse nod and leaned back in his seat. "Okay. But please make it fast. This place is already starting to have a bad influence on me. I feel the need to buy polo shirts and shorts. Maybe some Man Sandals."

Grinning, I unbuckled my seat belt. "Anything but Man Sandals! Although, not gonna lie, a polo shirt wouldn't be a bad addition to your wardrobe."

David made a face at me and tugged at the hem of his sweater. "This is a classic," he informed me, and I leaned over to give him one more quick kiss.

"Sure it is."

Across the street, a group of boys came stumbling out the

front door of the redbrick Sigma Kappa Nu house, one of them breaking away to puke in the azalea bushes.

Charming.

"Abigail and Amanda, the things I do for you," I muttered as I got out of the car, shutting the door behind me.

Pushing my shoulders back, I did the best I could to saunter across the lawn, projecting confidence while also trying not to draw too much attention to myself. That's why I'd picked this dress. Should things get . . . out of hand, "girl in a black dress" wasn't all that memorable of a description.

The door to the frat house was hanging open as I approached, thanks to the puking guy and his friends, so I was able to slip inside unnoticed.

If the bass had been pounding from outside, it was like a physical presence in the house, rattling my teeth and starting an immediate headache behind my eyes.

And the smell . . .

Beer, boy, old pizza, and carpet that probably hadn't been cleaned since they'd built this place back in the sixties.

Ugh. Frats were the worst.

But I was here on a mission, and I switched my purse from one shoulder to the other as I scanned the crowd, looking for Abigail and Amanda's twin blond heads.

A few months ago, I wouldn't have been caught dead here. I mean, don't get me wrong, there are some fraternities worth hanging out with, but Sigma Kappa Nu was not one of them. These were, on the whole, big dumb party boys, and I was not into that. At all.

But back in October, I'd killed my history teacher with a shoe, and everything had changed.

It turned out I was a Paladin, a kind of superpowered warrior, charged with protecting the Oracle, aka David Stark, aka my new boyfriend. Being an Oracle meant that David could see the future, which obviously made him a pretty valuable commodity to a lot of people. And not good people, either. The Ephors were a group of men who had owned Oracles for years, using their visions to get ahead in the world. To predict the outcome of everything from wars to financial investments. Because David was a male Oracle, the Ephors had wanted to kill him—the only other male Oracle had been nowhere near as powerful as the traditional female ones, plus he'd become super unstable. But David had been rescued by his first Paladin, a guy named Christopher Hall, and by his Mage, Saylor Stark.

I hadn't exactly done a bang-up job of protecting David at first—people had died, including Saylor, and David had undergone a spell that gave him stronger powers than ever. Not only did he have much clearer visions, but also, he'd been able to make Paladins, giving the same powers I had to a group of girls at Cotillion. Oh, and did I mention my ex, Ryan, was our new Mage? So, yeah, complicated, but we were all trying to make the best of things.

That's part of why I was here, walking carefully among plastic cups and Ping-Pong balls, dodging puddles of beer. Before she'd died, Saylor had told me there was a possibility of David becoming a danger to himself, that the world-changing, super-intense visions would "burn him up."

Ryan and I had only helped him have two of those big types of visions. The first one, in the newspaper room at our school, had started a fire in a trash can, and short-circuited every computer in there. The second had resulted in David staying home for nearly a week, his eyes glowing brightly, his head aching. After that, I decided we should start small. Besides, it's like my mom always says: Charity begins at home.

What better way to use David's powers than to check on the futures of friends and family, and see if there was anything I could do to help them should those futures turn out not so great?

So far, we'd kept my Aunt May from accidentally using salt instead of sugar in a batch of brownies for the Junior League bake sale (an act that would have gotten her kicked out of Junior League), and we'd saved David's friend Chie from forgetting to save the final copy of *The Grove News* to her hard drive.

And now Abigail. Her future would take a hard left turn tonight when she met some douche-y frat brother named Spencer. They'd date for the rest of Abi's high school career, then she'd marry him instead of going to college. From there, David hadn't been able to see much more, only that Abi's future with Spencer felt "sad," and would lead to her and her twin, Amanda, becoming estranged.

Saving people from future earthquakes or volcanoes seemed daunting—not to mention almost impossible to get people to believe—but keeping a friend from falling for the wrong guy? Oh, that I could handle.

Provided I could find Abigail, of course. A set of French doors opened into a big backyard, and I headed in that direction, hoping to see the twins. As I kicked a crumpled Bud Light can out of my path, my phone vibrated. Pulling it out of my purse, I saw it was a text from David. "This is how I feel about fraternities right now." Underneath was a picture of him pulling the worst face—nose wrinkled, mouth turned down in a huge frown, eyes narrowed. I smiled, unsure of what was funnier: the picture itself or the idea of David Stark taking a selfie.

"Goofball," I texted back before sliding my phone into my purse and stepping outside.

A giant keg had become a sort of fountain in the middle of the yard. Two boys were holding another guy up by his legs so he could attempt the dreaded keg stand, and I sighed, wondering what the appeal of these dudes even was.

And then, thank God, I saw two identical blond heads close together by a cluster of coolers.

"Abigail! Amanda!" I called, making my way over to them. That involved stepping over more beer cans, and at least two unconscious dudes, and I frowned. *Ew.*

The twins both raised their eyebrows at me, surprised. "Harper? What are you doing here?" Abi asked. She wore her signature fishtail braid loose and over one shoulder, while Amanda's hair was pulled back from her face with two little clips. They were both wearing red dresses, so I was glad the hair made it easy to tell them apart.

I gave them my sternest look, propping my hands on my hips. "I should ask the two of you that. Now come on. We're leaving."

This is a secret I learned from cheerleading and SGA. If you act like you're in the right, people will fall in line without really questioning. I'd never bothered to come up with an excuse as to why I was looking for the two of them at Sigma Kappa Nu, and it wasn't like I could say, "My boyfriend has psychic powers, so tonight I'm saving one of you from a terrible future." Instead, I relied on two years of being their head cheerleader to make Abi and Amanda follow me.

And it worked.

They both studied me for a minute. Abi screwed up her mouth like she might argue, but Amanda shrugged and took her twin's arm with a muttered "I'm over this place anyway."

I made my way toward the French doors, pleased. That had gone so much easier than I'd—

A figure suddenly reared up in front of me. "Whoa, whoa, little lady, what's the rush?"

The guy who blocked the doorway looked a lot like my ex-boyfriend, Ryan. Tall, nicely built, reddish hair that was just a little too long. But while Ryan's smile was charming, this guy's was smarmy, and I was not in the mood to deal with him right now.

"We're leaving," I said, smiling but saying the words firmly enough for him to know I meant business. "My friends are ready to go."

"No, I'm not," Abi said, one strap of her red dress sliding off her shoulder. Amanda kind of shook her head, too.

Man, what I wouldn't have given for Ryan and his mind-control powers right about now. But all I had were my powers of persuasion, which *I* thought were still pretty great.

"This place is super gross, Abi," I told her, gesturing around at the crushed cups on the lawn, the stained couches inside, the random depressions knocked into the walls by heads or fists, "and if your parents knew you were here, they'd die. Heck, you're not even related to me, and *I* kind of want to die. Now let's go."

But Frat-enstein over here was still looming in the doorway, arms braced on either side of the frame, a red plastic cup in one hand. "'Super gross'?" he repeated. He pressed a meaty paw over the Greek letters on his shirt, and his blurry eyes tried to focus on me. His cheeks were red, and his nose was kind of shiny. Honestly, what did Abi even see in a guy like this? "Sigma Kappa Nu is the best frat on campus."

I snorted. "Please. Alpha Epsilon is the best frat on campus. You guys are the *biggest* frat on campus, and that's because there's so many of you without the grades to get into decent fraternities. Now get out of our way."

He was blinking down at me, like my words were taking a while to penetrate the haze of beer and dumb that clearly clouded his mind. Then, finally, he slurred, *"You're* super gross."

"Zing," I muttered, turning back to Abigail and Amanda with eyebrows raised. "Can we please go now?"

Amanda nodded this time, thank God, but Abi was still chewing her lower lip and looking at the guy. "It's not even eleven," she said, fiddling with the end of her braid. Now the guy was looking back at her, blinking, and, ugh, this was going to be harder than I thought. "I mean, we could stay for a little while."

Biting back a sigh, I made myself smile at Abi. "No, we can't. Now kindly get out of our way . . ."

"Spencer," the guy offered with a flick of his hair. "And I think your pretty friend is right—she *could* stay for a while."

There was no real danger here, but everything in me ached to go super Paladin on Spencer's fratty butt. And then, thankfully, he gave me the chance.

His hand came down on my shoulder, hard enough that I actually winced. "Hey, there—" was as much as he got out before my fingers curled around his hand, holding him in place while my other hand shot out, heel of my palm smacking him solidly in the solar plexus.

He let out a whoosh of air that smelled like stale beer and sour apple Jolly Ranchers, making me wrinkle my nose even as I hooked my foot around his ankle and sent him crashing to the ground. The dude was built like a tree, so he went down hard, and I didn't give him the chance to get up again. Still clutching his hand, I pressed my shoe to his chest and slid my fingers down to circle his wrist. I only had to pull the littlest bit before he whimpered. And, I mean, I didn't want to break his wrist or anything.

I just wanted to scare him a little bit. It occurred to me that once upon a time I could do that with a mere icy smile or an eye roll. These days, things were a lot more . . . physical.

"When a lady says she's ready to leave," I told him, applying pressure, "she is ready to leave. And you do not get in her way. Is that clear?"

When he didn't answer, I gave another little tug that had him nodding frantically. "Right, yes. I'm sorry, I—I won't do it again."

I tossed his hand down, dusting my palms on the back of my skirt. "I would hope not."

Lifting my head to the twins, I saw them watching me with mouths agape. Luckily, most of the party was still outside, so only a couple of guys—also dressed in the maroon and blue of Sigma Kappa Nu—saw me with Spencer, and they were so drunk that they barely noticed me.

I glanced back at the twins. "Self-defense class," I told them with a little shrug. "Now can we please go?"

Spencer was sitting up now, holding his wrist and watching me with wary eyes, but I saw Abi hesitate before following me out of the room, and I wasn't sure if I'd done my job here tonight or not.

"You're not the boss of us, Harper," Abi said once we were out of the frat house and marching down the front steps toward the street. She'd grabbed her cardigan off the back of a chair on the way out, and was shoving her arms into it, scowling.

Then why are you following me? I thought.

What I *said* was, "I'm just looking out for you. That's what friends do."

"Abi's right," Amanda said, and they both stopped there at the edge of the yard. "We've all known you were a control freak, but this is kind of nuts."

I stopped then, turning to glance between them, wishing their words didn't . . . bug.

It was too close to what David had said when I'd first come up with this idea. "People have to live their lives, Harper," he'd said.

But, as I'd reminded him, what was the point of having

superpowers, superpowers he could actually use now—safely—if we didn't, you know, use them?

"Ladies," David said with a little wave, and they both scowled at him.

"What is *he* doing here?" Abi asked, and I rolled my eyes.

"He's my boyfriend. He drove me here, obvs."

The twins were looking at David's car like it might give them a disease, and while I was irritated, I couldn't really blame them. David's Dodge was a total clunker, full of dents and dings and scratched paint, and . . . the truth was, I might have done some of that damage myself during a car chase last fall, but the point was that it barely looked drivable. I didn't know why David insisted on hanging on to that thing. He still had his aunt's car, and while Saylor's Cadillac was of the old-lady variety, it certainly wasn't in danger of having its engine drop out.

Abi opened the back door, delicately kicking a stack of books off the backseat and onto the floor. David winced as the books fell, and the corners of his mouth jerked down as he cut his eyes at me.

However, when Amanda tossed his ratty messenger bag out of the way, he twisted to look into the backseat. "Hey," he started, and then he winced.

I wondered if Amanda had pushed his bag onto something and broken it—there was no end to the random stuff in David's backseat—but then I felt my own chest seize up in pain, and knew we were in for something way worse.

A vision.

But those didn't just pop up the way they used to. David's

powers were under control now. Thing was, David didn't know that me and Ryan were using the wards to keep his powers under control. But it was for his own good. The smaller visions didn't leave him sick and shaking.

Or looking so scary.

"What the hell?" one of the twins squawked from the back-seat, and David fumbled with his door handle, shaking his head.

"David," I said, reaching across the car to grab his arm.

Fingers closing around the handle, David shoved the door open, spilling out into the street.

Chapter 2

I WAS ALREADY out of my seat and moving around to him, barely paying attention to the twins, who were climbing out of the backseat.

David fell to his knees, hands pressed to his head. Golden light poured out of his eyes, so bright it hurt to look at, and from behind me, I heard one of the twins make a sound somewhere between a gasp and a breathy scream.

"What is wrong with him?"

There was a part of my mind already on the phone with Ryan, asking him to work his mind-wipe mojo on the twins ASAP, but for right now, David was the only thing that mattered. I didn't know if it was my Paladin powers or the way I felt about him that made my chest hurt, but I knelt down next to him, taking his hand.

His skin was clammy, but he grabbed my hand tight, fingers curling around my palm. "It's all right," I heard myself say, even though the power coming from him was making my teeth ache. I'd only seen him like this once, the night of Cotillion. Right now, light in his eyes, body vibrating, he looked a lot less like my boyfriend, and a lot more like a powerful supernatural creature.

Which, I had to remind myself, was exactly what he was.

But still, he shouldn't have been having visions like this, not anymore.

"We have to go," he said, his voice sounding deeper and echoing slightly, like there were two people talking. "Now. We need to go to them."

I'd never known cold sweat was a thing people could actually feel, but that's exactly what popped out on my forehead.

I held his hand tighter. "Where?" I asked. "Is Bee there?"

David's head swung toward me, and I flinched at the glare.

My best friend had gone missing the night of Cotillion, kidnapped by Blythe and taken who knew where. Of everything that had happened that night, even Saylor's death, losing Bee had been the worst. I couldn't stop feeling like I'd failed her.

"Bee's at cheerleading camp."

Glancing over my shoulder, I saw that the twins were still frowning at us. Well, Amanda was. Abi was just staring at David, shocked.

"Seriously, what is *wrong* with him?" Abi asked, and I winced.

"It's nothing," I said, lifting my and David's joined hands to look at his wrist. I never wore a watch, but David always did, so I checked it now. It was nearly eleven, and I'd promised my parents I'd be home by midnight.

David's vision was already fading. I could feel the power draining out of him, and his breathing was starting to slow, the light in his eyes going dim. "Pres?" he croaked, and while there was still a little echo, he sounded more like himself than like the Oracle.

Sucking in a deep breath through my nose, I forced myself to think. First things first, I needed to get the twins home and dealt with. I could worry about my parents and where David was meant to be taking me once Abi and Amanda were handled.

"Okay," I said, overly bright, as I clapped my hands together and rose to my feet. "Everybody back in the car."

David stood, too, lurching for the driver's side, but I caught his arm and steered him back toward the passenger seat. The twins stood there, arms folded over their chests.

"What the hell was that, Harper?" Amanda asked, and Abi echoed, "The. Hell."

It had been a long night already, and I had a feeling it was about to get a lot longer. I shook my head, shooing the twins back toward the car. "I'll explain later," I promised, even though I had no intention of doing anything of the sort. What I did plan on doing was calling Ryan.

Even though last year I spearheaded the Campaign Against Texting and Driving—I signed a pledge and everything—I was already starting the car when I pulled up Ryan's number and texted, "Meet me at the twins' house. 911."

"Harper," David said, his voice low and rough. "We don't have time. We have to go *now*." I didn't take my eyes off the road to look at him, but I did drop my phone in the change tray under the radio, reaching out to put my hand on his knee.

"It's okay," I said, even though my heart and mind were racing at a million miles an hour.

I had no idea what was going on, but I did know that to handle it, we had to ditch the Not-So-Wonder Twins and hope to God that Ryan had gotten my text, since he didn't seem in any hurry to reply.

But when we pulled up in the driveway, Ryan was leaning against his car outside the twins' house. "What's he doing here?" Abi said from the backseat.

"Don't know!" I chirped, throwing the car into park. "Stay here," I told David firmly, pointing at him in case he wasn't clear how serious I was.

He gave a weak nod and waved his hand, still slumped against the door panel. Maybe this will make me sound like a terrible person, but seeing him like that, much as it worried me, also made me feel kind of . . . relieved. Vindicated, even. This was what Ryan and I were protecting him from, this kind of pain. I knew it had bummed David out that his visions weren't as big as he'd hoped, but surely he could understand that a little disappointment was better than *this*.

I started to open the car door, but before I could, Ryan was suddenly there in the open window, folding his arms on the door, chin resting on his forearms. As always, he looked like he'd just stepped out of an Abercrombie & Fitch catalog, auburn hair curling over his brow, hazel eyes kind of sleepy and lazy, his T-shirt showing off the results of plenty of time in the gym. I could practically feel the twins swoon in the backseat. Ryan used to make me swoon once, too, but now I frowned and waved him back from the door so I could get out of the car.

"What's the emergency?" he asked once we were on the lawn, and I glanced over my shoulder at the car.

"David had a vision, and the twins saw," I said in a whispered rush. "So now I need you to do your Mage thing and wipe their memories, okay?"

By now, the twins were getting out of the backseat, muttering to each other. I heard David's name, and also mine, along with a few words that, were I not so concerned with other things right now, I would have lit into them for. Honestly.

"What kind of vision?" Ryan asked, his brow wrinkling. "About what?"

"It doesn't matter right now," I told him, already making to move back to the car. "Do the mind wipe, and—"

Ryan caught my elbow before I could rush back to David. "It seems like it matters. It's Oracle stuff, which means I'm involved, too. Harper, if he's having visions without us, after all that we did, that's . . . that's kind of an issue."

That was true, but right now, I needed him to erase the twins' memories of tonight so I could get back to David. Luckily, at that minute, the twins wandered up, and I saw Ryan's eyes flick to them.

"We'll talk later!" I called, both to Ryan and to Amanda and Abigail, before hurrying back across the lawn.

David was out of the car, moving to the driver's seat, and I stopped him with a *Whoa whoa whoa. What do you think you're doing?"*

Under the street lamps, he was looking a little bit better, but not much. There were still shadows underneath his eyes, and he was moving gingerly, like something inside him was broken. But his jaw was set when he looked at me, fingers on the door handle. "I'm driving."

I put my hands on my hips, shifting my weight to one foot. "Um, okay, except you're not?"

Now was not exactly the time to be arguing over who had control of the car, but I was not about to let a guy who looked like his brain might actually start leaking out of his ears get behind the wheel.

But David wasn't budging. "You heard what it—what *I*—said. I'll lead the way."

Behind me, I could hear the low murmur of voices as Ryan talked to the twins, but I ignored that, focusing on David with my arms crossed tightly.

The twins' street was quiet, the lawns almost identical green squares, glowing in the security lights. Azalea bushes lined the brick walls, and every yard had either dogwood trees or magnolias planted smack-dab in the middle of the grass. "Right, but you could, like, lead the way by telling me where we're going. Like a GPS."

David's eyes blinked behind his glasses, and he shook his head slightly. "Pres, for once, can't I be in charge of some aspect of this whole thing? I'm telling you, I need to drive us there. I'm fine now"—the slight trembling of his hand seemed to make that a lie, but whatever—"so please get in the car."

I thought about arguing with him again, but David was right;

I did tend to put myself in charge of all of these things, but how could I not? Wasn't that my responsibility now that Saylor was gone?

But then I thought again of his visions, and the lies I'd told.

Couldn't I give him this one thing?

Dropping my head, I pinched the bridge of my nose between my fingers. "David—" I started, and he dropped his head, trying to meet my eyes.

"Trust me, Pres," he said. "Please."

The twins were walking toward their house, and Ryan gave me a thumbs-up, so I figured that was settled, thank goodness.

But then Ryan walked over to us and grinned.

"So," he said, opening the door to the backseat. "Where are we headed?"

Chapter 3

"It's NOT that I don't want you to come," I explained for what had to be the third time in five miles. "But David and I have this."

From the backseat, Ryan snorted, and when I glanced over my shoulder, he was sitting back, his arms folded, legs spread wide. I'd always hated when he sat like that, taking up too much space, but there wasn't anything I could say to him. That was a Boyfriend Complaint, and Ryan wasn't my boyfriend anymore. Of course, *what* he was now, I couldn't even explain. We'd never been friends, exactly, so saying we were didn't feel true. Maybe we were coworkers.

Which was part of why I didn't want Ryan on this little expedition. He'd never liked the idea of not telling David about how we were limiting his visions, and I was worried that all of the weirdness of tonight was going to make him feel worse, maybe even give him the urge to confess.

"The other day you were bitching—sorry, complaining," Ryan amended, catching my look, "that I wasn't doing enough Mage stuff." He spread his big hands wide. "Isn't this Mage stuff?"

I looked back over at David. His hands were clenched tightly around the steering wheel, eyes on the dark road in front of us. We were driving out of town, in the opposite direction from the college where we'd been earlier, and the houses were starting to be few and far between.

I caught Ryan's eyes in the rearview mirror. "When I said I wanted you to do more Mage stuff, I meant I wanted you to check on the wards Saylor made." David's "aunt" had put up all kinds of magical protection charms over Pine Grove to keep the Ephors from finding him, and we'd told David that they needed to be charged up from time to time.

"And," I added, twisting in my seat, "I think you may want to add wards farther out."

"Sure thing. Should I go ahead and cover the whole state?" Ryan asked, and I rolled my eyes.

"No," David said. "No more wards."

Surprised, I twisted in my seat, the seat belt digging into my hip. "What do you mean 'no more wards'?"

David shook his head, but didn't look at me. "I think the wards are screwing up my visions."

I could hear Ryan shift in the backseat, and willed him not to say anything. Luckily, he didn't, and David continued. "I mean, I had those two big ones, right? The thing about the earthquake in Peru, and then the one about that senator lady Harper likes becoming president. But then . . . nothing. For months now." He was talking faster now, fingers drumming on the steering wheel. "So maybe all the wards Saylor put up to protect me are, like, getting in the way of that."

I tried not to squirm in my seat since it wasn't Saylor's wards getting in his way.

"And now," David added, "the most important thing I've been able to see is that your friend will marry a douche someday. Not earth-shattering stuff."

"Which friend and which douche?" Ryan asked, leaning forward, but I ignored him.

"I happen to think that kind of thing is important, David." And I did. Sort of.

He did look over then, eyebrows drawing close together over the rims of his glasses. We'd started to move out of the city now, fields to either side of the road, and only the occasional streetlight. The green glow from the dashboard lights played over David's high cheekbones, making his eyes look slightly sunken in. "I mean, your friends are important," David said, even though I was pretty sure he didn't actually think that. There was something weird in his voice. "But bigger-picture stuff? Stuff that might actually help . . . I don't know, the world? At least more people than a handful of your friends. Tonight, for the first time in months, I had a strong vision, a clear one that I didn't need any help with. And it was a big one." He glanced over at me. "I saw the Ephors, Pres."

My heart thudded heavily in my chest. "What?"

He nodded and reached over to squeeze my hand. "The Ephors," he repeated, eyes still on the road. It was probably just the reflection of streetlights, but it looked like his eyes were glowing again, and I swallowed hard.

"Although why they've decided to set up shop all the way out here, I don't know," he said, and I jerked my hand back.

"Wait, we're going to see them? That's where you're taking us?"

"That seems like information we should've had from the start," Ryan commented, and when I caught his eye in the rear-view mirror, he was frowning, auburn hair hanging low on his forehead.

"If I'd told you, would you have come?" David asked, turning to glance at me. Now I could tell his eyes weren't glowing after all, but I didn't feel much better.

"Yes," I told him quickly. "But, you know, with . . . weapons. Grenades, maybe."

David shook his head and turned down a dirt road, the car thumping over bumps and ruts.

"There's nothing out here," Ryan offered, leaning up between us. He had his elbows propped on his spread knees, his hazel eyes scanning the road in front of us, the fields of tall grass on either side. "Me and some of the guys used to come out here to drink beer."

"When was that?" I asked, but now it was his turn to ignore me apparently.

"There used to be a house," he told David. "Big ol' *Gone with the Wind*-type place. My grandmother had a painting of it over her mantel. Apparently it was kinda famous or something, but it burned down back in the seventies. All that was left was a chimney. And we threw enough cans at it that I'm not sure much of that was left either."

"What a fabulous use of time," I muttered, and I think Ryan would have had a comment for that had the car not taken a curve in the road right then.

David brought the car to a shuddering halt.

"A house like *that*?" he asked, and Ryan gave a slow nod.

The house in front of us looked a lot like Magnolia House back in town, but while that was just a reproduction of a fancy antebellum home, this seemed to be the real thing. White columns rose from the front porch to a wraparound balcony above, and tall windows, bracketed by dark shutters, stood on either side of the massive front door. Lights glowed in those windows, throwing out long rectangles of gold on the neatly manicured lawn.

"Maybe someone built a new place," Ryan suggested, but his voice was faint. "In the . . . three weeks since I was out here."

"This is the place," David said, drumming his fingers on the steering wheel. "I feel it, don't you?"

I did. I wasn't sure how exactly, but I definitely did. I don't know what I was expecting the Ephor headquarters—if that's what this place was—to look like. I mean, they were an ancient society that started in Greece, made up of people who wanted to control the world, so I don't think I was too far off in imagining that they'd do business in something like a temple, or at least an old building made of stone. It looked like they'd decided to restore some of the local architecture instead.

So I thought I could be forgiven for doubting David. "Are you sure?"

David was still staring at the house, his wrists draped over the steering wheel. "Yeah," he said at last. "That's the place."

As the three of us got out of the car, it was all I could do not to shiver. The house might not have looked magical, but it sure as heck felt like it. I couldn't see any obvious markings, like the wards Saylor had put up around town, but power pulsed off the building in a steady beat that I could almost feel coming up through the soles of my feet. It made the hair on the back of my neck stand up and my teeth ache.

"That's intense," David said, and I glanced at him. Reaching over, I threaded my fingers with his, squeezing.

"Do you have any kind of plan here? Are we just marching in, or . . ."

David squeezed my hand back. "No plan," he said. "I *have* to be here. That's all I know. It's like . . . remember when you told me that if I'm in danger, you can't do anything except save me?"

I nodded. That was part of the Oracle/Paladin bond. Even if an orphanage staffed by kittens was on fire right next to him, I couldn't do anything but save David. So, yeah, I understood how mystical compulsions could make you do things that weren't good for you, but I still didn't like it.

I made myself smile at David. "We got this," I said, even though I had no idea what "this" was. But David and I had handled The Weird before and gotten through it. We could do it again.

Turning his head, he smiled down at me. Well, his lips lifted in something that I think was supposed to be a smile, but he was either too tired or too freaked out to give it his best shot.

I'd take it.

From behind me, I thought I heard Ryan blow out a long breath, but I kept my eyes on the house, waiting for . . . I didn't even know what.

The three of us approached the building cautiously, like we were afraid we'd be rushed at any second. My Paladin senses weren't tingling, so that probably wasn't going to happen, but I still didn't want to take any chances.

The porch steps didn't even creak under our feet although the potted ferns by the door rustled slightly in the night wind. Other than that, there was no sign of movement, nothing happening behind the windows or door, and we all stood there for a moment. I didn't see an intercom button or anything like that, and I wasn't sure if I was supposed to knock. Kick down the door, maybe?

Before I could do either of those things, the door slowly swung open.

"Cool," Ryan said from behind me. "I was starting to think this crap wasn't creepy enough."

David snorted, and when he cut his eyes at Ryan, he looked better. Less pale, for sure. Sharper, almost. "Sorry we got you involved in a Scooby-Doo mystery."

That made Ryan smile a little bit, and he shoved his hands in his pockets, rocking back on his heels. "That is what's happening, isn't it? Which obviously makes you Shaggy." He nodded at David, whose smirk turned into a grin.

"Then you're Fred," he told Ryan. "And Pres here"—he bumped me with an elbow—"is for sure Daphne."

"For sure," Ryan agreed, and I rolled my eyes at both of them.

"Okay, if y'all are done being boys, can we please go in and see what the heck is going on here?"

We walked inside. The house smelled nice, like furniture polish and expensive candles, with a hint of something warm and spicy underneath. Tea, maybe. And it certainly didn't look like a lair of evil. Overhead, a chandelier sparkled, and the wooden stairs gleamed. There were vases of fresh flowers on long, narrow tables, and pretty artwork dotted the walls. It looked like the inside of a lot of these old houses: The outside might be all vintage and historical, but there was clearly some twenty-first-century interior decorating going on.

"Maybe we died?" David suggested. "And ended up in Harper's version of heaven?"

"Well, the Ephors have good taste, even if they *are* evil." I turned in a small circle on one of the lush rugs, glancing up. The house was quiet, but people had to be here.

Bee might be here.

I'd gotten so used to my Paladin senses kicking in when they needed to that it was weird to feel so . . . blank. I couldn't get a read on anything, and not for the first time, I wondered if there was some kind of magic blocking my powers. "If they're evil, why are we here?" Ryan asked, and I had to admit it was a good question. We'd spent last semester trying to hide David from the Ephors, and now we were walking into their . . . house? Headquarters? For a meeting? Still, that didn't keep me from scanning the room for objects that could be used as weapons. There were several pretty hefty candlesticks on the mantel over the enormous fireplace. Those would work.

I turned to ask David more about his vision, but he was studying one of the paintings on the wall. "Whoa," he murmured softly, and I followed his gaze.

"Whoa," I echoed.

The painting depicted a girl in a flowing white gown, her body floating in midair, her eyes bright and golden. On either side of her stood a man, one in armor, the other in a white robe, and kneeling all around the three of them were shadowy figures, their hands outstretched toward the girl. The paint seemed to glow, and I fought the urge to run my fingers over the canvas.

"*The Oracle Speaks,*" a voice said from behind us, and David, Ryan, and I jumped, then whirled around.

A man was standing there, but I had no idea where he'd come from. I hadn't heard his footsteps approach or a door open. He was maybe forty or so, and handsome in the same old-world, expensive way the house was. Blond hair, high cheekbones, really nice suit. Like the house, power seemed to radiate from him, and I rubbed my hands up and down my arms.

But his smile was perfectly pleasant as he gestured toward the painting. "That's what this particular work of art is called. Felt appropriate to hang here."

"You're an Ephor," David said quietly, his hands clenching into fists at his side, and the man gave a slight bow.

"I am. My name is Alexander. And you are the Oracle and, I take it, *you* are his intrepid Paladin and Mage," he said, nodding to me and Ryan. There was a slight lilt to his words, an accent I couldn't quite place. "So good of you to come."

He was acting like he'd invited us here, like we were expected, and I wasn't sure why, but that gave me all of the creeps. Still, although I waited for my Paladin senses to kick in and tell me this guy was bad news, there was nothing. Magic, sure, a hint of power, yes, but none of the chest-tightening, muscletensing sickness I felt when David was in danger.

The Ephors had always been the greatest threat to David, so why wasn't I in attack mode? It suddenly occurred to me that they might be doing something to override my Paladin powers. Could they do that? After all, they'd somehow managed to break through the wards so that David could have an all-consuming vision. For probably the thousandth time, I wished Saylor were here to tell me what was going on.

"I'm so pleased to have you here," Alexander said, still smiling that bland smile, one hand extended toward a dim hallway off to the side. "Now, if you'll come with me—"

I was about to interject that we were staying right where we were, but before I could, David stepped forward, looked at Alexander, and said, "You people took a girl last year. Bee Franklin. I want you to tell me where she is."

Chapter 4

"WHAT? IS BEE HERE? Did you see her?" Behind David, I saw my own surprise reflected on Ryan's face.

With a sigh, David turned to me, ruffling his hand over his hair. "No. Or not exactly, but she's . . . close, or . . ." He opened and closed his free hand like he was trying to pull the words out of the air. "Something. I can feel it."

Sensing people's presence wasn't exactly part of David's bag, and I'd certainly never heard him talk about anything like this before. Was he able to sense Bee because he'd juiced her up with Paladin powers before Blythe had taken her?

But David looked back at Alexander, and the Ephor took a deep breath, his brow wrinkling slightly. "All in good time, I assure you," he said at last, and then swept his hand toward the hall again. "First, we need to talk about what occurred this evening."

"The frat thing or David's vision?" I asked, and Alexander's green eyes flicked to me. His expression was blank, but I could still feel magic or power or whatever it was oozing from him, and I made myself hold his gaze.

"They are connected," he said at last, then nodded. "Now, if the three of you will come with me, all will be explained."

"Where are the rest of you?" David folded his arms across his chest. "Aren't there other Ephors here besides you?"

Alexander gave a tiny smile, revealing a hint of teeth. "All in good time."

I thought David might argue with him some more—I knew I wanted to—but instead, he started off in the direction Alexander had indicated.

At my side, I felt Ryan gently take my elbow. "Come on, Harper," he said in a low voice.

The hallway was lit with pretty little sconces covered with tiny burgundy shades, casting pools of warm light on the hardwood, but all I could see in my head was Bee. Bee, laughing with me at cheerleading practice; Bee, handing me lip gloss; Bee, tears streaming down her face as she'd kept me from killing Blythe.

Bee, vanishing right in front of me.

I'd wanted answers about the fight at the frat party tonight, but now, the only thing I cared about was knowing if Bee was here.

Alexander opened a doorway off to the left, ushering us into what looked like some kind of study. The decor here was even more extravagant: antique furniture, Tiffany lamps, carpet that felt lush and deep underfoot.

And three chairs sitting across from a gleaming mahogany desk.

The three of us sat, David between me and Ryan, while Alexander sank into the much larger chair behind the desk. "Well," he said at last, fixing all of us with that smile again. "Here we are. Tea?"

There was a pot beside his elbow, I saw now, steam spilling from the spout, but tea was the last thing on my mind. "No," I said, sitting up as straight as I could. "What we want are answers. Why are we here, what the heck did you have to do with David's vision tonight, and where is Bee?"

Alexander flicked his dark gold hair out of his eyes, frowning as though I had disappointed him. "So we're to skip the pleasantries, I see."

"Pleasantries?" Ryan sat back in his chair, propping his ankle on his opposite knee. "I only came into this thing at the end last year, but didn't y'all try to *kill* David?"

Alexander tilted his head in acknowledgment. "I understand how that may have looked, but we were never trying to harm David, merely to remove his Paladin from the equation."

"Yeah, that's not really helping on the trust front," I said, suppressing a shudder.

Alexander ignored me. "We sent our Mage to perform Alaric's ritual on the Oracle in the hopes that he would not prove as useless as we'd feared."

Alexander turned back to David and spread his hands wide. "And now look at you! Everything we'd hoped for and more. Powerful enough to create Paladins, stable enough to have clear, helpful visions. All in all, the entire process went even better than we'd hoped."

I couldn't help but grit my teeth as I thought of Saylor, bleeding to death in the kitchen. Of Bee, vanishing before my eyes.

But I didn't say anything. If this guy had Bee, I'd hold my tongue for as long as I could.

David had other ideas. "I don't have 'clear, helpful visions' anymore," he said. "All I can see are . . . minor things."

Alexander's pleasant expression didn't falter, but something about him still made the hairs on the back of my neck stand up. Did he know what Ryan and I had been doing?

"You have these powers," he said, waving one hand, "but no idea how to channel them. You're using them for trivial things, like ensuring that Miss Price's friends don't get their hearts broken."

I started. If he knew about that, then surely he knew *why* those were the only sorts of visions David was having. But Alexander just kept going, his voice low and smooth. "With our help, you can reach your full potential, which is all we want for you, David."

On my right, David rubbed his hand over the back of his neck, his shoulders tight. "And I'm supposed to believe that? After you people spent months—no, my whole freaking life— trying to kill me?"

Alexander's green eyes blinked twice, and then he sat up abruptly, thrusting his hand out at David. "Take it," he said, nodding to his palm. "Take it and look for yourself."

David blinked at the outstretched hand, his eyes narrowed behind his glasses. "I can see the future, not read minds."

Alexander's smile widened the littlest bit. "Are you sure?"

Leaning forward in my chair a little, I studied Alexander.

"Who are you? Like, chief Ephor, or head Mage? You clearly have some kind of crazy magic."

Alexander kept his hand outstretched, his eyes on David. "Six of one, half a dozen of the other," he replied, and I wanted to point out that he hadn't given me much of an answer.

I could hear the grandfather clock ticking in the corner, could hear my own breathing, and as I watched, David reached over and very gently laid his hand on top of Alexander's. I couldn't see anything happen when their hands touched, but then David closed his eyes and there was the briefest hint of light behind his eyelids.

And then his hand fell back to his lap. "He's telling the truth," David said, almost wonderingly. "I . . . I don't know how I know, but I know."

I didn't like that. I didn't like it at *all*. How could David suddenly have new powers we didn't know anything about? Saylor had never mentioned anything about mind reading, and, ugh, I was in no way ready to handle a boyfriend who could read my every thought whenever we touched hands.

"There are all sorts of things we can teach you." Alexander sat back, his chair creaking. "All sorts of powers locked away in that mind of yours."

"David doesn't want to learn anything from you people," I said, crossing my ankles.

But David jerked his head to look at me, something like irritation in his face. "I think that's one of those things I get to decide for myself, Pres," he said, and in that second, he wasn't the

Oracle or my boyfriend—he was the annoying guy who wrote mean articles about me in the school paper, the boy who never stopped arguing with me.

"Saylor said—" I started, only to let the words die in my throat. Saylor had told me that David's powers could prove dangerous, and that the Ephors wouldn't care. That his power was the only thing that would matter to them. I didn't think she'd ever told him that, though, and this wasn't a conversation I wanted to have in front of Alexander.

Ryan was looking down, frowning a little, but Alexander only watched me with those green eyes, brows drawn sharply together.

Finally, he folded his hands on the desk, the cuffs of his blue shirt peeking out from his jacket. "The issue as far as I can see, Miss Price, is that neither you nor the Oracle nor your Mage"— Ryan's head came up—"currently have any sort of guidance. With the deaths of Christopher Hall and the woman you called Saylor Stark, any assistance you could have had in protecting the Oracle—"

"David," I interrupted. "His name is David." My voice shook the littlest bit, and I hated that. But I also hated anything to do with these people wanting to "help" David.

Alexander inclined his head the tiniest bit, lips pursing slightly. "As you say. David."

Manners and graciousness dripped off those four words, but I knew when someone was being condescending, and I didn't like it. Maybe that's why my voice was frosty when I replied, "We don't need your assistance. We have things totally under control.

We have a Mage, an Oracle, and a Paladin. We don't need any-one else." It wasn't true, not really . . . I was shaky and tired and completely in over my head. But I couldn't take help from these people. Not the people who kidnapped Bee. As for everything else . . . we'd figure it out as we went.

Alexander's expression didn't change, but a muscle ticced in his jaw and after a long pause, he reached for the teapot at the edge of his desk, filling a delicate china cup. Once he'd taken a sip, he fixed me with that gaze again.

"I'm unsure of how you could control *anything*, Miss Price, seeing as how you are not actually a Paladin yet."

Chapter 5

My mouth went dry. "Excuse me?" I finally managed to croak.

His fingers drummed on the mahogany desk. "Well, you have the powers themselves, of course. That's not in any doubt, as Michael's corpse attests."

"Michael?" I said, confused. Next to me, I could feel David tense, and out of the corner of my eye, I saw that he was sitting up straighter in his chair now.

"I believe you knew him as 'Dr. DuPont'?" Alexander's manner was still casual as he tugged at his cuffs, but there was a hard glint in his eyes.

Oh, right. The history teacher turned assassin who I'd killed. I glanced at Ryan. He'd heard the story—I'd told him everything once he became the Mage—but I knew this was the part he still had a hard time with. It had to be weird, knowing your ex-girlfriend killed somebody, even if it was in self-defense. But he was still watching Alexander, a wrinkle between his auburn brows, his leg jiggling up and down.

Alexander continued, "We don't doubt your Paladin . . .

prowess, Miss Price. But you have not yet earned the right to call yourself by that name."

I didn't like the sound of that one bit, and I crossed one knee over the other as I leaned in toward Alexander. "I gave up a lot to protect David. I lost my best friend, I lied to my family, and I watched a woman I loved and admired die right in front of me. So don't tell me I haven't earned being a Paladin. I've more than earned it, buddy."

"Hear, hear," David muttered next to me, and I felt his hand land on mine on the arm of my chair. I glanced over long enough to smile at him, and across the desk, Alexander sat back in his chair.

"So," he said, nodding at our joined hands, "is that how things are?"

I jerked my hand out from underneath David's, although I couldn't have said why. It was like . . . I didn't want this guy knowing about us. But obviously, it was too late for that.

David shot me a glance that was either pissed or wounded or both before facing Alexander. "What, is that not allowed?"

Alexander gave an elegant shrug, still kicked back in his chair. "It's not officially against any rule I've heard of. But it's never been an issue in the past."

Curiosity got the best of me, and I shifted in my seat. "Why?"

Drumming his fingers on the arm of his chair, Alexander looked up, like he was trying to think of the right words. "Oracles are usually very . . . dedicated to their duties. Having constant visions leaves little time for personal relationships."

I thought of how David was when he was in the grips of a vision. I couldn't imagine him being like that all the time. I didn't want to.

When I looked over at David, his face was almost blank, his eyes fixed straight ahead. His foot was bouncing, which meant that he was thinking hard, but about what?

"But what do you mean about Harper not being a Paladin?" Ryan asked. He was slouching again, but he tugged at his sleeves, his eyes never leaving Alexander. "Does that mean I'm not a Mage? I mean, Oracles are born, I got that, but if we were both made into . . . whatever it is we are—"

The Ephor held up a hand. "Every point on the triangle is different, comes with different responsibilities and duties. A Mage, once powers have been transferred, is a Mage, fully and completely. All the knowledge the previous Mage contained is passed on. But a Paladin is a horse of a different color, as it were. Paladins have a sacred duty. As do the Oracle and the Mage, of course, but the Paladin has an especially challenging role. To be sure Miss Price is up to the task, she would have to go through the Peirasmos."

The word rolled off his tongue in a pretty way, but there was power in those three syllables. I could feel it, and even David shuddered a little bit.

"Do you know what that is, Miss Price?" Alexander raised his eyebrows at me, still totally pleasant, and I hated to have to shake my head.

"No."

Alexander made an exaggerated moue of disappointment.

"What a shame. I hoped Miss Stark would have completed that part of your training."

"Things were a little rushed," I told him, scowling, "what with you people and your crazy Mage trying to kill us all the time. We didn't have time for . . . whatever that word was."

"Peirasmos," he repeated. "And in all fairness, Miss Price, we were using the Mage to kill *you*, not the Oracle."

"David," Ryan interjected, and I glanced over at him, throwing him a quick smile.

Now all pleasantness disappeared from Alexander's face, and he sat up in his chair. "Oh, for the love of the gods. Is it like that, too?"

My cheeks flamed red, and I looked away from Ryan, back toward the Ephor. "None of that is any of your business."

Alexander only wrinkled his nose, bracing his elbows on the desk. "Teenagers," he said on a long sigh. "Well, what can one expect, I suppose. In any case." He steepled his long fingers. "When Saylor Stark and Christopher Hall broke away from us, they rejected many of our traditions, it would seem. Which is a shame since the Peirasmos is vital."

"Says who?" I asked, crossing my legs at the ankle. "And why? I mean, I'm clearly a Paladin, I have all the . . . the . . ." I waved my hands in the air. "Superpowers or whatever. What would this Peirasmos change?"

Alexander sniffed, resting his elbows on the desk. "What would they change? For starters, by completing these trials, you get to live. Is that enough of a reason for you, Miss Price?"

It had been a long night. I'd had to go into possibly the

grossest frat house in Alabama, I'd watched my boyfriend go all mega-Oracle, and I'd gotten my ex-boyfriend to wipe my friends' minds; my life being threatened was the icing on a seriously crappy cake.

"So that whole 'Hey, we want to help you and be besties' thing lasted what, five minutes?" I asked. Next to me, I could feel Ryan go tense, and I nudged him with my elbow. I appreciated the chivalry, but dealing with death threats was kind of my area of expertise.

Alexander sat back in his chair, eyes narrowing even as he smiled. "You certainly have enough spark to be a Paladin. I can appreciate that. But let me make myself very clear, Miss Price. We are offering our assistance because you need us, and I think you know that. Work with us, and David stays safe and protected, as well as extremely useful as an Oracle. I think it should be clear by now that our powers are greater than yours. After all, I was able to penetrate your wards with hardly any trouble at all."

"Please don't say 'penetrate,'" I muttered, but once again, Alexander ignored me and kept going.

"You and Mr. Bradshaw here have some of the weight taken off your shoulders. But if you choose not to follow our rules, then you declare yourselves our enemies, and we will spend however long it takes to eradicate all three of you. Should the Oracle die, another will be called. Another Paladin will be created, and another Mage."

Leaning forward, he pressed his palms flat on the desktop. A strand of hair fell over his forehead, marring that whole men's-magazine thing he had going on. "You are expendable to us."

My heart was pounding, my mouth dry. On one side, Ryan was breathing hard, his fingers clenching and unclenching. On the other, David was glaring at Alexander. He wasn't jiggling his foot anymore, and had gone so still it was almost unnerving.

"Then why not kill us all now?" I asked Alexander, trying to keep my voice steady. "I mean, we're all here. It wouldn't be hard."

"Harper, could you not?" Ryan muttered, but Alexander only smiled.

"Because that's not what we want. It's true we can replace you, all three of you, but that's not ideal. Much easier to simply welcome you all back into the fold."

"I am not in your fold, buddy," I said, standing up. "And neither are Ryan or David."

On my left, Ryan rose to his feet, shoving his hands in his pockets. "Damn straight."

But David sat in his chair, his elbows on his knees, hands clasped tightly in front of him. He was looking at the ground, a muscle working in his jaw. "David?" I asked, hating how unsure I sounded.

"It's just . . . Pres, we need help. *I* need help."

"But," I faltered, "you have help. You have me and Ryan."

He nodded, almost too quickly. "I do, and you're great, both of you, but . . . Harper, if my powers could actually be used to help people, if this guy"—he nodded at Alexander—"can help me do that . . . it kind of seems worth it, don't you think?"

I stood there, my stomach twisting, my skin suddenly cold. "Saylor and Christopher gave up everything to protect you from these people. They tried to kill you, David. They took Bee."

"I know," David said, "but, Pres, I looked into this guy's mind. He's not trying to hurt me, and what he said adds up. The Ephors only wanted me gone when they thought I was a crappy Oracle. Now that the ritual has worked and it didn't kill me, they need me again. Hell, maybe . . ." He trailed off, tugging at his hair. "Maybe the *world* needs me. And it's not worth your lives"—he gestured at me and Ryan—"if I'm not doing something important. Plus, I'm . . ." Another hair tug. "I'm sick of running from this. Aren't you?" Behind his glasses, his eyes were very blue, and I could hear the plea in his voice.

"He's got a point, Harper," Ryan agreed, and I turned, surprised.

"Okay, what happened to 'damn straight'?"

Ryan gave one of those easy shrugs, and it was the weirdest thing, seeing such a familiar gesture in such a bizarre setting. "Our job is to protect David, right? If this is what David wants, it seems like we should go with it. If the alternative is us looking over our shoulders forever, this seems a hell of a lot better."

I had plenty of experience getting girls in line, but it seemed like boys were a way bigger pain in the butt. I couldn't believe I was being overruled by my boyfriend and my ex-boyfriend in front of a guy I was already pretty sure I hated.

Still, I wanted to present a united front. "Let's go home and talk about it," I said, smoothing my hands over my skirt. In the soft golden lamplight of the study, I could make out a little stain at the hem. Ugh, Spencer must have spilled beer on me when I grabbed him, and I suddenly felt exhausted. "No decision needs to be made tonight, and, hey, not to be rude, but it's not like either of you have to go through some kind of crazy Greek trials if we say yes."

"Oh, I'm sorry," Alexander said, his brows drawing together with what had to be fake concern. "I don't think I was clear. There's no 'deciding.' You are already in the Peirasmos, Miss Price."

I turned to look at him. "What?"

"The moment I arrived here, the Peirasmos began. It's not a choice you get to make, but rather a duty you *must* fulfill."

If I hadn't been so tired and rattled, I probably could've managed something better than "That's not fair!" But that's exactly what I said, and I sounded petulant even to myself.

Alexander only shrugged. "Has any part of this been fair to anyone?" he asked, and I realized I couldn't argue with that. Everything about this had been unfair from day one, but this seemed particularly awful. I was getting sick of not being offered a freaking *choice* in things.

"The Peirasmos have begun," Alexander continued. "And either you will pass, or you will die."

That seemed like a pretty steep grading curve, and for the first time in a long time, I felt something like real fear. Not the adrenaline spike I got when I was fighting bad guys or keeping David safe, but the scary kind. It was a cold, kind of sick feeling that made me want to go home and put my head under the covers, maybe forever.

But I couldn't do that right now, so instead, I stared Alexander down and said, "That seems kind of stupid. If I fail the trials, I die, and then David doesn't have *any* kind of Paladin, official or not, and how—"

"Ah," Alexander interrupted as he drummed his long, elegant fingers on the desk. "That actually brings me to my next point."

"I wasn't finished," I said, turning a glare on him, but he was already rising from the desk.

"We've made provisions for those circumstances." He lifted a hand and nodded at the doorway behind him. "Thanks to you, David, we have a spare."

I turned, my heart in my throat.

There, in the doorway of Alexander's study, was Bee.

Chapter 6

I'D THOUGHT ABOUT seeing Bee again for so long, but now that she was actually there, standing right in front of me, I felt frozen. Paralyzed.

I think I was afraid to believe she was actually there.

Ryan apparently did not have that fear, though, because he crossed the room in a few strides, swooping her up into a big hug. "Holy crap," I heard him say, and her hands came up to rest on his shoulder blades, hugging him back. Bee was only a few inches shorter than Ryan, so I could clearly see her heart-shaped face over his shoulder. Long blond hair pulled back in a braid, dressed in a simple black T-shirt and jeans, she looked so . . . normal.

"Easy there," she said, and her voice sounded exactly the same. "I like my ribs."

That's what did it for me, hearing her sound so normal, so Bee, and then I was across the room, too, shamelessly using my Paladin strength to push Ryan out of the way and throw my arms around her.

"You're okay," I said, squeezing my eyes against the sudden

stinging there. "You're okay, you're okay . . . wait." I pulled back, held her at arm's length. "Are you okay?"

There were tears in her big brown eyes, but she laughed shakily, nodding. "I am. I totally am."

"Miss Franklin was never mistreated in our care," Alexander said, and it was like I'd forgotten he was there. I turned to look over my shoulder.

"That doesn't exactly make up for kidnapping her," I said, and he gave another one of those rolling shrugs.

"She was not meant to be taken. That was all Blythe's doing, and I assure you, she was punished for it."

Something about the way he said "punished" made my skin crawl, but for right now, Bee was here, and she was fine, and she was smiling at me, and I didn't care what the Ephors wanted, so long as she was here.

But then I remembered what he had said, about how if I died during the trials, they'd made "provisions."

The night of Cotillion, David had transformed all the other girls into Paladins, too. He'd undone the spell on everyone else, but Blythe had taken Bee before then. Which meant that Bee—

"Miss Franklin is a Paladin as well," Alexander said, finishing my thought for me. "She's been with us, training, being very well cared for, as you can see." He gestured to Bee, and I had to admit, she didn't look terrible. Her cheeks were full, her skin was as clear and bright as it had always been, and while there was something in her eyes that I couldn't quite name, she seemed . . . fine.

"Should you fail in the trials, Miss Franklin will be here to take your place as the Oracle's Paladin." He lifted his shoulders. "Easy as can be."

It didn't sound all that easy to me. In fact, it sounded like a lot of BS. There were no Paladin powers racing through me, so I figured the prickling at the back of my neck was good old-fashioned anger.

"So you're using my best friend as my understudy in case I get killed?" I said.

Alexander sat back behind his desk, taking a sip of his tea. "When you put it that way, it sounds a great deal more mercenary than it actually is. We simply want to . . . hedge our bets, let us say." He nodded at Bee. "And Miss Franklin has been very well prepared for this."

When I turned back to Bee, she was looking at Alexander, but her gaze slid to me. She tried to smile, but it was shaky and I reached out to hold both her hands in mine.

"They did tell me about all this," she said, taking a deep breath. "That's why they took me, so that they'd have a . . . a spare, I guess."

"You're no one's spare," I told her, squeezing her hands. Relief and anger warred inside of me, along with a fair amount of confusion. I was so happy to have Bee back, but the last thing I'd ever wanted was for her to get involved in this, too. Bad enough that Ryan had been dragged in, but—

Suddenly David was at my side, taking my hand from Bee's. "What the—" I started, but he only shook his head, pressing his palm to Bee's. I saw his brow wrinkle in confusion, and he glanced over her shoulder at Alexander.

"That mind-reading trick. Why won't it work on her?"

Alexander lifted both eyebrows. "Oh, did I not mention? Once the Paladin begins the Peirasmos, the Oracle is stripped of her—well, *his,* in this case—powers. Can't have you looking into the future to help Miss Price face her trials."

David's hands clenched into fists. "You can't do that," he said, but Alexander only shrugged.

"I already have."

"And I didn't begin anything," I argued, dropping Bee's hands. I noticed Ryan moving a little closer to her as David and I approached Alexander's desk.

"You said that I have to do these things or die. It's not like there was a starter pistol or a ready-set-go that happened, so how—"

"They began the moment I summoned David," Alexander interrupted, giving me a smile that showed too many teeth for my liking. "Congratulations."

"No," I said, shaking my head. "No, you don't get to come here and tell us what to do. We were getting along fine without you."

"Were you?" Alexander rolled his eyes up toward the ceiling as though he were thinking something over. "David was squandering his godlike power while the two of you scrambled to keep the people in your lives from figuring out what had happened to you. You threw up wards around your town to keep people from remembering what happened the night Blythe performed the ritual. You acted like children, hoping pebbles would hold back the sea. And Miss Franklin," he finished, inclining his head toward Bee, "was missing—for all you knew, never coming back. And now we have come to help you."

He kept saying "we," but the house was empty except for him, as far as I knew. But then, as far as I knew, there hadn't even *been* a house here a few weeks ago.

I didn't like it. No, more than that, I hated it. Saylor would have known what to do here. The weirdest thing was that parts of it sounded okay. It sounded *right*. And there was Bee.

"I understand why you hesitate to trust us, Miss Price, I honestly do," Alexander said. "But right now, we are all you have. And believe me when I say we need you as desperately as you need us."

"What for?" David asked, but Alexander only shook his head.

"All in good time. Now, Miss Price, the Peirasmos began as of midnight tonight. There are three trials you will undergo before the end of this moon cycle. The trials may be physical in nature, or perhaps tests of the mind, of your spirit. You will not know when they are coming, and you will not receive any assistance. To do so violates the laws of the Peirasmos, and would be considered a failure of the tests. At the end of the trials, you will be stronger, quicker, better at being a Paladin, and Miss Franklin"— another nod at Bee—"will lose her own Paladin powers and return to life as before. Have I made myself clear?"

"As mud," I muttered, and he frowned again.

"Pardon?"

Waving that off, I took a deep breath. "I get it. I do these trial things, I get better powers, I *don't* die, and Bee gets to be de-Paladined." I looked back at Bee, still standing in the doorway. "Is that what you want?"

She didn't even hesitate, her head bobbing up and down quickly. "Yes. God. Like . . . a lot."

That was it, then. It's not like I'd ever had much of a choice in this thing—"do this or die" is not a choice, let's be real—but seeing the relief on Bee's face was enough to make me feel a little better about all of this. Go through these trials, get even more powerful, *don't* get killed, and Bee gets to be happy? That seemed worthwhile to me.

But that wasn't the only reason I found myself turning back to Alexander and saying, "I guess I'm in." It was that something twisting in my stomach, and I knew it was part nervousness, but more than that, it was a little bit . . . excitement. Look, I'm not saying I didn't feel terrible about this—after all, it was probably going to mean more lying, and definitely more danger, but for the past few months, I'd felt like I was in this weird stasis, waiting for something to happen. And now here it was.

And here was *Bee.*

I took her hand and started pulling her toward Alexander's office door, even as David said, "So that's it? We're leaving?"

"We need to get Bee home," I said. "And I think we've heard everything Alexander has to say." Flipping my hair over my shoulder, I looked at the Ephor with raised eyebrows. "Unless there's some other horrible thing you'd like to dump on us tonight?"

To my surprise, he replied, "No, I'm finished for now."

At least he didn't try to argue that this had not been horrible. That was something.

The four of us made our way back down the hall, me and Bee in front, the boys trailing behind. We weren't even halfway to the front door when David said, "So where did they have you?"

Next to me, Bee twisted to glance back at him. "Here," she said. "But . . . it's like it wasn't here. It was this house, but not in this place."

"But this is the house that was originally here," David said, walking a little faster so that he was right behind us, the toes of his sneakers nearly catching the back of my heels. "He . . . magicked it up or whatever. Are you sure it wasn't here?"

Bee's fingers were clammy in mine when she answered, "I never went outside, but I don't think it was here. Or maybe it wasn't this house." Stopping, she pressed her fingers to her forehead. "It was just a bunch of rooms, like a hotel. I never saw anyone but Alexander, but there was food, and all these books about Paladins and Oracles and—"

"What did the books say?" David asked, and that was enough for me. I stopped in front of the door, my hand already on the crystal knob.

"Okay, look. This has been a weird night. Bee has had a weird few months. Ease up on the third degree, please?"

David's blue eyes fixed on mine, his fingers flexing at his side. "We need to know this stuff, Pres."

Ryan's hand came down on David's shoulder. It was a friendly enough gesture, but it was firm, too. Unlike me, Ryan *could* be firm with David.

"Harper's right," he said. "We can talk about all this later, but for now, let's get Bee home."

"Home," she mumbled, following me out onto the porch in a kind of daze. "God, what do my parents think happened to me?" When she turned to look at me, her eyes were so big that I could see the whites all the way around her irises. "Are they okay? Are the police looking for me?" Her grip tightened on my arm. "Have I been on one of those true-crime TV shows?"

"No," I told her, covering her hand with mine. "No, everyone thinks you were at cheerleading camp. Ryan did a spell." I stopped suddenly, pulling Bee up short. "I . . . should probably explain that."

But Bee shook her head. "No, Ryan's a Mage and does magic. Alexander told me when I was . . . wherever I was." She frowned slightly, tugging her hand from mine and hugging herself. "But I have to be honest, I still don't totally get . . . any of this."

"We'll explain in the car," I told her.

So we did. The entire ride back into town, the three of us took turns explaining how all this had come about, starting with that first night in the school bathroom, ending at the frat party tonight.

By the time we were done, we were at my house, and the car was very quiet except for Bee's breathing.

"That's . . . a lot," she said at last, and all three of us muttered, "Yeah," in unison.

Her fingers were twisted tight in the hem of her black T-shirt as she lifted her eyes to me and said, "Do you think it would be okay if I slept over at your house tonight? I'm not sure I'm ready to deal with my parents yet. Especially since they didn't even miss me."

That would be weird, I realized, and I nodded quickly. "Of course you can, no problem."

David shook his head. "We need to keep talking about this,"

he said, drumming his fingers on the steering wheel. "About what they told Bee, and about how we can prepare for the Peirasmos, and about what the heck *I'm* supposed to do without any powers, and—"

I cut him off with a palm laid flat across his mouth. "Tomorrow," I told him. "Or the next day. For now, let me help Bee. Everything else will wait."

David mumbled something behind my hand, and I rolled my eyes.

"She's right," Ryan said from the back, leaning forward and bracing both his hands on the headrest of my seat. "It's late, we've had a lot to process, and Harper and Bee should have some time to themselves."

With that, he lifted one hand to slap the back of David's seat. "Don't try to come between these two, man, trust me," he said, his voice light and jovial even though I was guessing he didn't feel it. I'd known Ryan long enough to know that tightness in his voice when he was worried about something.

But thankfully David nodded. "Okay. Yeah, you're right, nothing we can do right now. We'll talk later."

With that, he leaned over like he was going to kiss me, only to pause, his eyes flicking toward the backseat.

Scoffing, I reached out and grabbed his face with both hands, planting a quick but firm kiss on his lips. I didn't like PDA, but Ryan and Bee weren't the public, and it wasn't like they didn't know we were dating.

Oh. Wait.

It wasn't like *Ryan* didn't know we were dating.

I looked back at Bee, who was watching me with her mouth slightly open. "Um. That is . . . another thing we should've mentioned," I said, a little meekly, but Bee was already reaching for the door handle.

"One trauma at a time, please."

David winced at that, but it made me feel better to hear a little of the old Bee in her voice. I gave him another quick kiss, this one on the cheek, and then stepped out of the car to stand next to Bee at the edge of my driveway.

Bee watched Ryan and David drive off into the night, and stepped close to me, our arms brushing. "Your life got weird," she said after a long pause, and I thought of Alexander, of everything that might be coming.

"And getting weirder."

Chapter 7

BEE WAS GONE when I woke up in the morning. A note left on my dresser said she'd walked home. Since her house was only a couple of blocks from mine, it wasn't all that weird, but I still wished she'd hung around a little longer. It was like I needed to convince myself that she was okay. But I reminded myself that she definitely needed some Parental Time, and probably wanted to sleep in her own bed.

Mom was already up and making breakfast when I went downstairs, which was surprising. It was Sunday, which meant we went to the earlier church service, then out for breakfast afterward.

"Eggs?" she asked, gesturing to the pan on the stove.

The sight of them made me a little queasy; I'd never been a big breakfast person. So I shook my head and grabbed an apple from the fruit bowl on the counter. "No, thanks."

Maybe it was my imagination, but I could have sworn Mom looked a little disappointed. Tucking her hair—dark like mine, but cut shorter—behind her ear, she turned back to the stove. "Okay. I could also make bacon? Ooh!" She set the spatula down on the trivet I'd made her at summer camp years ago. It was supposed to look like a frog, but something had happened in the kiln to turn it into more of a dark green amoeba. "How about pancakes?"

I glanced at the clock, then back at Mom, still in her robe. "Don't we have church?"

She gave a little shrug, turning back to the stove. "I thought we might skip this Sunday. Spend some family time."

With that, Mom turned back to the stove. The eggs had started to smoke a little, and she heaved a sigh as she scraped them around the skillet.

I frowned. Bad enough that things were weird with David right now. I wasn't sure I could handle family problems on top of that. Maybe Mom wanted us to hang out because she needed to tell me she and Dad were separating, or she was sick, or . . .

I stood up, putting the apple back in the bowl. "Mom, is everything all right?"

She glanced over her shoulder at me. "As far as I know. Why?

The eggs were completely burned now, and Mom made a faint "tsking" sound as she moved the pan off the eye of the stove. My mom was traditional in so many ways—in the Junior League, taught Sunday school, wore makeup even if she was just staying home all day—but she was not the best cook.

"You never skip church," I told her. "Or make breakfast. Or get up this early. So I thought maybe something was up."

Mom dumped the eggs in the trash and put the pan in the sink. "It just seems like I never see you." She crossed her arms, the delicate gold bracelet around her wrist flashing. It had belonged to my sister, and Mom had worn it ever since Leigh-Anne had died two years ago.

When I didn't answer, Mom gave a rueful smile. "I guess missing you is to be expected with as busy as you are, but . . ." She trailed off, her eyes moving over my face. "I worry about you, sweetie."

I crossed in front of the island in the center of the kitchen. "There's nothing to worry about," I said. I thought I sounded pretty convincing, given that I was lying through my teeth. I'd gotten good at lying over the past few months. It wasn't something I was particularly proud of, but I didn't see a way around it. The fewer people I loved who knew about Paladins and Oracles and Ephors and all the other crazy stuff that had taken over my life, the safer they'd all be.

"You've gone through so many changes recently," Mom said, the corners of her mouth turning down.

You have no idea, I thought. What I said was, "Nothing major, though."

Mom's frown deepened. "'Nothing major'? Harper, you broke up with the boy you'd been in love with for years, you started dating a boy we all thought you'd *hated* for years, and you hardly ever spend any time with Bee." For a second, her eyes got slightly hazy, confusion wrinkling her brow. "Where is Bee, anyway? Didn't she go somewhere?"

"She's back," I told her, not having to fake the brightness in my voice. "Remember, she was at cheerleading camp? She got back last night, actually."

Some of the wrinkles around Mom's brow eased. "Oh. Well, that's nice. But Bee aside, I'm still concerned about you and Ryan. You seem happy, but—"

I squeezed her fingers. "I am happy. And Ryan and I still hang out; we're friends. We just don't date anymore."

After a moment, Mom squeezed back. "Okay. But you promise everything is all right?" Smiling, she brushed my hair back from my forehead with her free hand. "You're not going to suddenly dye your hair blue or start piercing things, are you?"

I shook my head with a little shudder. "Okay, the very thought of that makes me want to vomit. No."

Mom laughed a little at that before wrapping me in a hug. "Well, there's the Harper Jane I know."

On Monday morning, I was heading out to my car when Bee's white Acura came roaring up to the curb. She sat behind the wheel, her curly blond hair a cloud around her bright, smiling face, music blaring on the radio.

I smiled back, but something about her grin bothered me. It seemed . . . fake. Still, I made my way out to the car. "You offering me a ride?"

"A ride and coffee!" Triumphantly, she held a Starbucks cup out the window, and I took it, still feeling uneasy. I barely slid into the passenger seat before she was pulling back into the street, her fingers drumming on the steering wheel.

"So did everything go okay with your parents?" I asked, holding the coffee tight to keep it from sloshing through the little hole in the lid as Bee took a corner a little too fast. I almost had to yell to be heard over the music.

"It was fine!" Bee said, and I wished she would take off her sunglasses so I could see her face. "I mean, weird. At first it was like they didn't even recognize me, or it was like they had just woken up or something." She gave a little shrug. "But then it was fine. Like you said, they think I've been at cheerleading camp this whole time."

We were almost to the school now—it wasn't very far from my house—and I put my coffee in the cup holder before reaching out to touch her arm gently. "You're sure you're okay?"

"Are you?" she asked, glancing over at me. I could see her brows rising over the tops of her aviators. "I'm not the one who could have super-dangerous challenges thrown at me at any moment. Although"—the corners of her mouth turned down—"I guess I will be if something happens to you."

"Nothing is going to happen to me," I said with a confidence I definitely did not feel. "I'll get through this, you can go back to being normal, and everything will be like it was before. Well, mostly."

Bee pulled into a parking spot and shut off the engine, turning to face me. She slid her glasses onto the top of her head and studied my face. "Nothing is ever going to be normal again, is it?" Then she frowned. "But it hasn't been normal for you in a long time."

Look, I definitely wasn't thrilled my best friend had been all magicked up, and was now my backup in case I got horribly killed during some supernatural trials. But I had to admit that Bee actually knowing what was going on, being able to talk to her about it and have her understand, felt good. One fewer person to lie to was always a nice thing as far as I was concerned.

"Don't worry about me," I said. "I've had months to get used to this kind of thing."

"That's what all the hanging out with Saylor was about, huh?" she asked, opening her car door. "The karate stuff?"

I nodded. "I'll tell you the whole story at lunch, promise."

We both stepped out of the car and into the bright spring morning. The smell of flowers hung in the air, and the grass sparkled with dew. It was a gorgeous day, and I took a deep breath, feeling a little better. On a morning like this, it seemed impossible to believe that anything bad could happen. I had my best friend back, a new pair of ballet flats on my feet, and a boyfriend heading toward me with a smile on his face and . . . what appeared to be bowling shoes on his feet.

"Where did you even get those?" I asked as he came up to stand beside me, and he held one foot out, turning his ankle.

"Salvation Army. They're cool, right?"

They *did* kind of match his shirt, which I guessed I should consider a win.

I turned to say something to Bee, but she was already heading off toward the school, shoulders held back.

Following my gaze, David nodded toward Bee. "She okay?"

I thought about Bee's bright smile, how fake it had seemed, and I gave an uneasy shrug. "She's not *not* okay, I guess," I finally settled on, and David nodded.

"Kind of the status quo around here."

I couldn't argue with that.

Bee wasn't in any of my classes that day, which wasn't a surprise since technically she wasn't registered for spring semester. Ryan had said he'd meet her at the main office to do the best he could, Mage-wise, to help out with that, but by the time lunch rolled around, I was getting a little worried about Bee. Stepping outside, I scanned the courtyard for her bright hair, but there was no sign of her. Ryan was out there, though, already sitting at one of the picnic tables with Mary Beth and the twins, but there was no sign of Brandon, Ryan's best friend and Bee's boyfriend.

Catching Ryan's eye, I mouthed, "Bee?"

He gave me a thumbs-up, then a little wave, inviting me to sit at his table. Mary Beth glanced behind her, and while she didn't, like, hiss or anything, I could see her eyes narrow. So, yeah, sitting with them was out.

I thought about going back into the building to look for Bee, but she was a big girl, and if she wanted to handle this on her own, I needed to respect that.

Taking a deep breath, I glanced around the courtyard again, and saw David waving to me, so I joined him and his friends from the newspaper, Michael and Chie. The three of them were sitting underneath the big oak tree on the edge of the courtyard, and when I walked over, David jumped up to pull a jacket out of his bag for me to sit on.

"Thanks," I told him, arranging myself on his tweed. Chie and Michael, who'd been laughing when I came over, now sat in silence, paying a lot of attention to their lunch.

Apparently I wasn't going to escape weirdness no matter where I sat.

"I like your necklace, Chie," I said, figuring flattery was always a good tactic. And seeing as how she was wearing a battered army jacket, an oversized black T-shirt, and a pair of leggings that I was pretty sure violated dress code, the necklace was about the only thing I *could* compliment.

But as Chie's fingers trailed over the gold chain, her dark eyes regarded me suspiciously. "I got it at Walmart," she said, almost like a challenge.

I nodded. "They have pretty stuff. Sometimes."

David shot me a look that was part exasperation, part amusement, and I gave a little shrug in response. I was all for making an effort to be nice, but I wasn't going to gush over Walmart. Come on, now.

After clearing his throat, David pulled an apple out of his bag, tossing it back and forth between his hands. "We were talking about what story the newspaper should tackle next." He nodded at his friends. "Chie has this great idea about how few people in Pine Grove actually recycle, and then Michael wanted to investigate allegations that the cafeteria is still using foods with MSG even after the school board told them they couldn't."

I took a long swallow of Diet Coke, hoping that would give me time to think of some reply. In the end, all I came up with was "Okay."

Chie flicked her bangs out of her eyes. She wasn't exactly glaring at me, but I was clearly not her favorite person right now. "What, you don't think those are valid stories?"

Next to her, Michael tugged his sleeves over his hands, his right foot jiggling. He was taller and skinnier than David, something that hardly seemed possible, and his dark hair was thick and shaggy, lying over his collar. In the few months I'd been working in the newspaper room, I wasn't sure he'd said more than a dozen words to me. I got the sense that I might have scared him a bit.

"It's not that," I said to Chie, tucking my hair behind my ears. "But . . . both of those stories seem depressing."

And boring, I thought.

David frowned and drew his knees up to his chest, circling them with his arms. "The news isn't always cheerful, Pres."

"I get that, but . . ." I looked around at the three of them, all regarding me seriously. "This is a tiny school paper read by a few hundred kids. If that. Gotta be honest, when y'all hand those things out, most of them end up in the trash can. Or the recycling bin," I hastily added when Chie's shoulders went up. "But my point is, maybe more people would read *The Grove News* if it were, like, cheerier. Funnier. When the SGA was doing a newsletter—"

"Maybe we should print it on pink paper," Chie muttered under her breath, and David sat up straighter.

"Hey," he said as he pushed his glasses up with one finger. "Harper is a member of our staff now, and she might have a point."

Michael nodded but Chie rolled her eyes and stood up. "David, please. She's on the staff because, for some reason none of us understand, she's your girlfriend. So sorry if I don't exactly feel like taking advice from her." Leaning down, she scooped up her bag and jerked her head at Michael. "Let's go, Mike," she said. "We can let our fearless leader and his first lady debate the principles of journalism without us."

Michael's blue eyes darted back and forth between me and David still sitting on the ground and Chie looming over him. Eventually, he gave a mumbled "Sorry," and the two of them walked back toward the building.

David and I watched them go.

"I'm sorry," I said at last, picking an imaginary piece of lint off my skirt. "I shouldn't have said anything. I mean, she's right. I'm only on the paper to be closer to you."

But David shook his head, his gaze still on his friends. "No, you have every right to an opinion. They shouldn't have been jerks."

Over at their table, Mary Beth and Ryan were laughing. As we watched, she rested her head on his shoulder and he slung an arm around her neck, pulling her in to kiss the top of her head.

"Get a room!" I heard Amanda cry as she tossed a napkin at them.

"It's not like my friends would be that much nicer to you," I reminded David.

The wind was blowing softly through the leaves over our head, and I remembered earlier this morning, thinking what a pretty day this was. It was still gorgeous, but I had to admit, my mood was not nearly as sunny.

Then the toe of David's ugly shoe nudged my thigh. I glanced up and David leaned closer. "Our forbidden passion has transgressed social boundaries, and now we pay the price," he intoned with a somber nod, and I giggled, batting his foot away.

"Shut up."

But David only released his knees and wrapped his arms around me, pulling me sideways. "We shall be shunned!" he continued, squeezing me tight. "Driven from the lands of our birth, forced to wander the wilds—"

I was laughing now, even as I reached down to keep my skirt from riding up my thighs. "You are insane," I informed David, twisting in his embrace.

He grinned at me, and in that moment, there was no gold in his eyes, no feeling of danger. No prophecies or powers or magic. Just us, laughing under a tree in the courtyard.

My laughter faded and I reached up to push a lock of hair off his forehead. "I like you kind of a lot," I said quietly, and David's arms tightened around me.

"You're not so bad yourself, Pres," he said, and I wondered when the nickname that used to annoy me so much had started sounding so sweet.

I was still pretty firmly anti-PDA, but when David kissed me—quickly, but firmly—I decided that every once in a while, it wasn't so bad.

I was still smiling when I saw Brandon come out the front door, Bee right behind him. "Oh, there she is," I said, standing up. I walked quickly toward the sidewalk where they were standing, and only then did I realize how pale Bee had gone, how big her eyes were.

And Brandon was staring at her in obvious confusion.

"Brandon, it's *me*," she said. "Why didn't you wait when I called you?"

He flicked his hair out of his eyes, shifting his weight uncomfortably. "Um, because I don't know who you are?"

Chapter 8

BRANDON WAS BLINKING at Bee, his handsome face scrunched up in a puzzled frown, one hand running over the back of his neck. "I mean, you're pretty hot," he said with a shrug, "so I'd think I'd remember you, but . . . yeah, not ringing any bells."

David had jogged up beside me, and I could hear him blow out a long breath. "Crap," he muttered.

People were starting to stare. There was a group of freshman girls sitting at a nearby stone table, clearly paying a lot of attention to what was going on right now. All three had dark, shiny hair, and I watched one lick yogurt off her spoon before leaning in to whisper something to her friend.

Taking Bee's elbow, I tried to draw her back from Brandon a little bit. "It's okay," I said in a low voice, but she looked at me and shook her head.

"It's not okay, Harper. Mrs. Carter in English didn't recognize me either. That didn't seem like such a big deal, but then on the way to lunch, Lucy McCarroll stopped to welcome me to Grove Academy." She reached out, wrapping her fingers around my wrists, her grip tight enough to hurt. "It's like I never existed." Her voice wavered on the last word, and there was real panic in her eyes. I stood there, helpless, and wondered where the heck Ryan was. This was *his* spell, after all. Maybe there was something he could do, some way to—

"Be a real shame if a girl as fine as you didn't exist," Brandon practically leered, and Bee whirled on him.

"God, shut *up*, Brandon!" She was scared and hurt and frustrated, and I think she only meant to swat at Brandon's shoulder, like she'd done a thousand times before. Trouble was, all those other times?

She wasn't a Paladin.

Her hand connected with Brandon's collarbone, and he went flying backward, tripping over his backpack and landing hard on the grass with a startled yell.

"Brandon!" she cried as I squawked, "Bee!"

If only a handful of people had been watching this scene play out before, I was now pretty sure that every single person in the courtyard was paying rapt attention to what had just happened. I could hear voices not even bothering to whisper. One very loudly asked, "Who *is* that girl?" and Bee visibly shuddered.

David stepped forward, offering a hand to Brandon, who shook it off with an irritated glare before rising to his feet. "What the hell, crazy chick?" he asked Bee, who could only shake her head, and stammer, "I—I didn't mean to."

"Whatever," Brandon said with a dismissive wave of his hand. He was a good-looking guy, all blond hair and cutest-boy-on-the-basketball-team face, but in that moment, his expression was one of the ugliest things I'd ever seen. He brushed past Bee without a word, and when she took a step after him, I pulled her up short.

"Wait," I told her. "We can . . . We'll talk to Ryan, and—"

Luckily, Ryan was already walking over to us, Mary Beth trailing in his wake. "What's going on?" he asked.

"It's your sp—" I started, only to stop when I realized Mary Beth was right there. "Your *spectacularly* dumb friend upsetting Bee," I covered as quickly as I could, then jerked my head toward the building. "Can we go inside and talk for a minute? All of us?"

"About what?" Mary Beth asked, and I practically groaned. I was getting used to the idea of her and Ryan together, but that didn't mean I liked having to factor her into things like this. Right now, my main priority was getting Bee out of the courtyard and somewhere private. Tears were leaking down her cheeks, carrying a fair amount of her mascara with them, and I didn't like the way that table of freshman girls was still watching her.

I nearly had to go up on tiptoes to wrap my arm around Bee's shoulder, but I did it anyway, tugging her close. "It's nothing," I told Mary Beth, then flicked my gaze up at Ryan. "Can we?"

With that, I started pulling Bee toward Nash Hall. Maybe it wasn't nice to let Ryan deal with getting rid of Mary Beth on his own, but that wasn't my problem.

As we walked back into the school, a blast of air-conditioning washed over us, making Bee shiver, and I chafed my hand up and down her arm. "It's okay," I said again. It was becoming my mantra, no matter how untrue it was. Bee only sniffled in response.

"The newspaper room," David said from behind us, and I started steering Bee that way. We were still getting a few confused looks, and I wondered if that was from Bee crying, or from no one remembering who she was.

I was going to *throttle* Ryan. Okay, so maybe it wasn't entirely his fault, and the spell was bigger than he'd thought, but I needed someone to be mad at, and he'd do.

Michael and Chie were in the newspaper room, but when David asked if we could have a second, they cleared out. Chie glared at me as she picked up her bag, but I ignored that. I had bigger things to worry about right now than one of my boyfriend's besties being hostile all the time.

Bee was still shaky when she sat down in one of the rolling chairs at the back counter, and David watched her with a slight frown, taking a seat on top of a desk. I went over to sit by Bee as Ryan walked into the room, closing the door behind him. He leaned against it, arms folded over his chest, the sleeves of his T-shirt tight over his biceps.

"Is there anything you can do?" Bee asked, raising her head to look at Ryan. She wasn't crying, but she was still kind of sniffly, and I got up to go get the box of tissues on Mrs. Laurent's desk.

I handed it to Bee as Ryan sighed and said, "I don't know. This Mage stuff . . ." Trailing off, he opened and closed his hands. "It's like I know how to use it, but it's all instinct or something. Not real knowledge. I can do spells, but undoing them, or fixing them when they get screwed up?"

Reaching up, he scrubbed a hand over his auburn hair. I wondered if that was a habit he was picking up from David. "That I'm not so sure about," he said.

Wiping her nose, Bee shook her head. "My parents remembered me. Not at first, but then after a minute or so, it was like I'd never been gone."

"Maybe that's because they're your parents," I suggested, leaning forward to rest my hand on her knee. Her skin felt clammy and cool. "You'd have a stronger bond with them than—"

"Than with my boyfriend?" she asked, her head jerking up. None of us said anything for a while, and the only sound was Bee's harsh breathing and the rattle of David jiggling his leg up and down on the desk seat.

Finally, Bee wadded up her tissue. "I thought once I was back, everything would be fine. That's all I thought the whole time I was with Alexander. That if I could get back home, this would all be over."

She looked at me then, and I felt a lump rise in my throat. "But it's not, is it? Hardly anyone can remember me, you're a superhero who has to go through these . . . these *things* that might kill you, and if you do die, not only will I have lost my best friend, but I'm stuck protecting *him*." Bee gestured toward David and then added, "No offense."

"None taken," he replied quietly. "Trust me, I'm used to being a pain in the ass."

"You're not," I said automatically, but even as I did, I was remembering how I'd felt when Saylor had told me that my sacred duty was to protect David. I'd told her that I didn't want to screw up my life to save someone else.

Once again, this helpless, choking feeling rose up in my

throat. I wanted to pass the Peirasmos because I didn't want to *die,* obviously, but looking at Bee, who, even though she was more than half a foot taller than me, looked so small and scared sitting in that chair, one knee drawn up under her chin, her eyes still red, I realized there was more than just *my* life at stake.

I hadn't been able to protect Bee the night of Cotillion, but if I managed to survive the Peirasmos, she would be free from all of this.

"We're going to get through this, Bee," I said, and her head shot up. She'd rubbed off most of the mascara with the tissue I'd handed her, but there were still dark flecks around her eyes, and her face was splotchy and damp.

"You can't promise that, Harper," she said, and then, as the bell signaling the end of lunch rang, she stood up, rolling the chair underneath the counter.

"I just . . . I thought you'd all know what you were doing," she said at last, and with that, she walked out of the room, leaving me, Ryan, and David in silence.

Chapter 9

"That is rude, Harper Jane."

I glanced up guiltily, lowering my phone back into my lap. "Sorry, Aunt Jewel."

After school, I'd decided to run by The Aunts' house. Bee had gone home early, so I'd gotten David to drive me to my house to pick up my car. After everything in the newspaper room, I hadn't gotten a chance to talk to Bee again, and while I was worried about her, I thought maybe she needed a little space. Plus, I wasn't sure what to say. She was right that Ryan, David, and I hardly knew what we were doing, but it had still stung.

So off to The Aunts' I went. I hadn't done the best job being a good niece over the past few months, and as Mom always reminded me, The Aunts were the closest things to grandparents I had, so I needed to appreciate them.

And that meant that when I went to see them, I shouldn't be messing around on my phone. But I hadn't been able to resist poking around the internet a little bit to see if I could pick up any information on the Peirasmos, especially since The Aunts had been distracted by discussing whether or not Jell-O salad was still a thing you could take to a church potluck. Preparation was the key to any test, after all, and even if Alexander had said that the whole point was for me to be caught unaware, I didn't think that had to mean, you know, going in *completely* blind. But it wasn't like it mattered. Google seemed to think I might have some kind of stomach issue, but there was nothing on the internet about Peirasmos, the trials. I had been fixing to text David to see if he'd found anything in Saylor's books yet, but from the way Aunt Jewel was looking at me, that was no longer an option.

Aunt Jewel was only a year older than Aunt May and Aunt Martha, but she took her role as the eldest sister very seriously. She regarded me now through pink-rimmed glasses fastened on a sparkly chain around her neck. All three of The Aunts were decked out in pretty pastel sweaters, the pale green of Aunt Jewel's almost matching her eyes.

My purse was sitting beside my chair, and I slipped my phone into it.

"Oh, leave her be, Jewel," Aunt May said, not glancing up from her own cards. "The children today need their technology."

"That's true," Aunt Martha said, nodding. She'd been to the beauty shop that morning, obviously, since her steel-gray curls were tight against her head. "I read it in the *New York Times*. People Harper's age are actually in love with those fancy-schmancy phones of theirs. Activates the same chemicals in the brain." Sighing, she discarded a card. "I went to look at one of those phones at the Best Buy, but I couldn't make heads or tails of it."

"You can't make heads or tails out of your cordless phone, Martha," Aunt May said, picking up the card Aunt Martha had put down. All three had skin that still glowed despite their age, and green eyes like mine.

Before they could get into too much of a fuss, Aunt Jewel gave a little smile and said, "Well, I don't think it's her phone Harper is in love with, so much as the boy at the other end of it."

Aunt Martha gave a happy grin at that, tugging at the lace collar on her lavender sweater. "That Ryan sure is pretty."

Both Aunt Jewel and Aunt May gave identical sniffs of disgust. "They're broken up, silly," Aunt May informed Aunt Martha. "Have been for ages."

"Four months," I clarified, getting out of my chair to grab the pitcher of sweet tea on the kitchen counter. As I refilled The Aunts' glasses, I added, "Remember, Aunt Martha, I'm dating David Stark now."

Frowning, Aunt Martha set her cards down and picked up the pack of Virginia Slims by her elbow. "Oh. That's right. Saylor's boy."

I stiffened a little, hoping they wouldn't notice. Just like with Bee's disappearance, there was a spell keeping the people of Pine Grove from knowing what had really happened to Saylor Stark. Bee's spell had clearly held—maybe too well—but Ryan should probably shore up the one that made everyone think Saylor was just on an extended vacation.

Making a mental note to talk to him about it later, I set the pitcher back on the counter and took a seat at the table. I still wasn't allowed to play gin rummy with The Aunts—only once I was officially an adult, i.e., married, would I get invited to that table—but I liked to watch.

"And how are things with David?" Aunt Jewel asked. Her voice was light, but I saw how closely she was watching me. I loved Aunts May and Martha, but I was closest to Aunt Jewel. And while it wasn't like I'd told her anything that was going on with me, I always had the feeling she somehow knew there was more to me and David than met the eye.

But I smiled back and gave a little shrug. "They're good." I thought it would be easiest to leave it at that.

Aunt Jewel nodded, taking a sip of her tea. "Well, that's good to hear. I wondered, since you've looked a little out of sorts lately."

Aunt May and Aunt Martha made humming noises of agreement, and it was all I could do not to roll my eyes. "Just busy," I said. "Spring semester of your junior year is an important time. College applications, all of that."

That got all three of The Aunts' attention. "Ooh, what colleges are you looking at, honey?" Aunt May asked.

Relieved that we were on slightly safer ground, I launched into an account of the top schools on my list. They were mostly all here in the South, and I thought I'd chosen a pretty good mix of big state universities and smaller private colleges. Of course, they were all schools I'd picked out last year, and I felt a little twinge of guilt that I hadn't done more on the college front lately.

Of course, I'd been kind of busy.

Aunts May and Martha smiled pleasantly, but Aunt Jewel asked, "And David?"

When I didn't answer right away, she took one of Aunt Martha's cigarettes, lighting it with a hot pink Bic. "Are y'all looking at the same places? I know you haven't been together long, but it still seems like something you should talk about."

The College Issue was one of those things David and I had trouble talking about. Obviously, going to the same college was a nonnegotiable, and had nothing to do with us being a couple. I couldn't even go that far out of town alone without feeling an aching weight in my chest. But I was convinced we could find a place we both agreed on.

Unfortunately, David never wanted to talk about it, always shrugging and saying, "We'll cross that bridge when we come to it." Problem was, that bridge was rapidly approaching.

To Aunt Jewel, I said, "We're talking about it." And I certainly didn't add that my dream college was a women's school that was completely out of the question, and that no matter how hard I tried, I couldn't help but resent that the teensiest bit. Or that Ryan probably needed to be factored into the equation now.

Closing my eyes for a second, I took a deep breath. One thing at a time. First we'd deal with the Peirasmos, and then I could worry about how to negotiate The College Issue.

Thankfully, Aunt Martha changed the subject, asking if any of my friends were going to be in the upcoming Miss Pine Grove Pageant.

I laughed, leaning back in my seat. "Not that I know of. Most girls at the Grove aren't into that kind of thing." The pageant, which happened every May Day, was held in the town's big rec center, and despite the name, it was open to any girl in the surrounding few counties. As a result, Miss Pine Grove was usually from Appleton or Eversley rather than Pine Grove itself.

The Aunts thought the pageant was tacky and nearly had a collective stroke when my sister, Leigh-Anne, had decided to be in it several years ago.

They'd been even more horrified when she'd won.

So when I said that no one I knew had anything to do with it, I could practically feel them all sag with relief.

"Good girl," Aunt Martha said, just as Aunt May muttered, "Trashy," under her breath.

Aunt Jewel only took a drag on her cigarette and commented, "Oh, like you both don't have *Toddlers & Tiaras* saved on the TV box thingie."

"That is different," Aunt Martha said with a lift of her chin, and Aunt May agreed with a fervid "Very different."

On that note, I decided to head out. I still wanted to run by David's before I went home, so we could go through some of Saylor's books together. I'd thought about asking Bee what books she'd seen, but after today's incident, I thought it might be best to let that drop for a while.

But just as I went to go, my phone rang. Glancing at The Aunts, I shook my purse at them. "May I answer?"

"Go ahead, honey," Aunt May said with a wave, and I smiled, reaching into my bag. It was Ryan, which was kind of a surprise. He almost always texted if he needed to get in touch.

I had barely said hello when he broke in, his voice tight and breathless. "Harper, you need to get over here. *Now*."

Chapter 10

I MADE IT OVER to Ryan's house in record time—one of the perks of being a Paladin is the ability to drive like a stunt person—and Ryan was already waiting outside the front door for me as I pulled up.

"What took you so long?" he asked, and I noticed that he was the palest I'd ever seen him, almost gray.

Slamming the car door behind me, I hurried up his front steps, nearly tripping over a rocking chair on the porch. "I came as fast as I could," I said, moving past him into the house. "What is it? Is it Alexander? Is it one of the trials?"

That's what I'd thought when Ryan first called, and it had been the scenario I'd spun out in my head on the short drive over. But Ryan seemed okay, if shaken up, and now he shook his head at me, waving a hand toward the front door.

"Upstairs," Ryan said, scrubbing a hand over his hair. "It's MB." Misery was etched in every line of his body, and my heart took a sudden plunge as I started up the staircase.

There was a part of me expecting to see Mary Beth lying on his floor with a scimitar through her stomach or something, so I was actually relieved to see her sitting on the edge of Ryan's bed, seemingly completely okay, if a little . . . spacey.

"Hi, Mary Beth," I said, already trying to formulate a reason for being at Ryan's house. He'd called me to work on a school project?

But she didn't reply. In fact, she didn't even seem to hear me.

I shot a glance at Ryan over my shoulder. He was leaning against the doorjamb, nearly crying, his hazel eyes red.

Kneeling down at the edge of Ryan's bed, I snapped my fingers in front of Mary Beth's face. Her eyes slowly blinked once, then twice, but other than that, there was no sign that she'd heard me. Groaning, I turned back to Ryan. "What the heck did you do?"

The last time I'd seen Ryan this miserable was when he'd missed a free throw at a game against our rivals, the Webb Spiders. Now, like then, he was fidgeting, his arms crossed tightly across his chest. "I don't know. She was still pissed about me ditching her at lunch, so I wanted to . . . fix it."

"Ryan," I groaned, and he held up both hands.

"I know, I know. Anyway, I used some of that lip balm stuff on her. That stuff Saylor had."

Now that he mentioned it, there was a distinct rose scent wafting up from Mary Beth. "You kissed her with it on?" I was pretty sure my eyebrows were in my hairline, and when Ryan looked down at me, he scowled.

"Well, yeah. She's my girlfriend. And that seemed the easiest way to . . . apply it."

Still crouching in front of her, I studied her face. "Maybe

she wasn't meant to ingest it," I mused. "How much did you put on?"

Ryan knelt down next to me, and while he wasn't quite wringing his hands, he was close. "Not a lot," he said, a dull flush creeping up his neck. "I mean, I'm a dude, it would look weird if I slathered my whole mouth in a bunch of rose lip gloss, you know?"

There was nothing funny about this situation, but I couldn't stop a brief smile. Seeing it, Ryan smiled, too, giving a nervous laugh. "I need to go through Saylor's things, see if there's anything else that works for mind control, since I can't keep carrying lip balm everywhere."

"Maybe there's something you could work into an aftershave?" I suggested. "Or that gross boy body spray they're always advertising?"

He sniffed, shoulders rising and falling. "I don't wear that crap," he reminded me, and I nodded.

"I know. Trust me, you wouldn't have lasted long as my boyfriend if you had."

That made Ryan smile again, and he looked over at me with squinted eyes. "What is it you call David? That word he hates?"

"Boyfie," I answered, and Ryan laughed.

"Yeah, *you* wouldn't have lasted long as my girlfriend if you'd said that." He was still smiling, just the littlest bit, but then he looked back at Mary Beth and all the humor left his face. "She'll be okay, right?"

I leaned in closer to Mary Beth. Her eyes met mine, and I could tell she was trying to focus. "Mary Beth?"

Another blink, but nothing else. Next to me, Ryan stood up, chafing his palms against his thighs. "Oh God," he groaned. "I've lobotomized her. I've lobotomized my girlfriend with a— an effing *potion*."

He didn't say "effing," but I didn't bother admonishing him. We were in F-word territory for sure.

Crossing the room in two long strides, Ryan moved to his desk and snatched up the little pot of lip balm. "Screw this stuff," he said, and before I could stop him, he'd opened the window and thrown it out as hard as he could.

Now I shot to my feet. "Ryan!" I said sharply. "So you screwed up using it once. That doesn't mean you won't use it again. And what if someone else finds it?" Moving to the window, I ducked my head out, even though I knew I wasn't going to be able to see it.

"I suck at this," Ryan moaned, dropping his head into his hands as he sat down heavily on the bed. "I screwed up the spell with Bee, and now I've screwed up with MB, too."

I don't think I'd ever heard Ryan admit to being bad at something in his entire life. I wasn't sure he actually *had* been bad at anything in his entire life, now that I thought about it. Things had always come pretty easily to Ryan. It was one of the few things we'd had in common, and now, as I remembered how awful and confused I'd felt when I'd first learned I was a Paladin, I couldn't help but sympathize.

"Hey." My hand hovered over his shoulder as he slumped forward, elbows on his knees. Was I allowed to hug him? Even in a totally platonic, comforting way? I wasn't a hundred percent sure, so I did what seemed safest and patted his back a few times before clasping my hands in my lap. "You don't suck. You just don't know all the ropes yet."

Ryan dropped his hands from his face, swiveling his head to look at me. "Is this something where you can know the ropes, Harper? Because I'm pretty sure magic and potions and—and Oracles are always gonna be pretty effing confusing to me."

Considering the fact that I still had no idea when the Peirasmos was starting, that wasn't exactly something I could answer. Instead, I gave him another pat and said, "We'll all figure it out together."

Ryan seemed to sigh with his whole body, his hair ruffling with the long breath he blew out. "You say that all the time. 'We'll work it out.' 'Everything will be okay.'"

Stung, I dropped my hand from his back again. "We will. And it will be."

Ryan straightened, watching me over steepled fingers. "You've never been able to admit that you were in over your head."

I opened my mouth, but Ryan raised one hand. "No, I know you're going to say it isn't true, but it is, Harper. You know it. Only this time, it's not school dances and leadership committees and student government issues you're trying to balance. It's huge, life-or-death stuff, and you're still pretending it's another project. People are going to get hurt."

His gaze drifted to Mary Beth, slumped next to him. "People have *already* gotten hurt."

I moved over to Ryan's bookcase. It held a few sports biographies, but the shelves were mostly stacked with video games and a couple of picture frames. Once they'd held pictures of me and Ryan, but now he and Mary Beth smiled out at me from behind the glass. But in one picture frame, behind a photo of the two of them with their arms around each other on Mary Beth's parents' porch, I could make out a bright turquoise corner. That had been the backdrop for last year's Spring Fling. The theme had been Under the Sea. Ryan and I had gone together. Apparently, Ryan had shoved a picture of them on top of one of the two of us.

I fiddled with the frame now, half tempted to open it and see if I was right. "You think I don't know that?" I said at last, not looking at him. "Saylor Stark died the night of Cotillion. Bee was kidnapped. And now the Ephors suddenly want to be besties, and I'm apparently going to face some kind of trials, but I have no idea what they could be. And if I don't do them, we spend the rest of our lives trying not to get killed."

My voice broke on the last word, and from behind me, I heard Ryan sigh.

"I'm sorry, Harper," he said softly. And then he gave a little huff of laughter. "It's weird, my impulse is to hug you, but I don't know if that's something we can do anymore."

Turning around, I smiled and put the picture back on the shelf. "I know what you mean. But we should probably do without hugging."

Ryan was still wringing his hands in front of him, glancing over at Mary Beth. "It's gotta wear off eventually."

"I'm sure it will," I said, even though I wasn't exactly. Saylor had used that stuff a lot, but I'd never asked questions about how it worked. After she'd died, we'd handed all her various potions and elixirs over to Ryan without thinking. He'd inherited Saylor's skills, but that didn't necessarily mean he knew exactly how to use every little tool she'd had. Not for the first time, I wished that she were here.

Mary Beth's eyes started to flutter a little more, and Ryan was off the bed like a shot, kneeling in front of her. "MB?"

"My head," she slurred, her fingers going to her temple. Her dark red hair swung above her shoulders, and the freckles across the bridge of her nose stood out against her pale skin.

"You're okay," he said, cupping the back of her neck in one big hand. "You're fine." I wasn't sure if he was trying to use magic to convince her of that, or if he was just saying it in the normal, comforting boyfriend sense. In any case, Mary Beth didn't *look* fine. She was still blinking, her face flushed, her gaze muddled.

But it occurred to me that I might want to skedaddle before she came back fully and realized I was standing in her boyfriend's bedroom.

I didn't think that would go over particularly well, so I gave Ryan a little wave and mouthed, "Gonna go." He gave a distracted nod as I walked away.

Once I was outside, I took a minute to dig in the bushes around his house, trying to find the little pot of lip balm (and hoping no one saw me prowling around in Ryan Bradshaw's front garden). I finally felt it behind a camellia bush, and, pulling it out, rose to my feet. Ryan would definitely want the balm again, although maybe he'd be a little more careful with how much he used next time.

Chapter 11

"So, THE MALL?" I asked, starting my car. Bee sat in the passenger seat, her sunglasses on, elbow resting on the open window.

"Yup," she replied. "I need some normalcy."

Bee's second day back at school had been better than her first—fewer of the teachers seemed to think she was new, and Abi and Amanda had totally recognized her, which seemed to cheer her up. Brandon was still keeping his distance, though, and when I'd mentioned his name at lunch, Bee had cut me off with a shake of her head. "I don't want to talk about that."

After school, I'd planned on going home and doing a little more work on college stuff. That talk with The Aunts had reminded me that I'd been meaning to add at least two more schools to my application list. But then Bee had caught up with me and asked if we could have a "girls' afternoon," so here we were, heading toward the Pine Grove Galleria.

"Are you weirded out by Ryan and Mary Beth?" Bee suddenly asked, and I glanced over at her.

"Why would I be?" I asked, and she cut me a look.

"Okay," I acknowledged, turning right so that we could take

a shortcut through downtown, "it's a little weird, sure, but . . . not necessarily the bad kind of weird."

"Mary Beth hardly speaks to you." Bee twirled one long blond curl around her finger, still watching me, and I rolled my eyes.

"She barely spoke to me before except to be rude, so her dating Ryan isn't making much of a difference. And why does this bug you so much anyway?"

Bee shrugged, pulling up one leg so that she could wrap an arm around her knee. "Doesn't bug me. I'm just . . . curious. And an invested party, what with being your best friend and all."

That made me glance over at her. "Ryan, David, and I are all superheroes—as are you, I might add—and it's our romantic entanglements you wanna talk about?"

She laughed a little, more a huff of breath than a real chuckle. "I'm starting small."

"Are you sure things are—"

"They're fine, Harper," she said, and then shrugged, pulling her knee in tighter. "As fine as they're going to be, I guess."

I didn't know what to say to that, so instead of saying anything, I turned up the radio.

We were rounding the main square when Bee suddenly sat up in her seat, pointing to the statue of Adolphus Bridgeforth, one of Pine Grove's founders, that looked out over downtown. "Oh, man, someone vandalized poor Mr. Bridgeforth!"

I glanced over quickly, then did a double take, slamming on the brakes. Someone hadn't vandalized the statue. Someone had gouged marks into the stone around the base.

Wards. Right next to the other ones, the ones Saylor had put up to keep David safe.

My heart pounding, I turned the car so that we were heading toward Magnolia House.

"Harper?" Bee asked, twisting in her seat. "We're going the wrong way."

"Tiny detour," I promised.

Magnolia House, the huge mansion where Cotillion had been held, stood on a shady, oak-lined lane, but as we passed, I was able to see more marks on the wooden columns of the front porch. Another place where Saylor had her wards. They were still there, but now there were new ones next to them.

It had to be Alexander, or whoever he had working for him. But what did those wards do?

An hour or so later, I was the owner of two new pairs of shoes, a dress for Spring Fling, some new jeans, and a gorgeous Lilly Pulitzer skirt. Too bad none of that made me feel much better.

"You're making that face again," Bee said, nodding at me over a rack of cute rugby-striped shirts.

I shook my head, like that would somehow change my expression. I'd explained to Bee about the wards, but they were still on my mind. When Saylor had talked about the Ephors, I'd always pictured them in this more . . . administrative role, I guess. Guys in suits, pulling the strings, not guys with actual powers of their own. But Alexander had somehow managed to blow through the wards we'd put up, and now he was apparently setting up the Peirasmos all on his own. Were the new wards to help him, then? Or could wards, like, cancel one another out?

Adding to my irritation, I'd texted Ryan like five times about it, and had yet to get a reply. Funny how the one time I needed him to step up to the plate, he was missing in action.

"Lots on my mind," I told Bee.

She gave a sympathetic frown. "Nothing new on the trials?"

"Nothing," I said on a sigh. It had been a few days, and I knew we only had twenty-eight days—one full moon cycle, Alexander had said—to complete the Peirasmos, but other than Ryan's false alarm, nothing weird had happened at all.

Which felt weird in and of itself.

Now, I walked around the rack of clothes and looped my arm through Bee's, tugging her out of the store. "Come on. I have an angst only Cinnabon can cure."

When we got to the food court, Bee went off in search of drinks while I grabbed us a couple of cinnamon rolls.

By the time I got back, Bee was already at a table near the carousel, two Diet Cokes in front of her, and she pushed mine toward me as I sat down, along with a pale pink flyer.

"Look what I found!"

I took the flyer from her, raising my eyebrows. "The Miss Pine Grove Pageant?"

Bee took a sip of her drink and nodded. "We should do it."

Blinking, I chewed on the end of my straw and tried to think of the best way to answer that. A group of girls I recognized from school walked by, their arms laden down with bags, and Bee watched them pass with a wistful expression on her face.

But then she shook her head quickly, and turned back to the flyer, tapping it with one manicured nail. "Look at the date."

I did. "May first?" I read, and Bee nodded. "Last day of this moon cycle. Didn't Alexander say that the trials would take up one full moon cycle?"

He had, but all that had meant to me was that we had a nice timeline—almost a month. I hadn't considered what might be happening on any of those days.

"The Ephors are big drama queens, right?" Bee said, still looking at the flyer. "Look at what happened on the night of Cotillion." When she lifted her head, her eyes were brighter than I'd seen them in a long time. "The trials are going to be connected to *you*, which makes me think they'll be at school, or involve the town somehow. Stuff like that since that's, like, your whole wheelhouse."

Bee definitely had a point, and I wasn't sure what bugged me more: the idea of something big going down in front of my whole town again, or that she had had that idea and I hadn't.

When I didn't say anything, Bee gave a little shrug. "And, hey, if I'm wrong, it'll still be something kind of fun we did together. Something normal."

I couldn't help but snort at that. "Okay, Bee, I love you, but the Miss Pine Grove Pageant is far from normal. There is nothing normal about parading around in bathing suits and high heels." I didn't add that when my sister, Leigh-Anne, had done the pageant years ago, my parents had practically had a stroke over it. I didn't even want to think how they'd react to *me* wanting to do it.

Flashing me a look, Bee stirred her drink. "Oh, come on. It'll be fun. And it's not that much different from Cotillion."

It was worlds away from Cotillion, and I started to say that, but then Bee stabbed at her drink and said, "And, hey, maybe more people will remember I exist if I have a big honking tiara on my head."

She was joking, but the words still cut pretty deep, and I chewed on the end of my straw, thinking. I couldn't blame Bee for wanting some normalcy in her life after all that had happened to her. Besides, if she was right that this was when the last trial would happen, best to be prepared.

"It might look good on a college application," I acknowledged. "Showing a broad interest in things."

Bee smiled, her teeth straight and white. "Is that a yes?"

I thought of how The Aunts would react to the sight of another one of their nieces parading around in a swimsuit at the rec center and shuddered. "Do you promise I won't have to sing?"

Bee beamed at me. "Of course not." Then a dimple popped up in her cheek as she narrowed her eyes and added, "Besides, you're supposed to have an actual talent for the talent competition, Harper, and no one could call *your* singing a 'talent.'"

I tossed a balled-up napkin at her. "Ha-ha."

"Sign-ups for this are next week," I told Bee, tapping the flyer. "So you prepare answers about world peace, and I'll brush up on my baton skills."

Bee took the paper and folded it up, putting it in her purse. "Good deal." She glanced up then, her face brightening. "Oh, look, it's Ryan!"

I turned in my chair and our eyes met across the food court. For a second I thought that maybe he hadn't gotten my texts, but then I saw the guilt flickering across his face. I could tell he wanted to bolt, but it wasn't like he could pretend he hadn't seen me.

"Be right back," I said to Bee, then I walked as quickly as I could to where Ryan stood. He already had his hands shoved in his pockets, so I knew what he was going to say before he said it.

Still, I tried. "Did you get my texts?"

"Harper—"

"There are new wards set up around town, and I don't know what the heck they do."

"Yeah, I put them up."

I don't think my jaw has ever literally dropped before now. "What do you mean *you* put them up?"

"Alexander asked me to. It's part of the thing," he said, waving one hand. "The . . . peripatetic . . . peri—"

"Peirasmos," I hissed back. "And what do they do, exactly?"

Ryan's shoulders rolled underneath his shirt. "They just make sure David stays here. Like how Saylor's wards kept other people out, these keep him in."

The hairs on the back of my neck stood up. "Why would Alexander want to do that?"

"I don't know," Ryan admitted. "He just said it had something to do with the trials, and—"

"So Alexander has been in touch with you, but not me? And you . . . didn't bother to tell me?"

"It was literally two days ago, Harper. I was going to tell you, I promise, but . . . look, Mary Beth is weird about me spending time with you, and I'm trying to respect that."

It was one of the biggest struggles of my life not to roll my eyes at him right that second, but I managed admirably.

"I understand," I said, "but I've spent the past few days jumping at shadows over this thing. If you know anything about Paladin stuff, you have got to tell me. Especially about stuff that could be dangerous to David."

Ryan heaved a sigh, shoving his hands in his back pockets. "I'm trying, Harper. I seriously am, but—"

"This isn't easy on any of us," I reminded him, but Ryan shook his head.

"No, it's not, but you have to admit, it's a little easier on you and David than it is on me."

I looked up at him. "How do you figure that? David's visions make him feel like his head is splitting open, I'm worried about him, worried about me, and you, and Bee—"

Ryan leaned closer. "Look, I didn't say it was a freaking cakewalk for y'all, but at least you have each other. When you get your weird"—he waved his hands in the air around me— "Paladin feelings or David gets one of his visions, you can tell each other. David knows exactly what's going on with you, and you know exactly what's going on with him. You don't have to lie, either of you."

On the other side of the food court, the carousel was starting up again, the sound of tinkly calliope music filling the air. A little girl was tugging her mother toward a purple painted horse, and as I glanced over at them, I caught a glimpse of two blond heads making their way through the crowd.

Abi and Amanda. *Shoot.*

Grabbing Ryan's elbow, I tugged him into the little hallway where the bathrooms and water fountains were. "I understand that this isn't easy for you," I said once we were out of sight. "It isn't easy for me, either, and if you'd like a list of all the reasons why, I could make that for you. With annotations."

Ryan flicked a glance at the ceiling that wasn't quite an eye roll, but it was pretty close. Still, I kept going, tightening my fingers in the crook of his elbow. "You can't not tell me things, Ry. This whole . . . thing. None of it will work if we're not honest with each other."

Ryan looked down at me, his auburn brows raised. "Really? You wanna play that card when we've been lying to David about his visions since day one?"

I shook my head. "That's different. That's for his own safety."

Ryan blew out a deep breath. "You can keep saying that, Harper, but we can't keep lying to him. This Alexander guy is already promising David he can help him, but he doesn't *need* help. He couldn't have strong visions because *we* kept him from having them."

He reached out and covered my hand still resting on his arm with his own, his fingers curling around mine and squeezing. "We have to tell David the truth."

"Tell David the truth about what?"

Chapter 12

MARY BETH stood there, arms folded, mouth pressed into a tight line. As much as I hated myself for it, the words "This is not what it looks like" actually came out of my mouth, and from the way Ryan's eyes practically turned into hazel lasers, I could tell that he hated me for saying it, too.

I won't get into the details of all that happened next. Have you ever seen teenagers fight embarrassingly in public? It basically went like that. There was yelling and tears and Ryan trying to hug her while she yelled things like, "Don't touch me!"

Honestly, I tried to leave, but they were both blocking the entrance to the hallway, so in the end, I just stood there by the water fountains, wanting to die of humiliation. I mean, people were looking at us. Lots of people. And if Mary Beth hadn't finally ripped off her necklace, thrown it at Ryan's feet, and stormed off, I think a mall cop would've shown up, and then I would have had no choice but to change my name and leave town—heck, leave *Alabama*—forever.

Ryan didn't try to follow her this time. I guess once someone has thrown jewelry at your face and hollered about forgetting you exist, you sort of figure that ship has sailed. Instead, he squatted down and picked up the necklace, then stayed there, the chain dangling from his fingers, thumbs pressed against his eyebrows.

Bee came around the corner, arms full of bags, her eyes widening when she saw Ryan crouched on the ground and me standing right behind him, worrying my thumbnail with my teeth. As soon as I realized what I was doing, I made a disgusted sound and dropped my hand, wiping it on my skirt. I must've picked that up from David; he was always doing stuff like that.

Raising her eyebrows at me, Bee jerked her head toward Ryan.

"Mary Beth" was all I said, and she nodded.

As if his new ex-girlfriend's name was some sort of magic word, Ryan stood up abruptly, dropping the necklace into his pocket. "Well, that's effing great," he said, scrubbing his hands over his face.

Of course, he didn't actually say "effing," but it didn't bother me.

Tentatively, I laid a hand on his shoulder. "At least you don't have to worry about lying to her anymore?" I offered. We were still standing in the cramped little hallway, my hip almost right against a water fountain, and beyond us, people were still milling through the food court. Of all the places to go through a breakup, it was definitely low on glamour.

Lifting his head, Ryan looked at me. I'd known him almost my whole life. He was the first boy I'd ever kissed. The first boy I'd done . . . other stuff with, too. But in that moment, his handsome face drawn tight, he could've been a stranger.

"Whatever," he said, the word flat and heavy all at once.

I winced like he'd slapped me. Okay, maybe I hadn't been all that sympathetic to his issues with Mary Beth, but honestly, how did he think it was going to turn out? David and I were all tangled up with him, and there was no getting out of that. I was sorry he was hurt, but if he hadn't gotten involved with her in the first place, then none of this would have happened.

I think I might have actually said some of that, and probably ruined any chances I had of Ryan and me ever being friends again, but luckily, Bee stepped forward. Putting the shopping bags down, she laid her hand on Ryan's arm.

"Hey," she said, her voice warm and sweet. "Would you mind giving me a ride home? Harper drove us here, and she has to run back up to the school."

I didn't, and for a second, I frowned at her, confused. And then she gave me a little nod.

"Sure," Ryan said, his voice still blank, and as he turned to go, Bee looked over her shoulder at me, mouthing, "I'll talk to him."

That was good. Bee and Ryan had always gotten along, and if anyone could bring him back around to Team Harper, it was Bee.

I watched them walk off, then gathered up the shopping bags Bee had left with me and trudged out to the parking lot.

To my surprise, David's car was parked outside my house, and when I came in, Mom glanced up from the couch.

"There you are. David's in your room. Said the two of you had some kind of school project to work on?"

"Oh, right," I said, hanging my purse on the coatrack by the door next to my dad's truly heinous University of Alabama jacket. "Totally forgot, I was out shopping with Bee."

"Hope my American Express isn't smoking," Mom joked, and I pulled a face behind her back. I had indulged in a fair amount of retail therapy today.

As I jogged up the stairs, Mom called, "Door open, please!" and I rolled my eyes even as I called back, "Yes, ma'am!"

My parents had gotten pretty lenient with me and Ryan, I guess because they'd had a long time to get used to him. But something about David had made them hypervigilant on the propriety front, which was ironic, seeing as how me and David weren't . . . doing those things yet. I mean, we wanted to, and it's not like the subject hadn't come up, but the timing had never been right, and now with the trials and the Ephors, I wasn't sure when exactly things would get all consummated.

Certainly not now while my parents were downstairs, though. Gross.

When I pushed open my door, David was sitting in my desk chair, spinning idly. He stopped when he saw me, holding up his phone.

"So apparently you and Ryan caused a scandal at the Pine Grove Galleria today?"

Groaning, I dropped to the end of my bed. "It's already on Facebook?"

"Yup." He was looking at me from over the rims of his glasses, eyebrows raised. It was a familiar expression, and I'd always thought it was cute, but today, I wasn't sure what it meant, exactly.

With an exaggerated wince, I leaned back and put my hands

over my face. "That is so embarrassing. Almost as embarrassing as your shirt."

I heard the chair creak and then felt something nudge my knees. When I lifted my hands, David was leaning over me, his hands braced on either side of my head. There was still some space between us, but if my parents had walked in right then, well, let's just say David probably wouldn't have been allowed in my room anymore.

I didn't care. I let my hand rest on the back of his neck as he nuzzled the underside of my jaw.

"I happen to like this shirt."

"You happen to like all sorts of ugly things," I reminded him, even as I closed my eyes and let him dot kisses along the side of my neck. "That shirt, your car, like ninety-nine percent of your shoe collection—hey!"

I broke off laughing and rubbing the spot he'd poked on my ribs. "No fair," I said, lifting my head to give him a quick kiss. "You know I can't poke you back."

Smiling, David eased off me and sat on the floor. I slid down, too, sitting next to him and linking our hands as we both leaned back against my bed.

"So you aren't mad or jealous or weird?"

"I'm always weird," he acknowledged with a twist of his lips. "But mad or jealous? Nah. What's Ryan got that I don't have? I mean other than height and fabulous hair and cheekbones carved from granite."

I laughed and shook my head, tugging at his hair. "I like this. Most of the time."

David's lips brushed mine, briefly again, and I know I said I wouldn't do anything with my parents right downstairs, but I'd be lying if I said, in that moment, I didn't want to.

There were times things with David were weird—and I don't mean the Oracle stuff. We'd spent all our lives arguing, so this sudden shift to coupledom had been a tough transition in some ways. But when it was only the two of us, hanging out alone, we almost felt normal.

He pulled back again, returning to his chair. "Anything else happen at the mall?"

"I might have figured out at least one of the trials," I told him, handing over the flyer. "Same date as the last night of the moon cycle. Seems like a possibility, at least."

David's eyes scanned the paper. "They do seem to like picking big events for maximum damage, don't they?" he murmured. He glanced up at me then, quirking an eyebrow. "Will you twirl a baton?" he asked. "Please promise me a baton will be involved. And, like, huge hair."

I swatted at him. "You know I despise pageants. But I'm doing this for the greater good. And, hey"—I shrugged—"maybe it will make me look even more well rounded on my college applications."

"Well, as long as that's the only reason," he said with a shudder, and a little sizzle of irritation buzzed through me.

"It's not like the pageant is that big of a deal," I told him. "And Bee wanted do it."

That wiped the smirk off his face. Brows drawing together,

he shifted so his elbows rested on his knees. "How is she? After the other day?"

I picked up one of the throw pillows from my bed, tugging at the embroidery. "She's . . . okay. Obviously still shaken up and trying to come to terms with all of this."

David nodded, then reached up to scratch his shoulder through his ugly T-shirt. "I'm sorry," he said.

I looked up, surprised. "What do you have to be sorry for?"

He frowned, clasping his hands in front of him. "If I didn't suck so much at being an Oracle, maybe I could've found her earlier, you know?"

I dropped my gaze from him, watching my fingers as they traced over the little flower on the pillow. Aunt Martha had made this for me. Or had it been Aunt May? One of them. And maybe if I stared hard enough at the stitches, David wouldn't see the guilt on my face. If I hadn't messed around with his visions, could he have seen Bee?

David sat back in my chair, and it creaked slightly. "And of course now, I'm completely useless."

There was a bitterness in his voice I hadn't heard in a long time, and I set the pillow back on my bed, getting up to go to him. "Hey," I said softly, brushing a hand over his jaw. The stubble there was rough against my fingers, and when David looked up, I moved my hand to the back of his neck. "Just because you can't see the future right now doesn't mean you're useless."

One corner of his mouth kicked up in a smile. Or a grimace. "I guess I could make a dirty joke about what uses you might have for me," he said, and I rolled my eyes, letting my hand drop away from his neck.

"What I *meant*," I told him, going back to sit on the edge of my bed, "is that David Stark the person is worth a lot more to me than David Stark the Oracle."

Snorting, David crossed his feet at the ankle. "Yeah, well, David Stark the person just annoyed you. He didn't ruin your life."

There it was again, that bitterness I definitely didn't like. "Could you not say stuff like that?" I snapped. "I think I can decide who and what ruins my life."

Downstairs, I could hear pans rattling as Mom started dinner, and Dad's low voice talking on the phone. David glanced toward the door and heaved a sigh.

"I'm sorry, Pres," he said before standing up. "I'm embracing my inner emo, I guess."

I stood up, too, crossing the room to wrap my arms around his waist. "Well, that would explain the T-shirt."

He smiled then, a real smile, and after he kissed me, I said, "Why don't you stay for dinner? I don't like the thought of you in that big house alone."

David's expression didn't change, but I could feel his hands tighten on my waist. Then he shook his head and stepped back. "Thanks, but I'm not great company tonight. Besides, I have some stuff I need to work on for school."

I was going to ask what stuff exactly, but David was already picking up his bag and heading for the door. I walked him down, stopping so that he could say good night to my parents, and then followed him out to where his car was parked in the driveway. He opened the door and threw his satchel inside before turning back to me, that familiar wrinkle between his brows. "Sometimes I wonder what would happen if I just drove out of town, you know?"

His tone was casual, but something about those words made goose bumps break out all over my body. "You can't," I told him, my voice stiff. "I mean, right now, you literally can't since Alexander had Ryan put up all these wards, but—"

Shoving his hands in his pockets, David leaned forward a little. "What? Why?"

"I don't know," I confessed. "Apparently the one time Ryan decided to take the initiative, it potentially screwed us over."

With a groan, David tipped his head back. "It would be awesome," he said, "if people would stop doing things that affect me without, you know, asking how I might feel about those things."

I swallowed hard.

David tilted his head back down and gave me a steady look, his hands still in his pockets. For a moment, I thought my guilt must show clearly on my face.

But he didn't ask me anything about his visions. Instead, he studied me and asked, "If you could do it all over again, don't pretend that you never would have gone into the bathroom that night."

I blinked, thinking about Bee. About Saylor and the Cotillion and all the lying I'd done to my family.

Smiling as best as I could, I raised up on tiptoes and kissed him. "Of course I would have."

Chapter 13

"So THIS IS a thing that's happening?" David asked as he sat against the fence in my backyard.

Pulling my hair up into a high ponytail, I sighed around the rubber band in my mouth. "Yes," I mumbled. "And if you mock it, I'll never ask you to come back."

"No mocking," David replied, laying his arms on his upraised knees. His wrists looked bony underneath the cuffs of his (both ugly and seasonally inappropriate) plaid button-down. "You're going to train for whatever trials the Ephors may have coming your way by . . . spinning a baton? Because I was honestly kidding about that earlier."

Hair secured, I propped my hands on my hips. "It's not like I can practice dagger swinging or karate kicks in the backyard. But baton twirling is totally socially acceptable, and it lets me both work on my agility and wield what *could* be a weapon." I gave the baton a few experimental twirls, and David laughed.

"Your ability to multitask is truly extraordinary, Pres."

He looked back at the book he had spread open on the grass, and I tossed the baton up, catching it easily. "What are you reading?" I asked, and he raised his head, sunlight flashing off his glasses.

"Still looking through some of Saylor's books for stuff about the Peirasmos."

"Anything?" I asked, but he shook his head.

"Not yet. But Saylor had a *lot* of books."

I kept twirling, but watched him out of the corner of my eye. "And you? You feeling okay?"

"Sure," he said, the word clipped off and sharp in his mouth. He didn't look up at me, and something in my stomach twisted.

"David," I said, and he sighed, tapping his pen furiously against the page.

"It's just irritating, that's all. Being completely useless, power-wise. If I could just see something . . ." He broke off with a frustrated noise. "My visions might have been stupid before, but at least I could have them." Shaking his head, he leaned back against the fence. "No idea why everyone is working so hard to protect me when I'm not exactly worth much."

It was the second time he'd said something like that, and I still didn't like it. Part of that, I knew, was the guilt. But warding him had been for his own good, I thought again. To keep him safe and keep him . . . well, *him.*

But I'd tried to ignore how that was making David feel, especially when he was all alone in Saylor's house, with nothing but his own thoughts to keep him company. David was a smart guy, and ever since I'd known him, he'd had a bad tendency to over-think things. I knew he'd been sitting there at night, brooding over all of this.

Now, he tipped his head back and studied the sky, bright blue through the oak leaves overhead. "I'm trying to help by going through all these books, but nothing there is all that helpful, and I . . ." Trailing off, he pushed his hands under his glasses, scrubbing his face. "If something happens to you during all of this, Harper—"

I set the baton down and walked over to stand in front of him, catching his chin in my fingers and tilting his head up to look at me. "Nothing is going to," I told him. "We got through Cotillion, and we'll get through this, too."

David's eyes were nearly as blue as the sky above, and as they searched my face, I could tell he didn't believe me. But he dropped the subject, picking up the baton I'd laid down on the grass.

"I'm still having trouble wrapping my mind around you twirling this thing in a *pageant*," David said, idly toying with it as he stood up.

I took it from him with a skeptical frown. "It's a traditional choice," I admitted. "And my Paladin skills mean that I'm weirdly good with it."

David laughed at that. "Seriously? Thousands of years of knowledge and training have resulted in the ability to spin a baton?"

"Yup," I replied. "Check this out." With that, I tossed the baton from hand to hand, spinning it furiously as I did. The metal rod slid easily through my fingers, and I realized that in the right circumstances, this thing could actually be a pretty impressive weapon.

But I hoped that the right circumstances never occurred.

Braining someone with a baton was not on my agenda any time soon.

Tossing the baton high in the air, I added a backflip before coming down solidly on both feet and catching the baton with one hand. I used the other hand to give a little wave, and David looked at me with a grin.

"Okay, now you're showing off."

"Little bit," I admitted, glad that we were talking like normal people again. I tossed him the baton.

"Maybe you should start carrying one of these things," he mused as he inspected it.

He looked at the rubber end over the top of his glasses, squinting slightly, and I leaned over and smacked a kiss on his cheek. That was one of my favorite David faces.

"I'll stick with my dagger," I told him as he let the baton drop back on the grass.

He laughed. "I think the baton would be a little less conspicuous."

I shook my head. "No way. And then I'd have to join the marching band as a majorette to make up an excuse for carrying it around all the time." With a dramatic sigh, I tipped my head back to look at the sky. "And I've already had to join the paper and now I'm going to sign up for a pageant . . ."

David closed his notebook. "Admit that you kind of like the paper."

Wrinkling my nose, I shuddered. "No. It is a necessary evil."

But I couldn't stop smiling a little bit, and David pointed at me. "Aha! You do like it! In fact, you *love* the paper."

"Do not!" I insisted, but he was fully dedicated to teasing me now.

"You love the paper so much you're thinking of studying journalism at college instead of poli-sci."

"Ignoring you," I said in a singsong as I scooped my baton off the grass and started twirling it again.

David sat back down on the grass, wrapping his arms around his knees as he watched me. "It's too late. I know your secret heart."

Feeling better, I kept spinning the baton, tossing it and catching it, watching the sunlight glint off the silver. I was still practicing when the back gate opened and Bee walked inside, also dressed in a T-shirt and shorts.

"Have you come to mock with David?" I asked, and she shook her head, a few tendrils of hair coming loose from her own ponytail.

"I actually thought we should join forces on our talent. Do some kind of dual baton thing. Especially if I'm right about the pageant being one of the trials."

"That was Bee's idea?" When I glanced back, David was sitting up a little straighter, his eyebrows raised. "I thought you put that together, Pres."

Irritation bubbled up in me, which was probably stupid, since what did it matter whose idea it had been? But I didn't like the sharp, interested way David was looking at Bee. He was thinking . . . something. I wasn't sure what, but the wheels were clearly turning.

I shrugged, sweat rolling down my spine. The late afternoon

was getting warmer, and I was about to suggest going in when Bee held out one hand. "Here," she said, nodding toward the baton. "Let me try."

The baton was a little slick with my sweat—more from the warmth of the day than from any real effort—but I tossed it to her.

The baton turned end over end in the air, but before it had even completed one full rotation, Bee had launched into a forward handspring unlike anything I'd ever seen her do in cheerleading. Heck, Bee had been so bad at jumps that it was sort of a joke. She'd always said it was because she was too tall, but apparently that wasn't a problem anymore.

Bee was a blur of motion, and then the baton was in her hands before rising back into the sky. Another series of easy, effortless flips, and she caught it again, beaming at me triumphantly.

And then from the fence, I heard David breathe, "Holy crap. She's better than you."

Chapter 14

"Okay, well, let's not go that far," I joked, and Bee stepped up beside me, frowning at David.

"No, I'm not," she said, but David was already standing up, shaking his head.

"No, no, I didn't mean, like, *better* better," he said as he shoved his hands into his back pockets. "I just meant . . . you're good. It's one thing to know you're a Paladin, but it's another to see it in action, I guess."

David was still watching both of us, eyes bright behind his glasses. "What if . . ." He stopped, holding up both hands even though neither Bee nor I had said anything. "Hear me out," he added, and I knew that whatever was going to come next was not going to be something I'd like.

"Okay, so if Harper fails the Peirasmos, you become my Paladin, right?"

Bee shifted her weight, looking at David like he'd started speaking a foreign language. "Harper can't *fail* the trials," she said, and I noticed her fingers tightening around the baton. "She'll die."

"I know that," David said. "But is there any way she could maybe, I don't know, opt out? Let you take over?" He lifted his hands. "Not that I want *you* to die, obviously."

The words hit me square in the chest. "You don't want me to be your Paladin?" I asked, and David's gaze swung to me.

"Don't you get it?" he asked. "It's *perfect*." David was practically bouncing on the balls of his feet, his blue eyes bright when they looked over at me. "This is the solution to everything, Pres. *Bee* can be my Paladin, she can do this"—he waved one hand in the air—"Peirasmos thing, and we can just be us."

He was smiling so big, looking happier than I'd seen him look in a long time, and all I could do was stare at him, suddenly cold despite the warm afternoon.

"But . . . Bee doesn't want to do those things." I turned to her, pushing a stray strand of hair off my forehead. "You have powers, and that's awesome, but this is my problem. I'm not going to foist it off on you to make my life easier."

David blinked rapidly, like I'd smacked him in the face. "Pres," he said, shaking his head again, "we're not talking about making Bee do anything she can't do."

Now the cold was fading, and I felt something hot and angry rise up inside of me. "She was kidnapped," I said, gesturing toward Bee with my baton, "and she just got back, and you want her to go through something that might kill her?"

He frowned, eyes darting to Bee. She was still standing there, arms folded over her chest, watching the two of us. Even though we were talking about her, I had the sense that she wanted to stay out of this.

"Of course I don't, but I don't know why you're being so stubborn about this. If Bee can be my Paladin, that makes things less complicated for us."

"And totally screws up her life," I argued. "My life is already screwed up, so we might as well leave things the way they are."

Tugging at his hair, David tipped his head back to look at the sky. "Or maybe you *like* doing everything in the whole freaking world."

"Like?" My voice got louder. I wasn't shouting, not yet, but we were getting close. "No, I don't *like* having to do all of this, but that's the way it goes. Sorry that I won't throw my best friend away so you can have a regular girlfriend. Not that *you* could ever be a regular boyfriend, so what does it even matter?"

"Everything okay out here?"

I turned to see my dad sticking his head out the back door. His expression was fairly mild, but I saw the grip he had on the doorknob.

Taking a deep breath, I made myself smile. "Yup!" I called brightly. "Practicing for debate club!" I gave Dad a little wave, but he jerked his head, beckoning me over.

Hiding a sigh, I jogged away from David and Bee, up the porch steps and into the kitchen.

It was cooler in there, the air-conditioning nearly making me shiver. "Harper Jane, I know you're not in the debate club," Dad said as he walked over to the island.

I tried very hard not to fidget as he braced his hands on the counter and fixed me with a look, his eyes as green as mine. He was wearing a polo shirt and khaki shorts, plus there was a slight sunburn on his balding head, so I guessed golf had been on the agenda earlier.

"It's nothing," I told him with a little toss of my head. "Typical me-and-David stuff."

Dad frowned. "You never yelled at Ryan like that."

"Sure I did," I said, even though when I thought back, I realized that was a lie. "You just never heard me. And seriously, Dad, this is no big deal. Promise."

Another lie. I was furious, nearly shaking with anger at the idea that David wanted me to offer up Bee like some kind of Get Out of Paladin Life Free card. And if there was a part of me that didn't necessarily like giving up control, well . . . I could think about that later.

Now, I just smiled at Dad. "I'm going to head back out there now," I said. "I promise not to bean David with my baton. But if I do, luckily I know a good lawyer."

Dad rolled his eyes, but I could tell he was trying not to smile. "I'm a tax attorney, honey. You murder someone, that's on you."

I grinned back, then thought of Dr. DuPont, my shoe sticking out of his neck. What would my dad think if he knew I already *had* killed someone? That I was about to go through some kind of tests that might end with me killing more people? Or someone killing *me*?

When I went back outside, David and Bee were sitting near the fence, talking. As I approached, whatever conversation they'd been having died, and David nodded at the house.

"Is your dad going to kill me?" His thin shoulders hunched forward, one ankle crossed in front of the other.

"Not today," I said with a cheer I didn't feel.

David's eyes met mine, and I could tell there was more he wanted to say. This argument wasn't over yet, and that made me feel a weird combination of sad and frustrated. Why couldn't he see that this was the best way to handle things?

Leaning down, David grabbed his bag. "So I'm gonna head home," he said. "See you tomorrow, Pres?"

"Yeah," I told him, walking over and slipping an arm around his waist before going up on tiptoe to press a quick kiss against his lips, willing him to let this go, to let us be okay.

He kissed me back, but when I pulled away, that wrinkle was still between his brows. "See you tomorrow," I said, ignoring the wrinkle. "Don't forget, we have an assembly bright and early, and I want to see you in the front row."

Nodding, David smiled the littlest bit. "Got it. See you then." He waved to Bee, then let himself out the back gate.

After he was gone, I turned back to Bee. "So you want to work on more baton twirling?"

A wide grin split Bee's face, and overhead, the sun filtered through the leaves, leaving pretty dappled shadows on her skin. "Or we could practice something else."

With that, she lunged at me.

Instinct took over, and I dodged, dropping to sweep my leg underneath her feet. But she was quick, and leapt away from my kick with a laugh.

And then it was on.

In a weird way, it was like we were back in cheerleading

practice. Bee and I had always been a great team, and nothing had changed. Every punch she threw, I countered. Every kick, I matched. And when she caught me by my wrist, flipping me over her back, I actually laughed at the sheer *fun* of it. Not only did I have my best friend back, but I finally had someone who could train with me, who could let me release my abilities to their full extent.

When Bee and I were done, we were both sweating and breathing hard, but we were also smiling, so much that my cheeks ached.

We sat on the grass, and from beyond the fence, I could hear a car driving down our street. The wind rustled through the leaves overhead, and birds were singing. It could not have been a more perfect spring day, but I couldn't help the little chill that went down my spine. It wasn't the sense of dread and pain that came when David was in trouble—it wasn't nearly intense enough for that—but I frowned anyway.

"Bee," I ventured, "you know what David said . . . I'd never want you to do that for me. I wouldn't ask you to."

She glanced over at me, the breeze blowing wisps of blond hair into her face. "I know that, Harper. But I would. If you needed me to."

I shifted on the grass, scratching a spot behind my knee. "Bee, I know this isn't something you really want to talk about, but . . . when you were with Alexander, did he train you?"

I couldn't tell if the look in Bee's eyes was wary or embarrassed, but in either case, her gaze slid away from me and she gave a little shrug. "Sort of. There was a room there with these dummies I could kick, but no weapons."

"Makes sense," I muttered, then leaned closer to her. "And you never saw anyone but Alexander?"

She shook her head. "That girl who took me, Blythe. She was there at first, but she was gone within a day or two. Other than that . . ." Trailing off, she shaded her eyes, studying a bright blue bird perched on our privacy fence. "It was just him."

I frowned and settled back against the tree trunk. "I don't get it. The Ephors are supposed to be this . . . group. Like the Illuminati or something. Why is he the only one who seems to be in charge of anything?"

At that, Bee looked at me, resting her cheek on her raised knees. "Maybe he's an overachiever," she suggested, and that dimple appeared in her cheek again. "*Maybe*," she added, "he's the *you* of the Ephors and doesn't like delegating."

I bumped her with my own raised knees. "I guess that's possible, but still, it seems weird, right?"

With a long sigh, Bee leaned her head back, the sunlight and the leaves casting shadows on her face. "What about this isn't?" she asked.

She had a point.

For a while, we were silent, both lost in our thoughts, and I was actually a little startled when Bee said, "I feel sorry for him."

"Alexander?" I asked, wrinkling my nose, and she shook her head.

"David. Having powers you don't really get, people trying to kill you, people trying to keep you safe, and not being able to do anything about any of it. I mean, it's not easy for you or Ryan, either," she added, tucking a loose strand of hair behind one ear, "but y'all get to be *active* instead of waiting for other people to fix things."

Stretching out my legs, I let my head drop back against the trunk, too. "I never thought of it like that, exactly. Is that what y'all were talking about earlier?"

Bee unfolded her legs, mimicking my posture. "Kind of. He was apologizing for asking me to do the Peirasmos. Said he's spent a lot of time trying to come up with solutions, and that one just occurred to him before he really thought it through."

I definitely felt better about that, but it was still a little weird to think of David and Bee, like, sharing confidences and stuff.

"I don't think there is a solution to all of this," I told her, and Bee looked over at me.

"That's . . . depressing."

I laughed, but it sounded a little forced. "It's not so bad," I said. "Once David gets his powers back and under control, I'm sure having a future-telling boyfie will be the best, plus I get to be a ninja, and that's always fun—"

Bee reached out and laid a hand on my shoulder. "Harper," she said, and I recognized her "don't give me that BS" look. It was something about the way she tilted her head down, making me meet her eyes.

"Okay," I conceded, crossing one ankle over the other. "It sucks. It sucks a lot. But it's the way things are, and there's no way to change it."

Her hand fell away, fingers playing in the grass between us. "If David did just leave . . ."

I sat up, looking at her more sharply. "Did he mention that to you, too?"

She didn't look up, using one nail to split a blade of grass. "A little, but apparently there are wards keeping him here for the time being?" Now she lifted her gaze. "What would happen if he broke them?"

Surprised, I blinked at her. "I . . . don't know, honestly. I guess it would hurt him, or do something bad."

It was a little embarrassing to admit that I knew so little about something so major, but Bee only gave a slight hum and split another piece of grass.

Chapter 15

I GET THAT most people think that school assemblies are totally boring, and they're not always wrong—if I never have to sit through another meeting on selling wrapping paper to raise money for the Grove, it will be too soon—but I was actually looking forward to Friday morning's. Maybe it was because I got to speak before it started, and I always enjoyed things like that, especially now. There was something comfortingly normal about walking up to the podium and speaking confidently to the other students, even if it was only about upcoming service projects and the Spring Fling. It reminded me that there were still things in my life I controlled.

Or maybe I was psyched because I got to talk about the dance. In any case, I sat in the folding chair next to Lucy McCarroll, the sophomore class president. I'd dressed nicely today, wearing a yellow-and-green Lilly Pulitzer dress Mom had gotten for me on a shopping trip to Mobile. Headmaster Dunn made his remarks first, reminding us about upcoming ACT dates and not to leave litter in the parking lot and to remember that "after last year's unfortunate incident with farm animals in the band room," senior pranks were expressly forbidden. It may not have been a display of great manners, but I scanned the bleachers in front of us as he droned on. I spotted Bee almost immediately, sitting next to Ryan, and I smiled.

She grinned back, giving me a little wave, and then leaned over to say something to Ryan. His gaze flicked toward me, but I couldn't read his expression. Apparently the Mary Beth incident was still an issue. Which was fine, since the whole defacing-the-wards-and-not-telling-me thing was very much an issue as far as I was concerned. So I let my gaze move away from him, searching out David.

Who was . . . not there.

I spotted Chie and Michael talking to each other on the very top bleacher, clearly not listening to Headmaster Dunn. So where was David? He always sat with them, and if he wasn't there, then I'd expect him to be next to Bee and Ryan. I'd told him I was going to speak this morning, and, hey, even if I hadn't, assemblies were mandatory.

There was no tightness in my chest, no sense that anything was wrong with him, but still, it was weird.

I racked my brain, trying to remember if I'd seen him this morning, all while studying the note card in my hand like I was going over my remarks. Okay, yes, he'd been in the parking lot, wearing some atrocious shade of green. So where—

Lucy's elbow nudged my ribs, and I realized the gym was quiet, Headmaster Dunn waiting expectantly by the podium.

Shoot.

Rattled, I stood up, smoothing my skirt down over my thighs with one hand while the other clutched my note card. I usually breezed right through things like this, but right now I was unsettled. When I stepped up to the podium, the microphone released a shriek of feedback as I adjusted it, and I winced, tucking my hair behind my ear.

"Sorry about that," I said with a pained smile. "Anyway, um, good morning, Grove Academy. As you know, I'm Harper Price, your SGA president, and I wanted to mention a few upcoming—"

It hit me like a brick.

One moment, I was fine, albeit nervous; the next, I was gasping and clutching both sides of the podium, my entire upper body in a vise. I could feel sweat break out all over me, prickling at my hairline and my spine, and when I managed to open my eyes, I saw that Bee had risen to her feet and was already moving toward me.

"Harper—" Headmaster Dunn said, laying a beefy hand on my shoulder.

I gritted my teeth, my knees feeling weak and watery, adrenaline racing through me, alarm bells going off in my head.

No, wait. Those weren't in my head.

It was the fire alarm.

Easing me out of the way, Headmaster Dunn faced the six hundred or so students in the bleachers. "All right, kids," he said easily enough, but I saw the furrows around his mouth deepen. "You know the drill. Orderly line, out the main doors and into the courtyard."

It was a drill we ran at least twice a semester, and Headmaster Dunn's calm baritone voice kept everyone from panicking as they began to file out of the bleachers.

Everyone but me.

I stood there, waiting until the last person disappeared through the big double doors, and then I turned, heading for the back doors of the gym. Those were the ones that led to the main school buildings, and that, I knew as surely as I knew anything, was where David was.

Headmaster Dunn's hand on my arm stopped me.

"Whoa there, Miss Price," he said with a friendly smile. "Wrong way, sweetheart."

"I need to get my bag," I said lamely, and he shook his head.

"You know the rules," he said, his thick eyebrows drawing together. Under the gym lights, his bald head gleamed. "Way more important that you get out okay than that your stuff makes it. Come on."

There was no thinking. I drew back the arm he was holding, fast enough that it surprised him, throwing him slightly off balance. I saw his eyes go wide for a second, and his mouth made an almost perfect O shape as he stumbled.

A knee to his outer thigh had him dropping lower, and then, with his hand still clutching me, I drew back my free arm and elbowed him in the temple, hard.

He dropped like a sack of rocks, eyes rolling back in his head, and trust me, I felt *super* bad about it.

But David came first, and every cell in my body was urging me to get to him, get to him *now*.

Alarms were still going off, and as I entered the main building, I could smell smoke, acrid and bitter.

Heart racing, I made my way to the English hall, where the journalism lab was. He was there, I could feel it, and underneath all my worry, all my Paladin senses going crazy, there was this little flicker of irritation.

I'd told him I was speaking this morning, told him I'd wanted to see him, and instead, he'd skipped the assembly to do stuff for the paper. It shouldn't have been as annoying as it was, but for whatever reason, it seriously bugged me. I did stuff that was important for him, right? I'd joined the stupid paper, and—

I rounded the corner, and all of my anger vanished. One entire end of the English hall was in flames. I don't know what I'd expected, but that was definitely not it. It seemed to be pouring out of the janitor's closet at the end of the hall, and for a second I froze, watching flames lick up against the walls, consuming the banners SGA had hung for the Spring Fling, racing along posters, flickering in a huge pool underneath the closet door.

My heart hammered against my ribs, my stomach twisting, and I felt legitimate panic surge through me, even underneath all my "David's in danger" feelings. The classrooms—

Were empty, I remembered with a wave of relief. The assembly had seen to that. But as I made my way farther down the hall, I couldn't help but think that if they *hadn't* been, if there had been students trapped in there, I wouldn't have been able to save them. Not until I knew David was safe.

It was a disturbing thought, and I made myself shove it away, trying to focus on what was happening.

There was another smell mixed in with the smoke, a heavy, chemical odor, and I wondered if some of the cleaning products had exploded or something. And then I looked again at that spreading pool of flame, and with a sudden jolt, I realized that it wasn't spilled bleach or ammonia. It was gasoline.

Someone had set that fire on purpose, and I thought I had a pretty good idea of who.

Of course, none of that mattered right now. Right now, the main thing was getting to David. Throwing an arm over my face, I ran to the journalism lab. The fire was only a few yards or so away, and the doorknob was already warm to the touch as I twisted it.

My eyes watered as I scanned the room, but there was no sign of David.

Still, he had to be here. I felt it. "David!" I called, rushing in and bumping into a desk. It screeched across the linoleum, and I called again. "David!"

And then I saw his messenger bag propped against the door of the darkroom.

Several years ago, some parents whose kids had been super into photography had donated the funds to have the darkroom installed in the newspaper lab, but hardly anyone used it anymore.

Except David.

The little light over the door was on, showing that it was in use, but I ignored that, flinging open the door to stare at David, who whirled around to glare over the top of his glasses.

When he saw it was me, the glare lessened a bit, but he still didn't seem thrilled. "Pres, you know you can't open—"

Then he stopped, lifting his nose. "Wait, are the alarms going off? Is that smoke?"

Without answering, I reached in, grabbed him by the sleeve of his ratty sweater, and tugged him out of the darkroom.

I could already hear the wailing of sirens as I pulled David through the empty halls of the school, heading for the doors that led to the courtyard. He was safe now, so I didn't feel like my chest was in a vise, but my stomach still churned. The English hall hadn't totally gone up in flames, but the damage was going to be huge. We'd probably have to move classes out of there for the rest of the semester, a thought that made me feel angry and sad and sick. My *school*. The place I'd spent so much of my time trying to make perfect. But since I couldn't even begin to process that right now, I turned to David.

"Why were you in there?" I asked over the various sirens, and David pushed his glasses up the bridge of his nose.

"I forgot that I had some photographs I wanted to develop, and the assembly seemed like a good time to get them done."

Now that David wasn't in imminent danger of becoming charcoal, I whirled on him right there by the front doors. "I told you I was speaking this morning."

He frowned, folding his arms over his chest. "Yeah, but just about the dance, right? You already told me everything you were going to say."

It was the worry getting to me, I think, the worry and the knowledge that my school had been attacked and pretty seriously damaged. I couldn't freak out about all of that right now, but I could snap at David. "So you didn't care?"

He blinked at me. "Are we seriously going to do this here?"

He was right; now was definitely not the time, but if I could have shoved him out the door, I think I would have. Instead, I opened it and steered him toward the steps. "Go to your car. I'll meet you there in a minute."

David ran a hand over his sandy blond hair, ruffling it. "You're going back in there?" he asked, and I nodded.

"I knocked Headmaster Dunn unconscious, so I should probably deal with that."

His eyebrows lifted up into his hairline, but he didn't say anything else, jogging down the steps toward the group of students milling around on the grass.

I darted back inside, running back for the gym, trying to tell myself that it wasn't that big of a deal that David hadn't come to the assembly. I was probably just mad because it had put him in danger.

But then, as I rounded the corner back toward the gymnasium, I realized: If this *was* one of the trials, why on earth would the Ephors put David in danger? They said they wanted him.

Unless this was all a trick, and I was right about Alexander being evil.

Man, I really hoped I was right.

When I got back to the gym, I was surprised to see Ryan there, kneeling next to Headmaster Dunn, who was trying to stand.

"You okay, Headmaster?" Ryan asked, easing a hand under the man's elbow. "You seriously whacked your head on that podium."

Ryan could annoy the ever-living heck out of me, but right now, I was so grateful, I could have cried. Somehow, he must've known I'd need him, and I smiled at him as I came to help him get Headmaster Dunn to his feet.

"It's these gym floors," I said. "Super slippy."

But then Headmaster Dunn looked at me, his expression dark, his face nearly purple. "Gym floors?" he repeated. "You *hit* me, Miss Price."

Panicked, I looked at Ryan, who was staring back at me, confused. He gave a tiny shake of his head, and I could smell the rose balm in the air. He'd used the mind-wipe stuff, so why wasn't it working?

"Young lady, you are coming to my office right now," he continued, shaking his head as though he couldn't believe he was saying those words. *I* couldn't believe he was saying those words.

I'd already told David to meet me at his car so we could get to Alexander's and find out what the heck had happened. If I went with Headmaster Dunn now, I had a feeling I'd be in his office for a while. They'd have to call my parents. Oh God, or the police. Or my parents *and* the police. Honestly, what was the point of having someone who could do mind-wiping magic if the freaking mind-wiping magic didn't work?

Two choices stared me right in the face. Either I stayed here and I dealt with this, or I took off for my car and got to David and Alexander. If I did that, maybe I could get some answers about why one of the trials involved nearly killing David, and why Ryan's magic wasn't working.

I took a deep breath and blurted out, "Headmaster, I'm sorry about all of this, and I promise there's an explanation." Behind him, Ryan was already shaking his head and mouthing my name. "But I . . . I have to go."

And with that, I took off running.

Chapter 16

We took David's car out to Alexander's and spent most of the drive in silence. I wondered if I should text my parents, but I figured the school had already called them. *Later*, I thought, turning my phone off. Whatever was happening, we'd get to the bottom of it, and soon this whole unpleasant morning would be wiped away, either by Ryan's magic or by whatever Alexander could do.

"If this is a trial," David said, lifting one hand so he could push his glasses up his nose, "why put me in danger? That seems counterproductive."

"Who knows?" I replied. "In case you forgot, they're insane killer people who sent crazy witches to murder you last year, so we shouldn't be that surprised when they do, you know, crazy murderous things."

My heart was still pounding, an intense mix of irritation and fear shooting through me, and I focused on the green fields flying past, trying to calm my temper.

My school. The place I worked so hard to make nice and safe, and they'd used it as one of their . . . their testing grounds. They'd damaged it, set it on fire, could've freaking *destroyed* it for good.

That was so seriously not okay.

Next to me, David drummed his fingers on the steering wheel. "I read Alexander's mind, Harper. He didn't want to hurt me, I could feel it."

"Maybe you were wrong," I answered, but he shook his head as he turned the car onto the dirt road leading to the house.

"I'm just saying, hear the guy out before you go in there guns blazing."

Twisting in my seat, I faced David. "*Hear him out?* Even if he set the Grove on fire?"

David didn't answer, but kept watching the road, and I flopped back into my seat with a huff.

"Well, if they did set it, they must have kept an eye on you and known you weren't where you were supposed to be."

I didn't exactly hear David sigh. It was more like I *felt* it, a shiver of irritation that ran through him. "I'm sorry I wasn't at the assembly," he said in the most even tone known to man. "But I had something I needed to do, and I didn't think you'd mind."

"Something you *wanted* to do," I countered, and I got the sense he was counting to ten in his head.

"Let's focus on the task at hand, okay?"

"Fine by me."

When we pulled up to Alexander's, the late morning sun was playing on the windows, making them sparkle, and I was struck again by what a pretty place this was. Had this been what the original house looked like, or had Alexander—or a Mage, I was guessing—made it to suit himself? In any case, I liked it.

Too bad the person inside was a total jerk.

The car was barely in park before I was out of it, heading up the front steps with David close behind.

"Should we knock?" David asked, and I glared at the big wooden door in front of us.

"Oh, I'm going to knock," I told him, and gave the door a vicious kick. Even if the magic on this place kept me from being able to break in, kicking it was still pretty satisfying.

But the door flew open with a splintering crack when the flat of my foot hit it. David stepped back with a muttered "Whoa," but I was already moving into the house.

"Alexander!" I called. "Hey! Anybody home?"

"There's no need for screaming, Miss Price," Alexander said, appearing on the landing. He was wearing another suit, this one black, and smiling pleasantly at me like I hadn't just kicked in his front door.

"I disagree," I told him. "I usually feel pretty screamy when someone attacks my school."

His brows drew together as he made an exaggeratedly puzzled expression. "Did I not tell you that the trials would be coming up very soon? Or are you confused as to what the trials entail?"

"Actually, yes, I am confused," I said, my heart still pounding. Even though David was safe now, I could still feel a sort of residual ache in my chest. "Because I expected someone to come after *me*. I didn't think you'd put my entire school in danger."

Alexander gave one of those little smiles I hated so much.

"Well, if we let you face the expected, that would hardly serve the point of going through trials, now would it?"

"You could have hurt innocent people," I told him, my face hot. "You could've killed them. You could have made our school a smoldering pile of ash, and all for what? For some test?"

The smile vanished from Alexander's face. "Not some test, Miss Price, I assure you," he said, coming down a few steps, his shoulders rigid. "The most vital test a Paladin can face. And, in case this has not been made perfectly clear, I do not give a tinker's damn about your school or the people in it. The main purpose of this exercise is to test whether or not you are an adequate Paladin for the Oracle. You passed that test today—quite well, I should add."

"Are you going to give me a gold star?" I asked, and from behind me, I heard David's warning: "Harper."

"No," I said, turning to face him. "You should be angry, too. What is the point of putting your Oracle in danger to prove that your Paladin knows her stuff?"

At that, Alexander sighed, straightening one of his cuffs. "Mr. Stark was never in danger," he told me. "The situation was closely monitored, I assure you. Had you failed in your task, the Oracle would not have come to harm."

I didn't even know where to start with that, so I latched on to something else he had said. "Monitored by whom? And I smelled gasoline, so what's up with that? Can't you just, like, magic up some fire?"

Alexander flicked a strand of hair from his forehead, and I got the feeling he was rolling his eyes at me, like, in his soul. "The details of how we conduct these tests is not your concern."

I moved closer, my shoes tapping on the hardwood. "You keep saying 'we,' but I gotta be honest, I'm only seeing *you*. If you're going to do stuff like set a building full of kids on fire, I'd kind of like to talk to your supervisor."

"Harper," David said again, but Alexander held my gaze.

"As far as you are concerned, I am the alpha and omega of the Ephors, Miss Price. You do not dictate the boundaries of our tests, and there is no one you can talk to above me, I assure you."

I shook my head and said, "School should be off-limits. Period."

"Hmm," Alexander said, narrowing his eyes and tilting his head. "I see. So when you protect the Oracle from people who may want to hurt him, there will be places in this world that are off-limits? When some despotic ruler learns there's an Oracle in the world, ripe for the taking, if he approaches you at, say, your family's home, you'll simply inform him that this is not one of the agreed locations where an Oracle may be in danger?"

Faltering, I shook my head. "No, it's . . . it's not like that, but if it's only for a *test*—"

"The tests are meant to assess your readiness for real-world situations, Miss Price," he said sharply, all trace of that lazy elegance gone from his voice. "If you cannot be ready, then you cannot be a Paladin. This is not a hobby or an extracurricular activity."

I wanted to argue that, but nothing I could think of seemed

to work. He was right, and, ugh, I hated that so much. Still, I could at least try to get him to fix some of this mess.

"Fine," I said. "You've made your point. Now if you could please"—I waved in his direction—"rustle up some magic or whatever so that my principal forgets that I hit him and my parents don't freak out, I'd appreciate that. Ryan's Mage skills are apparently on the fritz."

But Alexander gave a tiny, elegant shrug. "They're not 'on the fritz.' They're gone for the time being."

"What?" David asked, coming up to stand beside me, his sneakers squeaking on the hardwood.

"Gone," Alexander repeated. "A simple ward I myself was able to create to keep Mr. Bradshaw from using his magic to assist you. It isn't as though that particular use of magic benefited the Oracle."

I swore I could feel my heart skip a few beats. Next to me, David scoffed, throwing up one hand.

"It benefits me plenty. Him helping Harper would help *me*. So let him do his mind-wipe thing, and let's—"

"No," Alexander said, his voice icy. He began to walk down the stairs, footsteps silent on the thick carpet. "Miss Price needs to learn that you cannot magic your way out of every obstacle. You hit your principal to save the Oracle. That's what you should have done, but now there must be consequences. Being a Paladin means accepting the consequences that come as a result of doing your duty."

Seriously afraid I was going to throw up, I clenched my

hands. "So you chose to set one of the trials at my school, and now I'm probably going to be expelled, and there's nothing I can do about it?"

Alexander sniffed, coming to the bottom of the stairs. "You're a clever girl, Miss Price. I'm sure you'll think of something. The Mage's powers do not exist in order to make things more convenient for *you*."

Please, I thought, but wouldn't let myself say. *Please don't tell him.*

Alexander's eyes remained on mine, and while I didn't think he could read my mind, I had a pretty good idea that he knew what I was thinking.

But that didn't stop him from saying, "We removed his powers because he was using them to stifle the Oracle's visions. An instruction *you* gave him, I believe."

The hall was so quiet I could hear my own heart racing, could hear David suck in a surprised gasp. "You were doing what?" he asked quietly, and I turned to face him.

My clothes still smelled like smoke, which was probably why my eyes were stinging as I said, "We were trying to help you."

But David was shaking his head, backing away from me. "You used Ryan to keep me from having visions?"

"No," I said, walking toward him. The sun coming in the big front windows had turned his hair lighter, lining him in gold. "No, you still had visions, but not ones that were big enough to hurt you."

I could see David's throat working, and I hated the way he was looking at me.

From behind me, Alexander gave a sigh. "Well," he said, "it would appear you two have some things to discuss."

I looked back, and he was already heading up the stairs again. "And, Miss Price," he added before turning back to flash a wolfish smile, "congratulations. You're one step closer to being a true Paladin."

Chapter 17

We left Alexander's house in silence, me trailing behind David. He jangled his keys in his hand, his jaw set, shoulders forward. I knew that look. That was David's thinking look, and I had no doubt exactly what he was thinking about now.

Guilt is such a weird feeling, a combination of sad and sick that I was getting too used to feeling. I'd had Ryan set up the wards to block David's visions because I'd thought it was the best thing for him—I still thought that, if I was being honest—but I knew I should have talked to David, should have tried to make him see that it was only because I wanted to keep him safe.

I slid into the passenger seat without a word, still lost in my thoughts, and David started the car, heading back out toward town.

David's fingers were curled tight around the steering wheel, so tight that his knuckles were turning pale.

"I'm sorry," I told him, rubbing my eyes. "I . . . I should have told you what Ryan and I were doing. And I wanted to. I was *going* to, I promise."

"When?" he asked, a muscle working in his jaw.

I didn't have an answer for that, not really, and I didn't think "eventually" was going to cut it.

And then, David suddenly jerked the wheel, pulling the car off the road, gravel and dust flying up in a cloud behind us as he came to a stop right past the "Welcome to Pine Grove!" sign.

Throwing the car in park, David opened his door and got out, walking a little ways away.

I watched him pace for a few seconds before getting out of the car, too.

"I don't know what else you want me to say," I told him, leaning one elbow on the open door. "I'm sorry I wasn't honest with you, David, I genuinely am, but part of my job is to protect you, and that's what I was doing, okay?"

David had his back to me, and didn't turn around as he tipped his head to look at the sky.

"All that time, I thought I was a crappy Oracle. But it was *you*. You keeping me from being what I'm supposed to be. And the fact is, if you'd left me alone, I might have been able to help you before this whole thing even started." He shook his head, a quick, angry series of jerks.

It was weird, how quickly guilt gave way to anger. "Did you hear the part about how I was doing it to keep you from going insane? Did you look at any of those Oracle pictures back at Alexander's?" I flung my hand back in the direction of the house. "Not sure if you noticed, but none of them exactly looked like people anymore, David. They were . . . things."

David glanced over his shoulder at me, hands low on his hips, elbows jutted out to the side. "But I *am* one of those 'things,' Harper. And you made a decision for me that you had no right to make. And by making a decision like that without talking to me, you pretty much treated me like a *thing*, didn't you?"

It had been a very long day, and my head was still spinning with everything that had happened, so it took me a sec to say, "No, *right*? This is part of what being a Paladin means. Keeping you safe, making hard decisions—"

The lines around his mouth looked deeper than normal and he waved a hand between us. "Hard decisions you didn't bother letting me in on. Because why would you? This is what you do, Harper, you . . . freaking steamroll everybody. You decide it's the best thing to do because it's what *you* want to do."

Slamming the car door, I walked over to David, the tall grass brushing my ankles. "That's unfair, and you know it."

David watched me warily. "Is it? What about all the stuff you had me do for your friends? Saving Abi from meeting that guy—"

I blinked, feeling his words like a punch to the gut. "That will make her life better," I snapped, but David threw his hands up, looking at the sky again.

"Will it? You don't know. You don't ask people what *they* want."

I opened my mouth to argue, but he held up a hand. "Don't start on the Paladin duty thing again, please. If you want to argue that you were doing what was best for me as an Oracle, fine, whatever. But that's not all I am to you, and you didn't take that into consideration at all." He shook his head. "Pres, you have to admit, us being an *us* has made things more complicated."

I wasn't sure how my heart could be fluttering and sinking all at once, but that seemed to be what was happening, and I wrapped my arms tight around me.

"It's made things better, though," I said. "Or has being my boyfriend only been a chore for you?"

David rolled his eyes, looking back up at the sky again. "No, of course not. I'm just saying that maybe . . . maybe we should rethink some stuff."

"Rethink?" I repeated. This could not be happening. I could not be getting dumped by David Freaking Stark on a country road in the middle of nowhere.

But behind the disbelief was another emotion.

Anger. Lots of it.

"Let me get this straight," I said, holding out one hand. "I made a call to keep you from having visions that would burn your brain up, and you dump me for it?"

David dropped his head to look at me, eyes slightly narrowed. "I didn't say I was dumping you, I said—"

"No," I interrupted. "That's what 'rethink stuff' means, David. And it means you're letting the Paladin/Oracle thing get all tangled up with everything else we are."

David laughed, but there was no humor in the sound. "It's already all tangled up, Pres. It always has been, and it's making both of us crazy."

Now David's arms were tight across his chest, too. "You can't quit being my Paladin, and I can't quit being an Oracle, but maybe until all this is sorted with the Peirasmos and Alexander and Bee—"

"What does Bee have to do with this?" I asked, shading my eyes against the sun. It was warm out here by the side of the road, and I could feel sweat on my forehead, behind my knees. My stomach ached, and my chest hurt. From the pained look on his face, I thought David might be feeling something similar.

"She's wrapped up in this, too. Which, let me remind you, is another thing that I *might* have been able to see coming if you hadn't screwed around with my powers. Maybe I could have looked for her, or we could've brought her back sooner."

I stepped closer to him, wishing I could at least poke him in the chest or something. I'd have to settle for saying all the hostile stuff I wanted. "Are you suggesting that what happened to Bee was my fault?"

A car drove by, sending up a cloud of dust, and David glared at me. "You know I don't think that."

But I did. That was the problem. If I'd told Bee the truth from the beginning, if I'd been faster at Cotillion, if I'd tried to do something to keep her from even *going* to Cotillion.

If I hadn't been so scared of my boyfriend turning into a monster that I'd kept him from using powers that maybe could've seen her.

Could've saved her.

"Harper," David said, his voice quieter now. "Why can't you admit that you can't do everything?" He sounded so much like the David Stark I'd fought with for all those years that it was hard to believe I'd kissed him just yesterday. That I'd loved him.

"You can't let go of anything, can you, Harper? You can't admit that maybe some things are too much for you. You can't be Homecoming Queen, and Paladin, and SGA president, and my girlfriend—"

I spun away from him, heading for the car. "Yeah, well, we can go ahead and strike one of those from the list, no problem."

With an aggrieved sound, David caught my elbow, pulling me up short. "I don't want to break up."

I stepped back, shaking my head. "Too late."

With that, I stomped back to the car, my throat tight, my eyes stinging.

David was still standing a few feet from the car, one hand at his waist, the other rubbing his mouth as he watched the traffic. Then, after a moment, I saw his shoulders rise and fall with a sigh, and he walked back to the car.

When he slid back in the driver's side, he didn't even look at me, starting the car and staring straight ahead.

I took a deep breath, wishing it hadn't sounded so shuddery. So that was that. We were done. Less than six months as a couple, and now it was over.

Maybe David was right and it was for the best.

We didn't say anything else until David pulled up in front of my house.

"Both your parents are home," he said, the car still idling.

"Probably because the school called them, and I'm about to be grounded for the rest of my life, if not imprisoned."

"Right," David said on a sigh, drumming his fingers on the steering wheel. "Do you want me to go in with you, try to explain?"

I was going to cry. I could feel it in my throat, which suddenly seemed so swollen and painful I was surprised I could breathe. And the last person I wanted to see me cry right now was the boy sitting next to me.

"No," I said. "I need to deal with this on my own."

"Pres," he said softly. In the dim light of the car, I could make out the freckles across the bridge of his nose, see the slight wobble of his chin, and I fumbled with the door handle as tears filled my vision.

"We'll talk tomorrow," I said, getting out of the car as quickly as I could and slamming the door behind me.

I didn't look back.

Chapter 18

"Would it help if I apologized again?"

I was sitting between my parents in Headmaster Dunn's office on Monday morning, the leather of the chair sticking to my thighs underneath the white linen skirt I was wearing. I was all in white today, down to the thin ribbon headband in my hair, hoping to project an air of innocence, but so far, it didn't seem to be working.

Headmaster Dunn still had an angry purple bruise on his right cheek, and the top of his bald head was red with anger, a vein pulsing steadily there. I'd never seen Headmaster Dunn angry before. God knows I'd never given him any reason to be before today, and for the first time, I got that—as a principal—he was pretty scary.

"Martin, you know this was very unusual behavior for Harper," my dad said, resting his ankle on his knee. "And we don't understand it any more than you do."

"I panicked!" I insisted, wondering if going all wide-eyed would be taking the innocence thing too far. "There was a fire alarm, and—"

"And your boyfriend was trapped in the newspaper room," Headmaster Dunn said on a sigh, and I startled.

"What?"

Reaching for a pen, Headmaster Dunn looked at me over the top of his half-moon glasses and said, "David Stark came to see me this morning, saying that you'd saved his life on Friday."

"Oh" was all I could manage. I'd been punched and kicked and attacked with knives, but I wasn't sure any of those things hurt as much as hearing David's name. When I'd gotten in on Friday afternoon, I'd had my parents' complete and total freak-out to distract me from the fact that David and I were no longer together. The school had called, of course, and told them about both the punching *and* the running off, so I'd had to spin a story and fast. It was the same one I'd told Headmaster Dunn during this meeting—freaked out, had a panic attack, acted in a Wildly Inappropriate and Uncharacteristic Manner—and while I was still grounded for the time being, at least they'd stopped yelling.

But later that night, lying in my bed, all I'd been able to think about was David's face, the way his voice had cracked when he'd said, "Pres?" And then on top of that, there was the worry. Breaking up sucked no matter what. Breaking up with a person who you had a mystical and lifelong bond with? Yeah. I'd been awake most of the night wondering what this would mean for us on the Paladin/Oracle side of things. And would this have any effect on the trials? It wasn't like I could quit being David's Paladin, or quit going through with the Peirasmos, but at the moment, I didn't even want to see David, much less go through more crap like what had happened Friday.

"Harper?"

I was so lost in thought that I hadn't noticed Headmaster Dunn talking to me.

"Yes, sir?" I asked, sitting forward in my chair a little bit.

He heaved another one of those sighs, his watery green eyes flicking between me and my parents. "I could have had you arrested, you know." He tapped the end of the pen up and down on the desk. "Charged you with assault."

My stomach dropped, and I clenched my suddenly sweaty fingers in my lap. "Yes, sir," I said, as meekly as I could manage.

"At the very *least* I could have you expelled." The pen was tapping faster now, and next to me, I heard both of my parents suck in a breath. When I looked over at Mom, she had her legs tightly crossed, fingers linked over her knees. Like me, she was mostly in white, although her pants were houndstooth.

Headmaster Dunn sat back in his chair. "*But* since this was extremely uncharacteristic of you, and you were doing it in the service of helping your fellow students, I'm not going to do either of those things."

I let out such a deep breath that I'm surprised I didn't sag in my chair. "*Ohmygoshthankyou*," I said in a rush and then stood up, reaching across the desk to shake his hand.

Headmaster Dunn flinched back, and Mom tugged at the hem of my skirt. "Sit down, sweetie."

As I did exactly that, Headmaster Dunn added, "You're not getting off scot-free, though, young lady. I expect you to dedicate at least a hundred service hours to the school before the end of the year." His gaze flicked past me and toward the door; he was no doubt picturing the English hall. It was still standing, but the smoke and water damage were bad enough that classes had been moved into the cafeteria for the time being. "Lord knows we'll have plenty for you to do," he said on a sigh, and I stood up again, this time not reaching for him.

"Thank you," I said again. "I promise, nothing like this will happen again, and I'm going to do a *totally* great job helping out."

Headmaster Dunn gave a snort and went back to tapping his pen. "We'll see about that."

Once we were back in the main office, I turned to both my parents, giving them my best smile. "See? It all worked out."

Dad shoved his hands in his pockets, rocking back on his heels. He had this way of looking at me where he sort of tucked his chin down and raised his eyes. He'd looked at Leigh-Anne like that, too, and it was always a sign that we were in trouble.

That was clearly still the case now, since his voice was firm when he said, "Just because you managed to avoid expulsion doesn't mean you're in the clear with us, young lady."

Mom reached out, setting her hands on my shoulders. "We're still worried, sweetheart. You have not been yourself for . . ." She looked up toward the ceiling. "Months, it seems like. And if you're having panic attacks so severe you assault your principal—"

"It wasn't assault," I said quickly. "It was an instinctive reaction so that I could help people."

Mom was still watching me, a deep crease between her brows, and I gave her my best "I've totally got this" smile.

I could tell she wasn't buying it, though—that crease only got deeper—so I hurried on, adding, "So I should get to class, and I promise we can talk more about this after school. Or after I get back from the pageant sign-ups."

Mom frowned at that. "Pageant sign-ups?" she repeated, and I nodded.

"Miss Pine Grove. Bee wanted to do it. Anyway, we can talk later, love you!" I gave her a quick kiss on the cheek, did the same to my dad, and then skedaddled out of that office as quickly as I could, leaving my parents' shocked expressions and the smell of burned coffee behind me.

The rest of the day was kind of a blur. The fire had everything all discombobulated, so classes were meeting in different locations. I had English in the gym, and Mrs. Laurent had sent all of us an e-mail that newspaper would now meet in the computer lab near the math hall. I hadn't seen David all day, and assumed he was avoiding me. That was . . . good. I wasn't ready to face him, not yet.

But when I got to the temporary newspaper lab and realized he wasn't there, I got worried. Even if David was lying low between classes and at lunch, he'd never miss newspaper.

Chie and Michael were working on computers in the back, and I tried to keep my voice as casual as I could. "Have either of you seen David?"

Chie shook her head, dark hair swinging around her jaw. "He's not in school today." She looked over her shoulder at me, the light from the computer monitor glowing in her eyes. "Did it take you this long to notice your boyfriend's missing?"

Okay, so David hadn't told his friends we'd broken up. I hadn't told mine either, except Bee.

Nodding, I gave a little shrug and backed up from them. "Sure, but I thought he might still show up for this class."

Neither Chie nor Michael replied, and I went over to one of the empty desks, sitting down with my bag. I had no idea what to do here without David. I usually worked with him, going over articles, suggesting layouts, throwing away any unflattering pictures—yearbooks are forever, and no one deserves to have certain shots preserved for eternity—but without him I felt sort of . . . lost.

And still worried.

Mrs. Laurent was nowhere to be seen, so I pulled out my cell phone and moved to the very back corner of the room. It smelled like dry-erase marker back there, and weird as it seemed, I kind of missed the hot ink smell of the old newspaper lab.

Ducking my head down, I dialed David's number quickly, and when he picked up after the third ring, I turned to face the wall.

"Pres," he said, and I closed my eyes for a second, willing myself not to sound all shaky and teary.

"Hi," I said as brightly as I could manage. "Skipping school today?"

On the other end of the phone, I could hear him blow out a long breath. "Thought it was a good idea, yeah," he replied. "And I've been meaning to spend some extra time with Saylor's books."

Frowning, I tried to decide how I felt about that. On the one hand, I was glad he was getting some research done. Saylor had tons of old books, and we'd barely scratched the surface of Oracle/Paladin knowledge. On the other, there was something about the image of him in that house, going through Saylor's things, that twisted my heart.

"Have you found anything?" I asked, and he sighed again. I pictured him with his phone jammed between his shoulder and his ear, an enormous tome spread out before him. I could hear the rattle of pages, and figured my mental image wasn't too far off.

"A few things," he said. "Not much, but at this point, I guess anything is better than nothing."

"Right," I agreed, and then, before I could stop myself, added, "You could bring some of the books by my house later if you wanted. We should, um, make sure we're both prepared for whatever comes next. Especially since that first trial was so intense."

There was silence on the other end of the phone, but only for a few heartbeats.

"Sure," he said at last. "After school?"

I glanced around. Chie was still facing her computer, but she wasn't typing anymore, and I got the feeling she was trying to listen.

Lowering my voice, I said, "I have pageant sign-ups, but after that, yeah. If my parents aren't home, you can use the extra key to let yourself in. It's—"

"I remember where it is," he said, and in the ensuing pause, I imagined him tugging at his hair.

Could we do this? Still act as Oracle and Paladin and pretend our hearts weren't breaking every time we talked? Sitting there in the computer lab, surrounded by people who were David's friends, I wanted to wish we'd never even tried to be together. That we'd made a mature decision that things were too complicated as it was, and that dating would make it worse.

But that would mean wishing he'd never kissed me the night of Cotillion. Wishing we'd never laughed together and held hands and all the other things that I already missed.

I wondered if David was thinking that, too, but in the end, he murmured, "See you then," and hung up.

Chapter 19

THE AUDITORIUM at the rec center smelled like floor polish, upholstery cleaner, and that indefinable old-building smell. In this case, I thought the smell might be the bitter tinge of humiliation. So many major events in town happened at the Community Center, and I wondered how many lives had been ruined on that stage? In Leigh-Anne's grade, there had been a girl named Sydney Linnet who'd puked during her eighth-grade graduation. And at least one kindergartner wet his or her pants every year during the Christmas pageant. I'd suffered the sting of defeat on that stage in sixth grade when David had beaten me in the spelling bee.

And now I was about to be humiliated all over again.

"You know we're not walking to a guillotine," Bee said, linking her arm with mine. "Besides, you *like* being in front of people."

"I like *talking* in front of people," I said, bumping her hip with mine. "Being in charge, directing things, not . . . performing."

"Fair enough," she said, glancing around the auditorium. "Is that the only thing making you look like you missed being valedictorian by a half a point?"

I tried to smile at her, but I know it didn't look right. "I was just thinking."

Bee puckered her lips briefly, brows drawing together. "About David?"

Sighing, I nodded, and Bee gave me a quick squeeze. "Look, I get that breakups suck, but . . . I mean, doesn't this make things a little easier? Now it's more like you're coworkers."

"Coworkers who are magically bound to each other. Forever," I reminded her, and Bee's big brown eyes blinked. "And, not to mention," I added, "my *other* ex is also a Magically Bound Coworker. I'm permanently tied to two guys I used to kiss."

Bee blew out a long breath. "Yeah, okay, that does make it tougher than a regular breakup. But . . . what were you going to do for the rest of your lives, anyway? Were you assuming that you'd always be a thing, and, I don't know, get married, have little future-telling babies?"

"It doesn't work like that," I said, meaning David's Oracle powers, but Bee nodded and said, "Exactly. Look at me and Brandon and you and Ryan, and Mary Beth and Ryan . . . your parents may have met in high school, Harper, but for most people, it doesn't work like that. You and David were probably going to break up at some point."

"I guess I could always ask him," I tried to joke. "See if he knew this was coming."

There was no way to explain to Bee how fast everything had been, how complicated. For people dealing with a guy who could see the future, we sure hadn't spent much time thinking about it. We'd always been focused on the present, on getting through one day, and then the next . . .

And look where we'd ended up.

I turned back to the stage, where a girl was practicing what might have been a modern dance routine. There were a lot of jazz hands happening, and a costume that was way too short. She'd probably learned to dance at the Pine Grove School of Dance over by the highway. Mom had sent me and Leigh-Anne to the Pine Grove Performing Arts School for our dance classes, since, according to her, the performances at PGSOD were too risqué.

As I watched the girl onstage stick her leg up behind her ear, I had to acknowledge Mom might have been right.

Then I tried to picture myself in that girl's place. Me. Onstage, in front of the whole town, doing a "talent," twirling that stupid baton. Taking a deep breath, I pushed my shoulders back and made my way down the slight incline to the stage. There was a long table set up just in front of the first row of seats, and a woman sat behind it, stacks of paper in front of her.

"Miss Plumley?" I asked, Bee trailing beside me. The woman turned around, pushing her glossy dark hair out of her eyes with manicured nails. A ridiculously huge diamond sparkled on her left hand, nearly blinding me as it caught the lights from the stage, and I remembered hearing that Sara was engaged to Dr. Bennett, a new dentist in town.

Sara Plumley had been friends with Leigh-Anne when we were growing up, even though she'd been a few years older than my sister. Still, she'd gone to our church, and when Leigh-Anne had been on the cheerleading squad her freshman year, Sara had been a senior.

She'd also won Miss Pine Grove several years back, and now she seemed to be the main force keeping the pageant going.

When she saw me and Bee, Sara gave a good-natured eye roll. "Oh, for heaven's *saaaake,* Harper," she drawled. "Do *not* call me 'Miss Plumley,' please, not when I'm only a few years older than you. It's always Sara."

Her accent was so thick that it came out "Say-ra," and I smiled, hugging her when she stood up.

"Okay, fine, Sara, then."

"That's better," she said with a wink. Then she looked up at Bee.

"Beeee, darlin', how *are* you? Didn't your mama say you were at some sort of . . ." Her face clouded for a second. "What was it again? A camp?"

"Cheerleading camp," Bee said quickly, and I hurried on before Sara could ask any more questions.

"So how is all of this going?" I nodded up at the stage, where a handful of girls were milling around.

Sara gave a wave of her hand. "The Lord is testing me, as usual. I swear, I would rather wrangle kittens than try to get a bunch of teenage girls to follow instructions, but what can you do?"

Her brown eyes narrowed slightly, taking in the two of us. "Are you girls here to volunteer? Because I am not gonna lie, I could use some help, especially from someone as organized as you, Harper. From the way I heard it, you practically ran Cotillion back in the fall."

She shook her head, glossy waves falling over her shoulder. "Of course, not even you could hold off a freaking earthquake. What a mess."

That was one word for it. But I smiled at Sara and shook my head. "Actually, we're here to sign up. For the pageant."

Sara's heart-shaped face wrinkled in a frown. "Well, that's real nice, honey, but sign-ups were last week. You know I love you, but I can't let you join up this late. It wouldn't be fair."

I bit back a smart reply. There were maybe twenty girls in the whole pageant, so it wasn't like me and Bee joining up was suddenly going to tip the whole thing into chaos. But snapping at Sara wasn't going to get me anywhere, and Aunt Jewel always said you gathered more flies with honey than vinegar.

So I put on my most honeyed smile and let my own accent drag out a little as I simpered, "I knooow, I'm *so* late. But to be honest, I wasn't sure if I'd have time to do the pageant this year, and then I was dusting Mama's curio cabinet. You know, the one right by our front door?"

Sara nodded, a little hesitant, and I decided it was time to lay it on thick. "And I saw Leigh-Anne's picture in there, from back when she won, and I . . ." I let myself trail off before biting my lower lip. "I felt like it was something I needed to do. I've followed in her footsteps in so many things, and the Miss Pine Grove pageant seemed like the final piece."

It was loathsome and heinous and probably made me a bad person, taking advantage of Leigh-Anne's death. But being a Paladin sometimes meant doing things like this, no matter how yucky I found it. If Bee was right and the last trial was tied to this pageant somehow, I sure as heck was going to be in it.

And yucky or not, it worked, because a sheen of tears suddenly appeared in Sara's eyes. She looked up at the ceiling, dabbing at the skin under her eyes with those French-manicured nails. "Oh, honey," she said, her voice thick. "You are exactly right. I don't know why I was fussing about deadlines and sign-up sheets."

She pointed one of those sharp nails at us. "But promise me that neither one of you is planning on singing 'The Greatest Love of All' or 'Hero' as your talent. If I have to hear either of those two songs again, I will eat a gun."

When Bee and I shook our heads, Sara gave a relieved sigh and handed us sign-up forms. "Fill these out and get them back to me by next Monday. That's the next rehearsal."

"We can't rehearse today?" Bee asked, gesturing up at the stage. A girl I didn't recognize—she either went to Lee High, the big public school on the other side of town, or was one of the girls from a neighboring county—was tap-dancing like her life depended on it.

But apparently Sara had already broken enough of her rules today, because she gave a very firm shake of her head. "Absolutely not. Not until your paperwork is sorted out."

"That's fine," I said quickly. I needed time to prepare myself for pageant practice anyway. Just coming in here had been weird enough. But, hey, if my trial ended up being public humiliation, at least I'd given the Ephors a heck of a setting.

Agreeing with Sara made her happy, because she flashed that super-white smile at me again. "Good. So are y'all gonna do the Festival, too?"

I wrinkled my nose. The Azalea Festival was the big fair on the outskirts of town. We had it every spring, along with the pageant, a giant bake sale, and this thing where people drove around looking at old houses with girls in hoop skirts out front.

The fair was like any carnival—rides, fried food, cheesy games, and oversized stuffed animals. I'd never been that crazy about it, even as a kid, but I'd always gone. The last few years, it had been a double-date thing with Ryan, Bee, and Brandon, and I'd kind of been looking forward to skipping it this year.

"Ooh, I hadn't thought about that!" Bee said, slipping her arm through mine again. "We ought to go tonight." Her brown eyes were warm when she looked down at me and added, "It might cheer you up."

I was pretty sure a cheesy town fair couldn't cheer up anyone, but, hey, I was already doing this pageant. *In for a penny, in for a pound*, I thought, and smiled back at her. "Sounds great."

Chapter 20

When I got home, David's car was parked against the curb, and I took a deep breath.

My parents were still at work, so David must have used the extra key like I'd told him to.

He was already in my room when I came up, standing at my desk, fiddling with his phone.

"Hi," I said, and he glanced up quickly, fumbling to put his phone in his pocket.

"Hi."

I inwardly cringed. This was ridiculous. A few days ago, he had been my boyfriend. In fact, the last time he'd been in this room, we'd done a fair amount of making out, and now I was standing in my own room, feeling awkward and . . . oh dear Lord, was I blushing?

Shaking my head, I tossed my bag next to my desk and put on my most no-nonsense voice to ask, "So what's up?"

David blinked behind his glasses. There were circles under his eyes, and I wondered if he was still having trouble sleeping. I could ask him that, right? I mean, that was Paladin/Oracle business, not girlfriend stuff. And the more I focused on Paladin stuff, the easier it was not to feel angry or hurt or any of the other things I'd been feeling since that afternoon in his car.

But just to be on the safe side, I didn't mention it, and instead sat down backward on my desk chair, folding my arms on the back and resting my chin on top of them.

Clearing his throat, David gestured to my bed. "Can I sit?"

"Sure," I said with a wave of my hand, trying not to remember how the last time he'd sat on my bed, I'd been sitting with him, my arms wrapped around his neck, our lips—

Nope. Nope, nope, nope, not thinking kissing thoughts.

But I thought maybe David was thinking them, too, especially since his neck was red and he wasn't quite meeting my eyes.

He sat down on my purple comforter and pulled an enormous book from his messenger bag. "I think I might have found something."

I should not have been disappointed. Of course he came over to talk business. That was good. Hadn't he promised to keep looking for more information about the trials? So, yeah, not disappointed at all. Pleased. Proud. Happy things like that.

"There isn't much," he said, opening the book on his lap and flipping to a page marked with a yellow sticky note. "Apparently they wanted to keep it pretty secret."

"Makes sense," I observed, twisting one of my rings. "Isn't the element of surprise the whole point? See how quickly you can think on your feet without getting killed?"

David glanced up at me, his lips quirking. "Basically, yeah. But here"—he tapped the page—"there's a story about a sixteenth-century Paladin, another girl—er, woman—like you, who went through her Peirasmos. It seems like the trials themselves are geared toward the particular Paladin. So, like, the first one was specific to you because of . . . the school, I guess."

Taking a deep breath, I stood up and walked back to my desk chair, bracing my hands on the back. "Thanks for this, David."

He gave an uneasy shrug, shoulders rolling underneath his gray T-shirt. Wait, David was wearing a T-shirt? A regular one without, like, a dragon on it or an ugly pattern? Then I took in the rest of his outfit. Jeans, and regular jeans at that, not those super-skinny ones he liked so much. Even his shoes were plain sneakers.

"Was there a fire at the argyle factory?" I asked, nodding at his clothes, and hoping that didn't come out too mean. I wasn't sure if snarkiness was something we could still do, or if it came off as too flirty now.

David frowned at me, brow wrinkling before understanding dawned. "Oh, right. Yeah, I, uh, threw something on this morning."

I was probably reading too much into David's wardrobe. We all had days when fashion seemed beyond us, right? Surely his dull clothing didn't mean he was . . . bummed or anything. Why should he be? He was the one who had done the dumping, not me.

There was a sudden stinging in my eyes that I blinked away,

turning to study the calendar on my desk like it was the most important thing in the history of creation. "If you wouldn't mind, could you leave the book with me? I want to read a little bit more."

I'd been aiming for "breezy," but my voice was so tight it sounded like I was choking.

And then I felt a warm weight on my elbow. Glancing down, I saw David's fingers curled there against my skin, and I let out a slow breath.

"Pres," he said, his voice every bit as tight, and I turned to look at him.

His eyes were very blue, and the freckles across his nose stood out against his paler-than-normal skin, and all I wanted to do was tuck myself against his chest and breathe in that familiar smell of soap and printer ink that David carried on him.

Then I shook myself. No. He had called things off, and a girl had to have some pride.

I stepped back so that his hand fell from my elbow and folded my arms across my chest. "Thanks for your help," I said again, and this time, there was no choking feeling in my throat. "But you should probably go now. My parents will be home soon, and they'll freak if you're in my room with no one else here."

"Right," he said, turning away quickly to grab his bag off the floor. "Good. Well, um. I hope it helps."

"I'm sure it will," I told him, forcing a smile.

I picked up the book instead of turning to watch him go. I'd just opened it when my phone buzzed. It was Bee.

"Azalea Festival? When do you wanna come over?" I glanced at the book on my bed, and then at my phone.

"Be there in fifteen."

"Are you sure you're okay?"

It was already the third time Bee had asked the question, so for the third time, I gave her the same answer.

"I'm great!" Earlier, when she'd answered the door, I'd said it with a sincere look in my eyes. Then when we'd come up to her room and she'd asked again, I'd tossed it over my shoulder as I flipped through the latest issue of *US Weekly*. Now, I didn't even look up, pawing through my purse for mascara.

From behind me on her bed, I heard Bee heave a sigh, and I fought back one of my own. It wasn't that I wasn't thankful for her concern. I was, honestly. But I didn't want to talk about David to her or to anyone else right now. It was all . . . yucky. Stressing over the trials, worrying about David being an Oracle, dealing with Bee being back—happy as that last thing was. Thinking about the breakup was too much on top of all of that, and for now, I wanted to pretend it wasn't happening. That shouldn't be so hard, right? I mean, David and I had gone years and years practically hating each other. Surely, it wouldn't be that tough to downshift to not being in love.

Too bad my eyes stung as soon as I thought of the word "love."

I located my mascara and did my best to act like all the blinking I was doing had everything to do with makeup application and nothing to do with David Stark.

"I'm super excited about the fair tonight!" I chirped, and Bee met my gaze in the mirror.

She sat up, tossing her own magazine back onto her nightstand and frowning. "Okay, now I know you're not okay, because you are never 'super excited about the fair.'"

"What are you talking about?" I scoffed, sliding the mascara wand back into its tube. "There are rides and lights and cotton candy. You have to be some kind of Nazi not to like cotton candy."

Bee's brown eyes narrowed. "And there's also the smell of manure and dudes who wear trucker hats, and more chewing tobacco than you can spit at." She waggled her eyebrows. "Get it? Spit? Because chewing—"

Holding up a hand, I stopped her before the thought could make me any more nauseated. "I got it. And you're right, I'm not a fan of those things." With that, I turned, bracing my hands on the little vanity. Bee's room had been the envy of every girl we knew . . . when we were eight. For some reason, she'd never gotten around to redecorating, and while I definitely understood the allure of a canopy bed, it was always a little weird seeing all six feet of Bee on a pink swiss-dotted bedspread.

"What I am a fan of," I continued, crossing my ankles, "is spending time with you. I need a good girls' night."

Bee's eyes darted away from mine.

"What?" I asked.

"Don't get mad," she said quickly, "but I sort of asked Ryan if he wanted to come with?"

For a second, all I could do was blink at her. And then, when

I actually went to talk, my voice was way too high. "Ryan?" I all but squeaked.

"I didn't mean to," Bee replied, rising to her feet. She was fiddling with the ends of her hair. "I was talking about the fair, and he mentioned that he wasn't sure he was going this year because he and Mary Beth had planned to go, but obviously that's not happening, and then he looked so bummed and I felt bad for him."

Last year, Ryan and I had gone to the fair with Bee and Brandon. I could practically still smell the popcorn and sugary-sweet scent of candy apples. Could remember Ryan's hand warm in mine. It hadn't been a great night or anything—Bee was right, the fair wasn't exactly my fave—but it had been normal.

I tried to imagine walking around the fair tonight with Ryan, not just my ex but a freaking Mage, a walking, talking reminder of how weird my life had become.

Disappointment has a taste, I swear. Something kind of bitter in the back of your throat that you can't quite swallow. It seemed like I was tasting it a lot these days.

But now I smiled at Bee and said, "Oh no, I totally get that. No worries."

Bee tilted her head, watching me. "Are you sure?"

"Yeah." I waved one hand. "Ryan and I are okay for the most part, and it might be nice to do something with him that's not crazy-superpower related."

Bee nodded, her hair bouncing. "That's what I thought!" she said, and there was something about the brightness of the words that had me looking at her a little more closely.

"Bee," I said slowly, resting one hip back against the vanity, its lace skirt brushing my calves. "You're not thinking about *Parent Trapping* us, are you?"

Rolling her eyes, Bee flopped back onto the bed. "This Paladin thing is making you paranoid. I only want everything to be normal."

So did I. A lot. But the thing was, it was never going to be. And it was like every time I thought I'd achieved some kind of normal, there was some new wrinkle thrown in, some curveball I had to adjust to. "Excellent multitasker" might have been one of the skills I'd listed on college applications, but it was getting harder and harder to do.

Maybe tonight could be a start, though. If eating cotton candy with Ryan and riding a machine that had been put together by scary dudes for like twenty bucks would make Bee happy, I'd give it a shot.

Chapter 21

THE FAIRGROUNDS were set up on this big field the town had especially to host the festivities every year, about a fifteen-minute drive from Bee's house.

There was a little bit of weirdness when Ryan came to pick us up, since I had no idea where to sit. Once upon a time, I would have sat with him in the front, but now that felt too couple-y. Especially since we were both technically uncoupled now. So I surrendered the front seat to Bee, sitting in the back and trying to pretend that this wasn't all super awkward.

Once we were parked, I followed Ryan and Bee from the "parking lot"—another field with a few orange cones and pieces of twine marking off spaces—and wrinkled my nose at the smell of horses and hay.

"Remind me why we're doing this again?" I said to Bee.

She was walking a little bit ahead of me, and she smiled as she turned to look at me, flipping a handful of hair off her shoulders. "Because it's fun," she insisted, hanging back to loop an arm through mine.

April in Alabama is usually pretty close to full-blown summer. Hot, humid, all of that. But it was nice now with the sun going down, the breeze cool enough to make me glad I'd grabbed a light cardigan before I'd left. In front of us, the fair sparkled with brightly colored lights, the sound of music and screams greeting our ears.

Stopping outside the main gate, Ryan shoved his hands in his pockets and rocked back on his heels, a broad smile splitting his handsome face. "Now we're talking," he said happily, and I couldn't help but smile, no matter how awkward this felt.

In that moment, I would've given anything to be able to slip my hand into Ryan's and lean against his shoulder. Not because I wanted him to be my boyfriend, but because he was good at that, being a shoulder to lean on.

Instead, I hugged myself, walking toward the booth to pay.

Once we were inside, the three of us kind of stood in the midway, unsure of what to do first.

The fair was, as usual, way too crowded, and I was a little too out of sorts to deal with things like the smell of farm animals and too many people. Still, I was doing my best to pretend this was the Best Night Ever, so I smiled at Bee and looped an arm through hers.

"What should we ride first?"

But Bee was not that easily fooled. "It's okay, Harper," she said, patting the hand I had resting on her forearm. "I know you hate every second of this."

"I don't!" I argued, but that lasted all of five seconds before I let my arm fall back to my side. "Okay, I do, but it's honestly not as bad as I remembered. I mean, they banned smoking! So that's something."

Laughing, Bee rolled her eyes at me. "At least you're trying," she acknowledged.

At my other side, Ryan nudged my elbow, nodding toward the shooting gallery amid the carnival games that lined the center of the midway.

"You wanna try out one of those?" he asked.

I almost laughed and shook my head. I had never been a fan of those types of things, and honestly, how many giant stuffed animals does a girl need? But then Ryan grinned down at me and nudged me again. "Come on, I wanna see your Paladin skills in action."

That was right. Along with increased strength and speed, I had some seriously excellent accuracy now and, like any girl right out of a breakup, I saw the appeal of making things explode.

I approached the booth, going to pull five bucks out of my pocket, but Ryan waved my money away. "No, this is on me. Harper Price, shooting things? Totally worth it."

Rolling my eyes, I smiled anyway. "Shooting balloons with a bright yellow plastic gun," I reminded him. "Not exactly super-hero stuff."

He flicked his auburn hair out of his eyes. "I'll take what I can get."

So for the next ten minutes or so, I shot the heck out of some balloons with a dart gun. And to be honest, it was fun. Not just the shooting things—although I have to admit that was a lot more enjoyable than I'd ever thought something like that could be—but the joking and laughing with Ryan and Bee. It felt so good not to worry about Oracles or Ephors, or if a vision was suddenly going to come out of nowhere, making me have to lie to everyone around me.

Part of me felt guilty about that, like having fun wasn't allowed.

But then I reminded myself that David was the one who had broken things off, David was the one who had chosen the Paladin over the girlfriend, and if I wanted to have a good time with my best friend and my ex-boyfriend, I was more than allowed.

After the shooting gallery, we went in search of other games that might test my and Bee's Paladin skills. That thing where you throw balls into goldfish bowls, more dart games, even an archery booth with foam-tipped arrows—I did them all, grinning at the surprise on the barkers' faces when I hit target after target, laughing with Bee as she struggled to hold all my stuffed prizes.

Finally, when we'd hit pretty much everything we could, we headed away from the carnival games..

"Can I stand next to Bee so people think I won all those for her?" Ryan asked, making us laugh.

"No need to feel emasculated," I reminded him as Bee handed yet another one of her prizes to a passing kid. "You did win the basketball thingie."

"Only because you let me," he reminded me, and I shrugged.

"What can I say, I'm a good friend."

Ryan stopped, turning to face me. The lights overhead brought out the red in his hair, and once again, I was forced to acknowledge that he *was* handsome. Maybe he didn't make my stomach flutter anymore, but there was something nice about feeling this way about him now. Like I actually saw him for the person he was—loyal, stubborn, easygoing—and not the trophy he used to be for me.

"You are a good friend, Harper," he said. "And I kind of like being your friend."

"Same," I told him, smiling.

Over his shoulder, I caught Bee watching us with an expression I couldn't read. Probably thinking more *Parent Trap* thoughts, I decided, and went over to take more of the fluffy animals from her hands.

"Stop," I told her in a low voice, joking, but she gave me a sort of wan smile in return, handing her last prize, a bright green stuffed frog, to a little boy in an Auburn Tigers T-shirt.

Once we were out of prizes to hand out, we made our way to the food trucks. "Did all that winning work up a hunger for something super caloric?" Bee asked, tugging at the hem of her light pink blouse.

Look, I'd love to tell you I was totally disgusted by the fried food on display, but A) some of those trucks were raising money for various charities and schools, and B) deep-fried Oreos were sent from heaven to prove God loves us.

"Yes, please," I told Bee. "Preferably something covered in powdered sugar."

She laughed at that again, and started tugging me toward the cotton candy machine. As we made our way down the midway, I bumped into someone, and I turned, an apology already on my lips.

The man I'd bumped was wearing stained jeans and a Lynyrd Skynyrd T-shirt, so nothing unusual for the fair, but there was something about the way his eyes focused on mine that had the words dying on my lips.

"Paladin," he said with a little nod, and a jolt went through me. It wasn't the feeling I got when David was in trouble; this was just normal fear, slithering through me, making food the last thing on my mind.

The crowd swallowed the man, but I stood still, making Bee turn to look at me with a little frown. "Harper?"

"Something's wrong," I told her. "It's . . . I think it's a trial."

Chapter 22

BEE REACHED OUT, squeezing my hand. "I'll come with," she said, "whatever it is."

But I shook my head. "No, you heard what Alexander said. If anyone helps me, I'm disqualified."

Which I was pretty sure meant "dead," even though Alexander hadn't spelled it out that specifically.

I could see a white circle forming around Bee's lips as she pressed them together, but in the end, she nodded. "Okay. But is there anything I can do?"

"Leave," I told her immediately. "You and Ryan get out of here, and if you see anyone we know, try to get them to leave, too." The last trial had involved fire, after all. There was no telling what might happen this time, and the fairgrounds were full of people. Kids.

"Will do," Ryan said, already taking Bee's elbow and pulling her away. I turned from them, heading in the direction the man had gone. My heart was pounding, palms slick with sweat, and with every step I took, my knees seemed to go more watery. The colored lights that had seemed so pretty when we came in now cast weird shadows, making me jumpy as I kept pushing my way through the crowd.

I couldn't see the man who had called me Paladin, but I somehow knew where to go, walking down the midway before turning left, then taking a right. All the rides on this side of the fairgrounds were crowded, lines of people waiting to get on the Ferris wheel or ride something called the Galactic Centipede. But one attraction was completely deserted, almost like there was a bubble around it, making it invisible to the rest of the people here.

The Fun House.

Sighing, I studied the dark building with its garish green door. "Of course," I muttered, visions of possessed carnies dressed as clowns filling my head. I didn't have a weapon, and I'd worn low sneakers tonight, so my footwear wouldn't be of any use.

Glancing around, I looked for anything I could use, but the only thing I saw was a couple of corn dog sticks, batter still clinging to the ends, stamped in the dirt. Um, no, thank you.

Then I glanced to the right, dozens of bobbing balloons catching my eye.

Perfect.

The guy running the balloon dart attraction was too busy flirting with a redheaded girl I vaguely recognized from the pageant sign-ups today to notice me sneak up alongside the booth and snatch a few darts from the side. Their tips weren't all that sharp—that had to be a lawsuit in waiting—but I figured they'd do in a pinch. And when I saw a deserted spork lying on the ground, I grabbed that, too, grimacing as I wiped it off on my jeans. Desperate times clearly called for desperate measures.

Heading back to the Fun House, I saw that it was still deserted, people walking by it like it wasn't even there.

Taking a deep breath, I slid the darts into my pocket, keeping the spork in my hand.

"Okay," I muttered to myself. "Let's do this."

The Fun House had never been one of my favorite parts of the fair. I'd only gone in it once when I was about nine. Leigh-Anne had gone with me, holding my hand the whole time, pointing out how silly we looked in the distorted mirrors, giggling about how fake the lime-green skeleton dangling from a doorway was. Afterward, she'd told me I was obviously the bravest third-grader in the state of Alabama, and we'd gone to get another cotton candy as a reward.

I kept that memory in mind now as I slowly made my way through the deserted Fun House. It was eerily quiet, the only sound the creaking boards underneath my feet and my own breath sawing in my ears. What exactly was going to happen here? Were more brainwashed people going to jump me? Ugh, fighting off frat boys had been terrible, but fighting off carnies? Yeah, I definitely wanted to take a pass on that.

There were a few lights scattered here and there, but it was still dim enough that I had trouble making out the room I was in. Or was it rooms? I felt like I'd gone through a doorway, but I wasn't sure.

I turned left, only to run into a wall, but when I turned back the way I'd come, there was a wall there, too. Disoriented, I turned again, passing through a door narrow enough to scrape my shoulders.

I was in a bigger room now, but it was even darker, and I wiped my free hand on the seat of my pants, wishing my heart weren't thundering in my ears.

From the corner of my eye, I saw something move, and I whirled around, spork raised high, only to drop my arm immediately when I saw who was standing in front of me.

My parents were wearing the same clothes I'd seen them in earlier this evening, Dad in his sweatshirt and jeans, Mom already in her pajamas. They had their arms wrapped around each other, their eyes huge and faces almost gray.

"Harper!" my mom screamed, and I rushed forward, the spork falling from my suddenly numb fingers. Not my parents. The school had been bad enough, but if Alexander or the Ephors hurt my parents—

I reached out, but instead of grabbing my parents, my hands hit hard, cold glass. One of the mirrors. Confused, I stumbled back, only to watch Mom and Dad vanish, my own reflection staring back at me. I looked as gray and panicked as they had, my hair coming loose from its braid, my lips parted with the force of my breathing.

Another movement, and I spun again, this time seeing Bee across the room, still in her T-shirt and jeans. Even though I'd told her to leave, I practically sagged with relief when I saw she was there. "It's some kind of illusion thing," I told her. "Making me see things, and—"

My words broke off in a shriek as something suddenly thrust through Bee's right side. I saw the glint of light on metal, the circle of red that began to spread across her shirt, her mouth open in a silent scream.

"Bee!" I practically threw myself across the room, only to come up hard against another mirror. Now Bee was gone, and I could only see myself again.

Panting, I turned in a circle, looking all around me. Earlier it had seemed like there were two mirrors, but now it was like the entire room was lined in them, reflecting dozens of me, all terrified, all confused. And then I wasn't in the glass anymore. It was my parents again, crying out for me even though I couldn't hear them. It was Bee, a sword through her back; Ryan, lying in a pool of blood like Saylor at Magnolia House; my aunts, their eyes blank, their minds not their own. Even Leigh-Anne was there, dressed the same as she was that night we'd gone through the Fun House all those years ago. She was pale, but smiling like she always had been, and for some reason, that hurt the most.

Swirling pictures of people I loved, scared or hurt or dead, appeared over and over again until I wanted to put my hands over my eyes and curl up on the floor. I'd been prepared to fight someone, but this? This was more than anyone could handle, superpowers or not. The room seemed to have gotten colder, so cold I was shaking, and I felt like my mind was going to snap.

A glow filled the room, coming from somewhere at the end

of the corridor, and when I made myself open my eyes, I saw that there was one more horrible vision for me to take in.

David floated a few feet ahead of me, but I knew it wasn't actually David. It was another illusion. But it didn't feel fake. It felt entirely too real, watching him as he looked down at me, his face blank, his eyes nothing but glowing orbs.

Then suddenly *I* stood in front of me. I wasn't dressed like I was tonight—jeans, T-shirt, cardigan—but in a dress. A white one that looked like my Cotillion dress, but couldn't be, since I'd burned that thing. It had still had splashes of blood on it, and every time I'd looked at it, I'd remembered what happened to Saylor, how although I'd saved David that night, I'd lost so much else.

The me in the mirror was standing right behind David, and she was crying. Of course, the me *not* in the mirror was crying now, too, because I'd seen what was in the other me's hand.

A knife.

Not any knife, but a dagger, the blade shiny and bright, the hilt intricately carved. Somehow I knew that this was a ceremonial dagger, something special.

Something only used on one occasion.

I watched golden light spill from David's fingertips, his eyes, his mouth. I watched the me in the mirror step closer to him, one hand going to his hair, the hair that he always tugged and pulled when he was nervous.

The Harper in the mirror was tugging his hair now, too, but only to pull his head back.

The blade caught the light, almost sparkling and looking strangely beautiful.

It came to rest under David's chin, and I looked at myself in the mirror, feeling a jolt as the other Harper's gaze met mine. Her eyes were bloodshot and wet, but her expression was firm as she watched me.

"Choose," she said and, with one quick jerk of her arm, drew the dagger across David's throat.

Chapter 23

JUST LIKE that first night, the door to Alexander's house swung open the second I was on the porch, and I walked right in, making my way down the hall and toward his office.

Alexander sat behind his desk, a steaming cup at his elbow, a huge book spread out in front of him. Music was playing in the background, something soft and vaguely sad on piano that I thought might be Chopin. Even though it was past eight o'clock, and he was the only one here, Alexander was wearing another one of those beautiful gray suits, his tie cinched in a tight Windsor knot at his throat.

He glanced up when I came in but didn't seem particularly surprised to see me. "Ah, Miss Price." Gesturing to the teapot at the edge of his desk, he raised his golden eyebrows. "I'm assuming the latest stage of the Peirasmos went well, then. Tea?"

"He'll die, won't he?" I asked, and Alexander blinked once. Twice. Then, sitting back in his chair, he laced his fingers over his chest. The ring he wore on his pinky glimmered in the lamplight.

"Everyone dies, Miss Price," he said mildly. "I know American schools are said to be woefully lacking, but it seems this is a fact you would have learned at some point in your educational career."

I was seriously not in the mood for this tonight, so I folded my arms and glared at him.

Finally, with a sigh, Alexander sat back up, the chair creaking slightly. "It's true that Oracles seem to have a short shelf life."

"I don't mean it like that," I said, coming to sit in the chair across from the desk. The music switched to something full of violins, the sound scratching over my frazzled nerves. "I mean that if he fully does the Oracle thing, he won't be David anymore. The Oracle part of him might keep going forever, but the David part, the part I . . . care about. Know. That part will be gone, won't it?"

Alexander lifted his hands in an elegant shrug. "That is part of it, I'm afraid."

I shook my head. David might not have been my boyfriend anymore, but that didn't mean that I was willing to let him get all super magicked up and then forget about him. All I could think of was David in fifth grade, his hair a lot blonder, but his scowl just as fierce when I'd beaten him in the spelling bee. David, one corner of his mouth lifting as he'd called me "Pres." David, sitting too close to his laptop and leaning over it in a way that made my neck ache in sympathy as he worked on the school paper.

David, the night of Cotillion, crossing the room to kiss me.

Alexander sat forward again, bracing his elbows on the desk and pressing his fingers together. "This seems to be another part of your training Miss Stark has neglected. You see the Oracle as a person. It's high time you started seeing him as a vessel."

"David is a lot more than his powers," I argued, but Alexander was already shaking his head.

"He's a boy, Miss Price," he said, and while the word "boy" didn't exactly drip with disdain, it didn't sound much like a compliment either. "A boy with powers he hasn't even begun to understand. Clearly they are greater than *you* understand. Are you saying that you'd rather David be your prom date than a being with the powers of gods in his veins?"

With a *tsk*ing sound, he fixed me with those green eyes. "You think we only want to use him, but his entire existence is an exercise in being useful, Miss Price. You're meant to protect him from those who would wish to hurt him, not from himself. Not from who he is."

I thought of what I'd seen in the Fun House tonight, remembering the blank look in David's—no, not David's, the *Oracle's*—eyes in that vision. "Even if it means killing him?"

Alexander didn't say anything for a long time, and I couldn't make myself look up and meet his eyes. I had never been a coward, but after admitting that, I didn't feel much like being the tough girl right now.

Finally, he said, "Is that what you saw tonight?"

I sat up a little in my chair. "What, you guys didn't make me see that?"

Sighing, he leaned back. "We engineer the scenario, not the specific visions. This test was meant to be psychological in nature. You saw the things that you fear the most, not things that will necessarily come true. Being confronted with one's worst nightmares is both a way of testing your mental fortitude and seeing where your heart lies. If one of your fears is David dying—"

"Not just him dying," I broke in. "Me *killing* him."

Alexander inclined his head slightly. "Even so. If that's one of your fears, that seems to prove that you are the woman for this job."

For a moment, I saw something flicker in Alexander's eyes, but he looked back at his desk again before I could tell what it had been.

And then he said, "I know you care about the Oracle, Miss Price, but the more you deny what he truly is, the more hurt you'll be in the end. It will be easier if you accept it now."

His voice was tight, and he didn't lift his head to look at me, but there was a note in his voice that almost sounded like sympathy.

Curious, I sat forward a little bit. "What was the last Oracle like?"

Alexander sniffed and dropped his pen in a little brass cup that held about five more pens. It clinked against the side as he said, "She was obedient and functional and performed her duties as was required."

That was it, but I saw that flicker again, and how white his knuckles were as he laced his fingers on top of his desk.

"Did you know her?" I asked. "I mean, obviously you *did,* but, like, the actual her? Or was she always all Oracled up?"

Alexander kept his gaze on me, but I had the feeling he was almost looking through me. "Like most Oracles, there was a period early on where she was more human than Oracle, and, yes, I did know her during that time."

I'd been so focused on keeping David away from the Ephors that I'd never spent much time wondering how they worked. They were the bad guys, and that had seemed like the only important thing to know. But now I wanted to know a lot more. "Where did y'all keep her?" I asked. "And when did you become an Ephor? Do you apply for it like a job? And that guy tonight, the one who talked to me. Was he an Ephor?" He cut me off with a brisk shake of his head.

"The gentleman tonight was one of your own townsfolk, temporarily magicked into service. As for the rest, my affairs are none of your concern. My point is this, Miss Price. David is an Oracle. He can never *not* be an Oracle. Perhaps your friendship has kept him more . . . average for the time being. But you'll never be able to keep him from becoming what he *is.* A being whose sole purpose is to tell the future."

I had the sleeves of my cardigan tugged over my hands, and I suddenly pushed them back with disgust. I was not going to be a sleeve-pulling weirdo. Sitting up straighter, I pushed my hair back over my shoulders and faced Alexander.

"I don't want that, though," I told him. "I want to protect *David,* not some freakish thing with glowing eyes who only speaks in riddles or prophecies."

Alexander took a deep breath, nostrils flaring slightly. The music was off now, the scent of tea still heavy in the air.

Looking in my eyes, he smiled, the first genuine smile I think I'd ever seen from him. But it was sad, and his voice was low when he said, "Miss Price, they are one and the same."

Chapter 24

"HARPER!"

Sara's sharp tone snapped me out of my thoughts, and when I blinked at her, she made a sweeping gesture with one hand.

"It's your turn to walk." Clipboard propped on her hip, bright fuchsia lips clenched, Sara did not seem like my biggest fan at the moment, and I shook myself slightly, stepping forward and completing the circuit around the stage as quickly as I could.

Which was apparently not what Sara wanted, since her lips somehow got even thinner. She twirled her glossy dark hair and said, "It's not a race, Harper. And this is Miss Pine Grove, not Cotillion. You can remove the broom handle from your backside. Walk lightly. Float." She demonstrated, but whatever she was doing looked a lot more like prancing than walking. Still, I nodded and murmured something about doing better next time.

But that only made Sara glare and announce that the pageant was practically here. "There are hardly any next times left, Harper!" she all but shrieked, and I had a sudden, satisfying vision of using my Paladin powers to boot her perky little butt all the way to the back of the auditorium.

Taking a deep breath, I closed my eyes and tried to stop the orgy of violence currently unfolding in my mind. It wasn't Sara's fault that I currently hated everything. The night at the fair was a week ago, but the vision of slitting David's throat still had me rattled. Alexander had said that the second trial was about facing my worst fears, that what I saw there wouldn't necessarily come true, but that didn't make me feel any better. Especially when I thought of what David had once told me—that he'd had a dream of the two of us fighting. That we weren't angry but sad. And on top of that, I could still see Saylor's worried expression when she'd told me that David could one day become a danger to himself as well as to everyone else.

So, yeah, I had a lot on my mind, and almost none of it revolved around making Sara Plumley happy with my walk. Plus, I still had one more trial left to go, and with the way the previous two had gone, I was pretty much expecting this last one to make my house blow up or something. It seemed like with every trial, I was losing a little bit more and, if I were honest, I wasn't even sure what I was doing this for. Being David's Paladin didn't seem so great when he wasn't even David anymore.

"Are you listening to me, Harper?" Sara asked, and this time, I thought of clobbering her with my baton.

"Yes, ma'am!" I called as brightly as I could, taking immense satisfaction from the way her brows drew close together. The "ma'am" implied "old," which was clearly not okay with Sara, but it was also polite, which meant there was nothing she could do about it.

Honestly, not enough people know how to use good manners as a weapon.

But that thought wiped the smile from my face. If only good manners would be an effective weapon in whatever it was Alexander had coming next. After the fire, I'd been prepared for all the trials to be like that, dangerous and destructive. But then the Fun House had been a psychological thing, and, for my money, that had almost been worse. I wasn't sure I'd ever get over not only the vision of David, but also seeing my mom screaming.

Seeing Bee with a sword thrust through her stomach.

That's what would happen to her, I reminded myself, if I didn't get through whatever this last trial was. Maybe not any time in the near future, but as I'd learned, being a Paladin was a dangerous business. I had to pass the Peirasmos, not just for me, but for Bee.

But thinking of Bee reminded me that I hadn't seen her in a while. I'd driven her to pageant rehearsal, but I hadn't seen her in at least fifteen minutes. That was weird. Like me, she'd decided to stick with the baton twirling, and Sara always made us go last. She had a pretty rigorous schedule for talent practice: singers first, then musicians, then the "athletic talents," like dance or, yes, baton twirling. Jill Wyatt was playing the accordion right now, and she was the last of the musicians to go (although calling what Jill did "music" was charitable). We'd be up soon, but Bee was nowhere in sight.

I made my way off the stage, nearly bumping into Amanda as I did. "Sorry," I said, and she shrugged it off.

"Someone needs to sneak something into her Slim-Fast before the pageant," Amanda muttered, nodding toward Sara, and I snorted.

"Agreed."

Like me, Amanda was dressed casually in jeans and a T-shirt, but tottering around on the heels she'd wear on the night of the pageant, and she nearly stumbled now as she went to cross one foot over the other.

I caught her elbow, steadying her, and she flashed me a quick grin. "Thanks."

"No problem."

Amanda and I were pretty much the same height in our heels, so she looked me in the eyes as she said, "It's intensely weird that you're doing this thing, you know. Me and Abi can't figure it out."

"Bee wanted to," I told her as one of the girls from Lee High hustled past us to practice her walk onstage. "And as Bee go, so goeth my nation."

That made Amanda smile, and she jerked her head toward the wings. "I hear you. I'm only here because Abi insisted."

I was smiling as I glanced over to where Amanda had gestured, only to feel my smile freeze when I saw who Abi was talking to.

Spencer. The frat guy who would, according to David's vision, one day ruin her life. But we'd stopped her from hooking up with him. Ryan had even wiped her memory so that she didn't remember *meeting* him. So what the heck was he doing here?

"Who's that guy?" I asked Amanda, and she gave an extravagant eye roll. "Oh my God, the love of my sister's life, apparently. Everything is all Spencer all the time with Abi."

My stomach churning, I watched as Abi leaned closer, letting one hand rest on Spencer's chest. He was grinning down at her, tucking her hair behind her ear, and while he didn't look quite as gross as he had the night of the party—not having roughly a twelve-pack of beer in your system will do that to a guy, I guess—I still was not a fan.

Neither was Amanda, if the way she looked at them was anything to go by.

What if you can't change the future, Pres? What if you're only delaying it a little while?

David's words echoed in my head, making me clench my jaw. That couldn't be true. If you couldn't change the future, what was the point of being able to see it?

From the front of the auditorium, Sara called, "Harper!"

Amanda grimaced in sympathy. "Seriously, some kind of mood stabilizer, right in her caramel Slim-Fast," she said. "It's happening."

Sighing, I headed back out onstage. Sara was indeed drinking a Slim-Fast, with a bright green bendy straw poking out of the top of the can. "Can you do me a favor?" she asked. "Go and see if you can find some crepe paper. Pink, preferably. In the closet by the stairs."

I wanted to tell her to get her own darn crepe paper, but instead, I gave a forced smile and said, "Sure thing!"

The closet by the stairs was in the back of the rec center, down one of the hallways underneath the stage, and I rolled my eyes as I made my way down there, still holding my baton.

Of course there would be crepe paper. Streamers, probably. Before you knew it, Sara would have a balloon arch up, and then my humiliation would be complete. I almost hoped whatever was going to happen would happen before the pageant got started, so no one would have to see me in this stupid leotard, twirling a baton under freaking crepe-paper streamers.

The supply closet was next to the staircase, and I saw the door was slightly ajar. My mind was still full of crepe-paper streamers, balloon arches, and the looks of horror sure to be on The Aunts' faces, when I tugged the door all the way open.

But the closet wasn't empty. There were people in there. Two of them, and I rolled my eyes, wondering who the heck would pick a supply closet in the rec center for romanc—

And then I saw the girl's blond hair, saw the tall auburn-haired boy kissing her, and realized what I was looking at. *Who* I was looking at.

Bee and Ryan.

Chapter 25

FOR A LONG MOMENT, it was like my brain refused to process what it was seeing. Bee. Ryan. Bee and Ryan, their mouths pressed together, Bee's hands clutching his shirt at his waist, Ryan holding the back of her head. I mean, I saw all of that, but it was like I kept trying to tell myself I wasn't seeing what I was seeing. That she was, I don't know, giving him mouth-to-mouth or something. That it wasn't even Bee, but Mary Beth in a blond wig. That I had finally snapped and was having some kind of psychotic break.

But no. No, that was my best friend and my ex-boyfriend, and they were full on *making out* in the supply closet at the rec center.

I guess the natural thing to do would have been to freak out and start yelling like I was gunning for a spot on a tacky talk show, or maybe to quietly close the door and pretend I'd never seen anything, but I didn't do either of those things.

Instead, I just stood there in my stupid leotard, hand on the doorknob, and said, "Oh."

They broke apart, Bee's Salmon Fantasy lip gloss smudged on both her mouth and Ryan's, and if I hadn't been busy trying to keep my stomach from plummeting to my feet, I guess there would have been something funny about the way they both gawked at me with big eyes and equally shocked expressions.

"Damn," Ryan muttered, while Bee nearly leapt out of his arms.

"Harper," she said, but I shook my head. My face hurt, and I realized it was because I was giving them another one of those big fake smiles I hated.

"It's fine," I said quickly. "So super fine. I mean, we've been broken up"—I waved my hand between me and Ryan—"and you and Brandon are broken up, and Ryan and Mary Beth are broken up, and wow, there has been a lot of breaking up going on lately, I just realized that. I guess that's the perils of trying to date in the middle of a supernatural crisis, right? Right. Anyway, I'll let y'all get back to . . . that."

I shut the door with shaking hands and turned away, walking back toward the auditorium, my baton clenched tightly in one hand. My eyes were stinging, and I almost bumped into a Styrofoam tree propped against the wall. Dimly, I heard the door open from behind me, and Bee called my name again.

I didn't stop walking, but when she caught my elbow, it wasn't like I could shake her off. I turned to see her watching me with big eyes. She'd wiped some of the gloss off her mouth, but there was still a faint salmon smudge on her chin.

"Harper, I am so sorry I didn't tell you," she said, her hand squeezing my arm.

"It's fine," I said, but voice was shaking, and Bee sighed, stepping a little closer.

"It's not, I know it's not. But I promise, it hasn't been going on for very long."

For some reason, it hadn't even occurred to me that it had happened before at *all*. Like I'd thought the kiss I'd seen had been their first or something, which was stupid. If they had already reached the "sneaking around" stage of things, this had obviously been going on for a little while.

"How long?" I asked, and Bee's brown eyes slid away from mine. My stomach was still rolling, and I tried to tell myself it was the smell of the rec center, all furniture polish and industrial carpet cleaner, making me feel sick.

"The night at the fair," she told me, and I remembered now that Ryan had dropped Bee off last.

"We were both kind of freaked out by everything that went down that night, and it . . ." Tears spilled over Bee's lower lashes, and she scrubbed at them with the back of her hand. "It just happened. I didn't mean for it to, and I swear to God, I never looked at Ryan like that while y'all were dating."

The thing was, I believed her. Bee had always been loyal, the best best friend a girl could have. It wasn't jealousy that was making me want to cry. Ryan and I were more than done, and while things with me and David were not all that simple right now, there was still no one else I'd rather be with. So it wasn't the actual kissing bugging me, it was the secrecy of it all. Bee had always told me everything, but she'd been keeping this a secret from me. I got it, but I didn't like it.

"If you want us not to see each other anymore, I'd totally understand," Bee said, and then Ryan came up behind her, laying one hand on her shoulder.

"I wouldn't," he said, looking at me, but I was still staring at his fingers curled over her shoulder. Since the night of the fair, she'd said, but that had been just a week ago.

There was a lot of intimacy in the way Ryan's hand lay there at the crook of her neck.

"Ryan," Bee said, but he shook his head, a muscle working in his jaw.

"I was okay with Harper and David," he said, "so Harper can be okay with me and you."

"I am okay with you. Both of you," I replied, but the words came out too fast. I thought of me asking David if we were okay, how quickly he'd answered me and how fake his answer had sounded. I guess I sounded every bit as fake, if the matching frowns on Bee's and Ryan's faces were anything to go by.

But for now, I didn't care; I needed to get out of here.

"Seriously," I told them as I turned to hurry back down the hall. "It's fine. So super fine."

Luckily, neither of them followed, and I managed to get to the dressing room, shucking off my leotard like it was on fire. I threw my clothes back on, and hurried out the back door of the rec center before anyone could see me. I'd e-mail Sara and tell her I'd gotten sick or something.

Getting into my car, I pushed my hair back with hands that were still trembling. I needed to talk to someone, but I sat there in the driver's side, the air-conditioning raising goose bumps on my skin, and racked my brain for someone I could talk to. Not David; things were still tense with us, and I was afraid that I wouldn't be able to explain why Bee and Ryan were weirding me out so much without him thinking it was a jealousy thing. But if I couldn't talk to David, and I couldn't talk to Bee, who *could* I talk to?

When the answer came, I felt a wave of relief wash over me.

It only took a few minutes to drive to Aunt Jewel's, and when I got there, she was outside watering her roses, dressed in a pretty light green top that seemed to have some kind of bird on it, and matching polyester slacks. As soon as I pulled up, she turned the hose off and waved me inside.

"Well, isn't this a nice surprise?" Aunt Jewel led me into the living room, and I flopped on the flowered sofa while she went into the kitchen to get us something to drink.

I fiddled with the hem of my dress, and when Aunt Jewel came back in, I blurted out, "I have something to tell you."

Aunt Jewel had leaned down to hand me a glass of iced tea, and she froze in place, the glass halfway to me. "Oh, Harper Jane," she said on a sigh. "You're not in trouble, are you?"

I was, of course. In lots of trouble, and I almost said answered yes. But then I realized Aunt Jewel thought I was in *that* kind of trouble.

"No," I said quickly, taking the tea before she spilled it. "No, no, no. Not even a little bit."

Breathing a sigh of relief, Aunt Jewel pressed her hand to her chest, right over the painted hummingbird on her sweater.

"Well, thank heaven for that at least." She squinted at me, leaning a little closer, and I picked up the scent of Estée Lauder perfume and the slightest hint of baby powder. "But if you're not in the family way, why do you look so sick?"

I didn't know I did look sick, and when I pressed both hands to my cheeks, Aunt Jewel clucked, sitting next to me on the couch. "I've thought you looked peaked for a few weeks at least. You aren't doing too much at school, are you?"

The tea was cold and sweet, and I gulped nearly half of the glass before setting it back on its coaster. "It's not school, Aunt Jewel. Or it is, but not the way you're thinking. Last year, during the fall, something . . . something happened to me."

She was squinting at me now, reaching down to pick up the glasses suspended on a glittery chain around her neck. Once they were on her nose, she settled deeper into the sofa and said, "What, exactly?"

It all spilled out then. All of it. The night of the Homecoming dance, Mr. Hall, killing Dr. DuPont, learning what a Paladin was, David being an Oracle, all the training with Saylor, Blythe, how there hadn't been an earthquake the night of Cotillion. How that had been me. How Ryan could do magic, and I'd made him do a spell that had wiped everyone's memory.

When I was done, the living room was very quiet. I'd drained my tea during my confession, but Aunt Jewel hadn't touched hers. The ice was melting in it now, leaving a dark ring on the coaster in front of her. I could hear the grandfather clock ticking in the main hallway, but that was the only sound.

Aunt Jewel heaved a sigh, and I waited for her to tell me I was insane or to say she was calling my mom.

Instead, she got up and patted my knee. "Come on, baby girl. We've got somewhere to go."

Chapter 26

I figured Aunt Jewel was taking me home. Or maybe driving me all the way up to the psychiatric hospital in Tuscaloosa.

So when she pulled into the parking lot of the Piggly Wiggly, I was both relieved and confused.

"The grocery store?" I asked as Aunt Jewel attempted to squeeze her massive Cadillac into a teensy parking space.

I winced as one of the side-view mirrors clipped the car next to us, but Aunt Jewel didn't seem too concerned.

"I think better when I'm shopping, and you have given me a lot to think about."

I was fairly certain my mouth was hanging open, and I imagined my eyes popping out like something in a cartoon. "Aunt Jewel, I just told you that I have superpowers. That my current boyfriend is an Oracle, and my ex-boyfriend is more or less a wizard. And you want to do a little shopping? I'd hoped you wouldn't freak out, don't get me wrong, but I expected *some* freaking out."

Heaving a sigh, Aunt Jewel gathered her pocketbook in her arms and faced me. "Harper Jane, I am nearly eighty years old. I have lived through a world war, buried two husbands, and when I was eighteen, I told my parents I was going to a church revival, but I actually spent a weekend in Biloxi with a traveling salesman. In other words, young lady, I understand that weird crap—Lord forgive me—happens. Now get out of the car and stop overthinking things."

So a few minutes later, I found myself stepping into the overly air-conditioned, overly Muzaked store, trailing behind my aunt.

I pushed the buggy for Aunt Jewel while she scanned the shelves of the Piggly Wiggly, occasionally squinting at the yellow legal pad she'd pulled out of her purse. She had just put a bunch of bananas in a little plastic baggie and laid it in the buggy when she said, "So David can see the future."

"Shh!" I hissed, glancing around us. This time of day, the Pig was mostly deserted, but I still couldn't be too careful. "Aunt Jewel, that is a private topic."

But she tsked at me and lifted her glasses to her nose, the sparkly chain winking in the fluorescent lights. Over the sound system, Whitney Houston wailed about finding the greatest love of all inside herself.

I trailed Aunt Jewel into the coffee and cereal aisle. "Yes," I said as quietly as I could.

"Hmm." Aunt Jewel picked up a can of Cream of Wheat. "How far into the future?"

I stopped, startled. Weirdly, I'd never thought of that before. It wasn't like David was seeing spaceships or intergalactic wars. "I don't know," I told her. "We never tried that much, I guess."

Aunt Jewel took that in with a little nod before adding a package of coffee to her groceries, along with some nondairy creamer. "Okay. Well, how often does he see the future? And is it only his future, or yours, or everyone in the whole wide world's? Because it seems to me that that would be a lot going on in one brain. I know that Stark boy is bright, but I'm not sure anyone's mind could handle all that information."

"That's exactly what I thought!" I exclaimed, our buggy squeaking to a halt. "But apparently me trying to keep him from seeing too much means that I'm controlling or whatever, and—"

I broke off, aware that Aunt Jewel was watching me. "Oh yeah," I added, a little sheepishly. "I, uh, I may have done some things to be sure he couldn't have very strong visions. But it's only because I was trying to keep him safe, which is supposed to be the whole point of this thing."

Sighing, Aunt Jewel wrapped her fingers around the edge of the buggy and tugged it out of my grip, wheeling it in front of her. As she took the handle and steered us down the Asian and ethnic food aisle (which contained some ramen and spaghetti sauce), she glanced over at me. "Don't fret, honey. It seems like you and David have taken on more responsibility than most children should."

"We're not children," I insisted, but Aunt Jewel only laughed.

"Of course you are. You're barely seventeen, and you still have a whole other year of school to get through. That makes you a child as far as I'm concerned."

When she turned back to me, her blue eyes were soft and she

smiled. "But then you'll always be my baby, even when you're forty years old with babies of your own."

It was a sweet thing to say, but it still hit me squarely in the chest. Aunt Jewel must've seen it, because her smile faded. "Oh. Except you can't have babies, can you? Not if you have to run around protecting David. Doesn't exactly seem like a child-friendly environment."

I shook my head, but it wasn't like I'd thought much about all of that. I'd thought about college, sure, but that was as far as I'd let myself go. Thinking about all the other stuff—marriage, kids, a career—had been too hard. Too scary, too *much*. I wasn't proud of the whole head-in-the-sand thing I'd been doing, but I hadn't known what else to do.

When the buggy stopped this time, it was Aunt Jewel's fault. She stopped there in front of a row of Chef Boyardee, frowning. "And David is your boyfriend now, but what if you break up? Or find someone else?"

I put a couple of jars of spaghetti sauce into the buggy. "We already broke up," I told her. "But bringing someone else into this would be a disaster. It was hard enough dealing with Ryan and Mary Beth." I thought again about Bee locked in Ryan's arms in the closet, her lip gloss smeared on Ryan's face. "Not that they're an issue anymore, I guess."

I'd told Aunt Jewel about Ryan's powers, but I'd left out the part with him and Bee. I wasn't quite ready to get into that just yet.

But now Aunt Jewel was frowning at me, her eyes bright over the tops of her glasses. "How did Ryan even get involved in all this?" she asked. "How did he get . . . powers or magic or whatever you want to call it?"

"Saylor passed them on to him after Brandon stabbed her," I answered without thinking.

The box of pasta in Aunt Jewel's hand tumbled to the floor, the container breaking open and penne spilling everywhere. But she didn't even seem to see it. "Saylor Stark was murdered?"

Oh. Right.

A stock boy rounded the corner and, seeing the mess, jogged off, probably to get a broom. I scooped Aunt Jewel's purse up out of the buggy and took her gently by the elbow.

"Maybe we should shop later."

"Yes," she said faintly, giving a nod. "M-maybe that's for the best."

Fifteen minutes later, we were at Miss Annemarie's Tearoom, huddled in one of the corner tables and drinking chamomile. Aunt Jewel's pot of tea was half empty by the time she took a shuddery breath and said, "All right, Miss Harper Jane. I take it back. You are not overthinking this. I don't think anyone could overthink such a thing—goodness."

Pressing a shaking hand to her lips, Aunt Jewel shook her head. "And you've been dealing with this all alone."

"Not alone," I told her as I poured us both another cup. "I have David and Ryan. And Bee. Bee knows." I left it at that, rather than explaining Bee's new Paladin powers and her kidnapping and sudden reappearance. Aunt Jewel had had enough shocks for one day. We could always get into that later if needed.

"But no adults," she said, dumping a few sugar cubes into her cup. "And all of you running around, breaking up with each other, getting together, breaking up again, getting together with different people."

I thought about telling her about Alexander, but since I still hadn't made up my mind how to feel about that, I decided I could skip it for now. "I know, things are complicated, and the dating stuff probably doesn't help."

But Aunt Jewel only shook her head, the cubic zirconias in her ears winking. "You're children," she said again. "That's what children do, make things messier than they have to be."

I thought of Ryan and Bee in the closet, her lipstick on his face, his eyes daring me to say I didn't want them to be together.

Yeah, things were messy, all right.

Miss Annemarie stopped by the table, smiling down at the two of us. "Harper! I've seen your mama and your aunts in here, but I haven't seen you in forever!"

"I've been busy with school," I said, not adding that I'd been avoiding her since we'd tried to kill each other at Cotillion. It was still bizarre to look into her face and remember her coming after me with a knife.

After Miss Annemarie had gone back to the kitchen, promising to make some of her crab bisque, Aunt Jewel turned back to me, her eyes rheumy but sharp behind her glasses.

"Sweetheart, if anyone can handle all these responsibilities, it's you. I've never known such a determined little thing in all my life. Did you know, when you were about two, your daddy

built you and Leigh-Anne a sandbox. And every day, you'd tod-
dle out there and try to build you a castle, and every day, your
sister would knock it down."

Clucking her tongue, she took her glasses off, letting them
dangle down the front of her shirt. "I loved that little girl, but
Lord, what a pill she could be. Anyway, all those times she
knocked down your castle, you never once cried. Never com-
plained. You jutted that bottom lip out and got back to work.
You never quit, even when that would have been the smartest
thing to do."

Somehow, I didn't think that was supposed to be a compliment. But I was still about to thank her when Aunt Jewel reached
across the table and took my hand. "You are trying to be too
many things to too many people, Harper Jane."

Aunt Jewel's fingers were cold, the skin papery, but she held
me tight as she added, "And I think one day, one day soon, you're
gonna have to *choose*."

Chapter 27

"Your leotard is ugly."

I looked down at the little girl standing next to me. She came up to right above my elbow, but I was pretty sure that a solid foot of that was hair. The rest of her was covered in a sea of pale blue ruffles, so I wasn't sure how she had any room to talk about what was ugly.

Still, being mean to kids is never okay, so I made myself put on a smile. "That's not very nice," I told her, but the little girl shrugged.

"It's very true."

In front of us, another girl about the same age as this devil spawn standing next to me was practicing her "dance" on the stage. It mostly seemed to consist of some awkward shuffling and a few waves, and every now and again she'd glance down to where her mom was doing a much more enthusiastic version of the same dance in the front row.

I sighed and shifted my baton to my other hand. Normally the Little Miss Pine Grove portion of rehearsal was over by the time we got in, but Sara was running late today, so we were stuck waiting for the younger girls to finish. Which apparently *also* meant we were stuck getting harassed by second-graders.

"It's the sleeves," the girl next to me said, looking me up and down. There was something weird about the way she talked, and when she opened her mouth to yawn, I realized she was wearing those little fake teeth they use to cover a missing tooth or two.

Seriously, pageants were the *weirdest*.

"Well, I like the sleeves," I told her, tugging at the material in question. I'd used Leigh-Anne's old majorette uniform, a sparkly green number that was a little too big for me. Aunt Jewel had sewn on some sleeves for me to give it "a little flair." Apparently, to Aunt Jewel, "a little flair" meant a metric ton of sequins and fake jewels, so every time I threw the baton, my arms clattered.

"You shouldn't like them," the little girl told me, "because they're ugly."

"Okay, thanks, got it," I replied through clenched teeth.

"Get lost, Lullaby League," Abi said, sauntering up, and the little girl stuck her tongue out at us before heading down the aisle toward the front of the stage.

Abi's gaze slid over me. She was wearing a simple black dress, since her talent was playing the piano. Looking at her, I wished I hadn't begged my mom to let me quit lessons when I was twelve, because piano seemed like a totally unembarrassing talent. A thin gold chain winked around her neck, and when Abi noticed me looking, she grinned, lifting the necklace up. "Isn't it pretty? It's from Spencer."

That name made me want to shudder—a reminder that we

might have been wrong about David's visions, that we *couldn't* change the future. And if that was true, what was the point of all of this?

Abi misread my expression, clearly, because she scowled at me, letting the necklace drop back to her chest. "Okay, Harper, enough with the judge-y face. Just because you're boyfriend-less for the first time in, like, ever, it doesn't mean you can't be happy for other people."

"I am," I said, and the words might have been convincing had I not seen Bee walk in. She was practically running—worrying about being late, I guess—and while it's not like she was wearing a sign that said, "I was making out with Ryan!" I couldn't help but remember them locked together in the closet. She looked . . . suspiciously glowy.

Abi glanced over at Bee, and when her gaze swung back to me, both eyebrows were lifted. "Where were you at lunch today?" she asked.

I'd hid out in the library like a weirdo because I hadn't wanted to face Bee or Ryan yet. I'd thought about hiding in the temporary newspaper lab, but when I'd walked past, David had been in there with Chie and Michael. As I'd sat on the floor in the back stacks of the library, I'd reminded myself that a few months ago, I would've died before being one of those people who *hid* during lunch. Lunch was primo socializing time, after all, but with Bee and Ryan being . . . Bee and Ryan, and me and David being *not* Me and David, I hadn't known what else to do.

It was an icky feeling.

Bee's eyes met mine across the auditorium, and her smile

faded. This was ridiculous, not talking to her in the middle of everything that was going on, but I . . . couldn't. I still didn't know what to say. I had no right to be jealous, not of Bee for being with Ryan, and not of Ryan for taking Bee away from me. Abi was right; just because I was alone, that didn't mean everyone else had to be, too.

Turning away, Bee headed for the little stairway that led to the backstage area, undoubtedly to change, and I breathed a little sigh of relief.

One that, unfortunately, Abi saw. "So y'all are fighting?" she asked. "That's what Amanda thinks. Is it about Ryan? Amanda said she saw Bee getting a ride home with Ryan after school yesterday, and—"

"Oh, shut up, Abigail," I heard myself say. "I try to do nice things for you, like save you from a dude who will ruin your life, and all I got for my time was a ruined pair of shoes and a dress that still smells like beer, and now you're with him anyway, *and* you're giving me crap, so honestly, why do I bother? Why do I bother with *anything?*"

I hadn't realized that my voice was getting so loud, but from the way Abi blinked at me, I thought maybe I'd gotten close to shouty on that last bit. But I *felt* shouty. All I ever did was try to help, try to make things *better,* and it seemed like I was failing all over the place. Sure, I'd gotten through the first trials, but I was wearing a leotard in the rec center, I had no boyfriend, things with me and my best friend were intensely weird, and I'd been insulted by a munchkin wearing fake teeth.

There was only so much a girl could take.

Except apparently the universe wasn't through screwing with me, because when Abi glanced toward the back of the auditorium, I saw someone standing in the doorway.

David.

"I . . . I'm sorry for the yelling," I told Abi, ignoring her when she asked, "What did you mean about Spencer?" and moved up the aisle toward where David still hovered.

It was stupid to feel embarrassed, but David seeing me in my leotard left me feeling weirdly exposed, and not because of all the skin on display. The old David would have watched me with twitching lips before making some kind of annoying joke about how I clearly had a future in leading parades. But now, it was like he wasn't seeing the costume. He was wearing a long-sleeved shirt in a shockingly nonoffensive shade of blue that brought out the color of his eyes.

Holy crap. His *eyes*.

When I looked closely, I could see light glowing there. Not brightly, but still there and not a reflection.

With a sigh, David whipped off his glasses, replacing them with a pair of sunglasses that he had hanging in the front of his shirt. "I'm guessing you can see it?" he asked, and I stepped closer. Behind me, I could hear the stereo system blasting "Yankee Doodle Dandy," so I knew the little kids were still practicing.

Momentarily distracted by that, David gazed past me before shaking his head slightly. "This place is—"

"It's a total freak show," I confirmed. "But we can worry about that later. Why are your eyes all . . . like that?"

Reaching up, David ruffled his hair. "They just are, okay?"

"That is like the least acceptable answer in the history of un-acceptable things, most of which, I should add, involve your wardrobe," I told him, folding my arms and trying not to notice the clatter of plastic gemstones. "David, what's going on?"

For all that his eyes were freaking me out, I wished I could see them right now. I could read a lot in his face—the tightness of his mouth told me he was going to be stubborn about this, the tugging at his hair meant he was nervous—but his eyes would've told me more. How freaked out *he* was, for example.

"I've been trying some things," he said, and I blew out a breath that ruffled my bangs. A few days ago, I'd thought about how much I didn't like him alone in that house, obsessively going through Saylor's things. Hadn't I thrown myself into time with Bee and pageant practice to distract me from our breakup? What had David been distracting himself with? It wasn't like he could see the future anymore, after all. Alexander had seen to that.

But if that was the case, why the heck were his eyes Oracled out? Again, I remembered him in the Fun House, floating in front of me, his eyes nothing but that golden light.

My knife at his throat.

Pushing that image away, I leaned in closer. "What kind of things?"

He'd tugged his sleeves over his hands. The music had stopped now, and I could hear Sara calling for all the Miss Pine Grove girls, but I kept my gaze on David. "What. Kind. Of. Things?" I re-peated, and David looked straight at me. Even through the dark lenses of his glasses, I could see the twin sparks of light there.

"Visions," he said in a low voice. "Alexander's spell doesn't work anymore."

That startled me so much that my baton nearly slipped from my suddenly numb fingers. "What?" was all I could manage, and David's mouth turned down at the corners. For the first time, I noticed that he looked even thinner, paler. Almost like he was fading away right in front of me.

"I don't know why or how," he continued, "but the other night, I . . . I saw something."

I opened my mouth to ask what, but David held up a hand before I could. "It wasn't clear. It was like before, when my visions were all muddled and cloudy. But I think . . . I think with *help* . . ."

It was my turn to hold up a hand. "Even if Ryan and I did try to help you have a vision, Alexander would know, right? He'd . . .Who knows what he'd do? That could disqualify me from the Peirasmos. It could kill me. Or you, or—"

But David shook his head. "This will work," he insisted. "And think about it—if I can override his powers, maybe I could override . . . I don't know, *everything*. Maybe this could end. If Alexander doesn't have any power over me, he doesn't have any power over you either."

It was tempting. *Really* tempting. But if David was wrong . . .

Like he could read my mind, David reached out and took my hand. His skin on mine felt familiar and good, and I fought the urge to let my fingers curl around his.

"Pres," he started, then moved in closer. "*Harper*. Trust me."

Behind me, Sara called my name, and I thought of what this would mean. I'd have to talk to Ryan, of course, and Bee, too, probably, since this affected her. The four of us—my two ex-boyfriends and my maybe-ex-best-friend—would have to work together.

It would be scary and hard and, if David was wrong, quite possibly fatal.

But in spite of all that, I squeezed David's hand and nodded.

Chapter 28

I'M SURE there have been more awkward car rides than the one we took out to the golf course to have David's vision.

I mean, Aunt May once told me a story about a funeral where the limo company screwed up and sent the same car for her cousin Roderick's wife and his mistress, and they had to ride to the cemetery together. That was probably worse than this ride.

But not by much.

Ryan had agreed to drive since he had the biggest car, a nice SUV his dad had bought for him last year when the basketball team had managed not to come in dead last. But even with all that space, I still felt cramped, even though it was just me and David in the backseat. Apparently the weirdness between us took up a lot of space. Bee rode up front with Ryan, and she'd done a decent job of trying to keep small talk going, but after getting monosyllabic answers from most of us, she'd given up, and now we drove in silence.

Bee and I still hadn't talked about that afternoon at the pageant, which, to be honest, was fine by me. Nobody can repress better than a good Southern girl, and I wondered if the best thing to do was to forget any of that had ever happened. So Bee and Ryan were a thing. So she hadn't told me.

That was . . . fine. No big deal at all. I certainly wasn't watching the two of them, waiting to see if their hands touched or if they glanced at each other the way they had that afternoon. And I definitely hadn't spent a lot of time wondering if, no matter what they'd told me, there hadn't been a spark of something there before.

No, definitely not wondering any of that.

Next to me, David felt like he was strung so tightly that he nearly vibrated, and I couldn't blame him. There was this bizarre vibe in the car, like something bad was coming, but that could have been all the tension. Still, when Ryan made the turn onto the highway out to the country club, I almost told him to turn back. Which would have been dumb, of course. I'd promised David we could do this, but if I was being honest, I didn't expect anything to happen. Alexander had taken David's powers from him, and no matter how much David thought he could somehow overcome that, I didn't have particularly high expectations. If anything, this felt more like a favor we could do for him.

That thought in mind, I laid my hand on David's leg, trying not to notice how he flinched when I first touched him. But then he glanced over at me, his blue eyes bright behind his glasses, and he linked his fingers with mine. It had been a while since we'd touched, and I was surprised by how good it felt to have his hand in mine, even if it was only for a second.

The big stone and wood sign announcing the Pine Grove Country Club was lit up, but everything else was dark as we turned down the winding drive. Ryan rolled down his window, waving a card in front of a sensor, and the gate slowly swung open. Technically, the club closed at seven, but since Ryan's dad owned the place, he could come and go as he pleased. And if his dad asked him why he'd been out at the club on a Wednesday night at ten, Ryan could always say he'd been cleaning the pool or something. That's what he'd said on the nights we'd come out here after hours—memories I didn't want to dwell on right now.

From the almost embarrassed way Ryan's eyes met mine in the rearview mirror, I didn't think he wanted to stroll down memory lane either.

We'd decided to come here for a couple of reasons. One, in all of David's readings, he'd realized that the past Oracles were always having visions in nature-y places like caves or forests. There were a few woody places around Pine Grove—there was a reason the town was called what it was—but since none of us were in the mood to tramp through underbrush and risk snake bites, ticks, and God knew what else, we'd chosen . . . civilized nature. Plus it was a nice, private space still in town, but not too close to anything else, just in case this got out of hand.

The country club was a pretty building made to look like an antebellum mansion, and as we drove past it, spotlights on the tall white columns, giant tubs of azaleas by the front door, David snorted. "I feel like I should start humming 'Dixie.'"

"Have you never been out here?" I asked, and he shook his head.

"Saylor came out here for lunch sometimes, but it's not exactly my scene."

There were still shadows under his eyes and his nails were bitten almost to the quick, but in that moment, there was enough of the old David in his face to make me feel a little better about what we were about to do. David's powers still scared me, and for all that he wanted to use them to the best of his abilities, I thought they scared him, too. And with the Peirasmos still going on, what if him doing this . . . violated that somehow?

I didn't want to think about what the repercussions of that could be, but I felt like this was something I owed David. He was asking me to have faith in him, and the least I could do was try.

Ryan's SUV drove silently over the asphalt lane winding its way to the golf course. We'd decided to attempt this on the eighth hole. Well, Ryan had decided, pointing out that that part of the golf course was hidden from the main road by a hill, plus there was the lake to one side, and trees to the other.

Once the car was parked, we piled out, and for a moment, we all just stood there, looking at the fairway.

"We're really going to do this," Ryan said, his hands in his pockets.

At his other side, Bee nodded. "We have to." She looked over her shoulder at me, tucking a strand of hair behind one ear. "Right, Harper?"

I nodded without thinking. "Right. So let's get started."

All four of us tromped down the hill, and once we were near the eighth hole, I gestured for us to sit. We did, forming a semicircle with David in the middle, Ryan and me on either side of him, Bee across from us. Overhead, the moon was high, reflecting on the pond. I could hear frogs croaking and the occasional chirp of bugs, but there was no breeze. The night was still and warm, almost too warm, but I still felt chilled.

I think David felt the same sense of wrongness. "Maybe this is a bad idea," he said in a rush, and a sudden whoosh of relief shot through me. *Yes, let's go home,* I thought. *Forget this whole idea.* Again, I saw David like I'd seen him in the Fun House—his skin glowing, his eyes pure light.

My dagger at his throat.

But that was the girl thinking, not the Paladin. It wasn't my responsibility just to keep him safe; I needed to make sure he could do everything he was meant to do, fulfill his destiny as an Oracle. And that meant having visions.

So I reached out and took his hand. To my surprise, Ryan reached out and took David's other hand.

"It's what we came here for," I said softly.

David turned to look at me, his eyes already bright. The light cast strange shadows on his face, emphasizing his cheekbones and the dark circles underneath his eyes. "And if it goes wrong—"

"It won't," Ryan said, his voice firm. "Me and Harper are here, and it's . . ." His eyes met mine over David's shoulder. "It's going to be fine."

It was the first time since all of this had happened that I honestly felt like that might be true. It was nice, going through one of these with everyone. Even with the oddness that was Bee and Ryan, I felt better having her here.

Reaching over with my free hand, I took Bee's and gave it a quick squeeze before letting go and taking Ryan's other hand.

"Ready?" I asked both boys, and they nodded.

There was a feeling in the air, a slight electric tingle that I recognized but still hadn't quite gotten used to. My hair felt like it was crackling over my shoulders, and on the other side of David, I heard Ryan suck in a breath.

David closed his eyes, but I could see the glow brightening behind the thin skin of his eyelids, and his hand shook in mine.

The electric feeling in the air got stronger, almost uncomfortably so, and I opened my eyes to see the flag stuck by the eighth hole snapping like there was a breeze, but the air was totally still.

Frowning, I held David's hand tighter. The flag waved again, then stopped, almost like it was frozen. Another ripple, but there was something off about it, something unnatural.

"Harper!" I heard someone cry. I thought it was Bee.

And then I didn't hear anything else as the world shattered apart around me.

Chapter 29

THERE WAS a sound like something tearing, and I felt David's hand fall from mine, but I couldn't see anything. Nothing except this bright golden light, so bright that I had to turn my face away, covering my eyes and crying out. Underneath me, the ground rumbled, and I felt like my whole body was about to shake itself apart.

It was still so bright that I could barely see, but I held my hand over my eyes and I could make out David on his feet off to one side.

There was a sound like wind or the ocean roaring in my ears, and I gritted my teeth against the hammering in my head. I'd seen David have visions lots of times now, had seen Blythe's ritual take him over the night of Cotillion, but this was something totally new. Something terrifying.

I caught movement out of the corner of my eye, and saw that the little pond next to the fairway was roiling, waves splashing onto the reeds by the shore, its entire surface practically bubbling. Bee followed my gaze, her eyes huge. "Harper!" she called out, but I only shook my head, my attention focused on David.

He was standing up straight, his arms rigid at his sides. At some point, his glasses had fallen off, but that didn't matter since his eyes were just glowing orbs now.

David stared at me, and I waited for him to do his normal thing, spouting out a direction or a specific event we needed to beware of.

But he didn't say anything at all. He kept looking at me, and I felt everything inside me go very cold. It was like what I'd seen in the Fun House, that same amount of power and that . . . I don't know, *lack* of David. He wasn't a person; he was a thing, just like I'd always feared.

The longer he stood there, saying nothing, but with power rolling off him in waves, the colder I felt. He'd broken through whatever it was Alexander had done to him. What did that mean? And what the hell was he *seeing*?

But David just watched me, the light burning and hurting. Still, I wouldn't look away. I couldn't.

"What exactly do you see?" another voice shouted. Ryan.

He moved closer to me, the wind or whatever the heck it was blowing his shirt away from his body as he looked at David, one hand lifted against the light. "Give us something here, man."

David's bright gaze swung to Ryan, and I saw Ryan flinch against it, but he still stood there, his shoulders back, his eyes trying to stay locked on David's face.

"Harper, what's going on?" Ryan shouted, lifting one hand to shade his eyes. "Why isn't he saying anything?"

I could only shake my head, and then there was this feeling, almost like a surge of power. I felt my hair blow back, and swore

I saw the ground ripple. Bee gave a little scream, and when I turned toward her, I saw a small section of grass was on fire.

Bee rushed over to it, stomping out the small flames with her booted foot.

David's eyes swung to me, but they weren't his eyes, not even a little bit. He didn't say anything, but I could feel something happening. He was seeing something, something to do with me. I couldn't say how I knew it. It was more like I felt it, this certainty that whatever vision he was locked into, it involved me.

I thought again about my knife at his throat, the bright red of his blood when I'd jerked my arm, and felt my stomach roil.

There was another pulse of power, and the ground shuddered, a crack springing up a few feet away from me, snaking through the earth, sending up clumps of grass and red dirt. It was close enough to Bee that she had to scramble backward, tripping as the ground gave way underneath one shoe.

"David!" I screamed.

The power went out of him all at once, and he sagged to the ground so suddenly that neither Ryan nor I had a chance to catch him. David fell in a heap, and all three of us moved forward, but I got to him first, resting my palm against his cheek. "David? David, wake up."

His eyes slowly blinked open, still bright, but nowhere near as blinding, and without thinking, I gave a soft cry of relief and leaned forward to kiss his cheek.

"See?" I told him. "You're fine, it's all fine."

But it wasn't, and all four of us knew it. That much power . . .

It felt like everything Saylor had warned me about, and I could see just how much it had taken out of David.

If I'd thought the ride to the golf course was awkward, that was nothing compared to the ride home. David sat on my left, his knees drawn up tight, his head resting against the window. I was holding his glasses, and he kept his eyes closed the whole way back. I could still see the light burning behind his eyelids, though, and his whole frame shook with occasional tremors.

"Should we take him to Alexander's?" Ryan asked.

"No," David replied. His voice sounded so thin and weak that it broke my heart. "I want to go home."

"Fair enough," Ryan said, and I reached over to hold David's hand. He curled his fingers around mine again, but this time they felt cold and clammy, and all I could think of was him standing there on the grass, light and power pouring out of him.

David's house was dark as I let us in, and even though he seemed a lot better than he had in the car, I kept my arm around his waist as we walked up the stairs. His room was, as usual, kind of a wreck, and I kicked clothes out of the way, clearing a path to his bed. That was also cluttered, but with books, and when I swept them all to the floor, David winced at the thump.

"Be careful with those, Pres," he said, and I was happy to hear him call me that. Happy that he finally sounded like the David I knew and not some kind of mystical bigwig.

Now that we were alone, I had to ask. "David, what did you see tonight?"

When he turned to look at me, there were still dark circles underneath his eyes, and the hollows under his cheekbones seemed deeper. There were little pinpricks of light at the center of each of his pupils, and I had to try very hard not to shudder at that.

He shook his head, rubbing a hand over his mouth. "It wasn't anything," he said at last. "A jumble of stuff." He glanced up at me, brows lifted. "Alexander's spell must have worked in some way."

He was lying.

There was no doubt in my mind. I had known David Stark most of my life, and I knew that look, knew from the way his lips twitched that he wasn't telling the truth.

I didn't press him—tonight had been rough enough on him— but I decided I would do a little truth-telling of my own.

"I had a vision, too, you know," I said, crossing my arms over my chest. "The night of my second trial. I saw you like that, the way you were tonight. I . . . I saw me with you." I couldn't add the part about what I'd done to him in that vision. I wanted to, but the words were too awful, and I couldn't seem to say them. Instead, I said, "The me I saw in the vision, she looked at me. She told me to choose."

David blew out a very long breath, his shoulders sagging a little. "You've had a lot to choose between," he said, reaching out with one hand and idly pushing his desk chair in a slow circle. "Your regular life, or life as my Paladin. Me as a person or me as an Oracle." He glanced up then, the tiniest smile lifting one corner of his lips. "And of course the most important choice of all— plaid or paisley?"

I laughed, but it sounded a lot like a sob. "As if."

Sitting gingerly on the edge of the bed, I reached out and took David's hand, pulling him closer to me. As soon as he did, he wrapped his arms around me, pulling me in tight for a hug. He wasn't shaking now, and I buried my face in the crook of his neck, breathing him in. I knew this was definitely not something we were supposed to do anymore—we were in boyfriend/girlfriend territory for sure with this kind of hug—but it felt so nice, and I'd missed it so much that I couldn't make myself stop. Not when every time I closed my eyes, I still saw him as the Oracle, not the boy.

"I'm sorry," he choked out, and I let my hands drift up and down his back.

"Sorry for what? You didn't do anything wrong tonight. We knew it might go like this, and—"

But he shook his head and pulled back. "No. I don't mean for tonight. I mean, I am sorry for that. I know it was scary. But I'm sorry for all of it." His hands came up to cup my face, fingers cold against my skin, but I leaned into him, resting my forehead against his.

"I'm sorry I told you we should take a break. I liked you for such a long time," David continued, making me huff out a laugh even as I reached up to curl my fingers around his.

"Even when I was beating you in spelling bees?"

David closed his eyes, a smile lifting his lips. "Especially then," he told me, his hand cupping the back of my neck. "And I feel like I finally got everything I ever wanted, and I screwed it up."

"You didn't," I promised him. "I mean, it's not like any relationship between the two of us was going to run smoothly. Making the shift from mortal enemy to boyfie was bound to be difficult."

He huffed out a laugh, opening his eyes. "I told you not to call me—" he started.

I kissed him.

It was stupid, probably. I never wanted to admit that Alexander was right, but if David couldn't be saved and he would eventually be that glowing, powerful creature all the time, I'd only get my heart broken.

But maybe it was too late for that, anyway.

"Pres," David said softly when we parted. "Is this, like, the absolute worst time in the world to tell you I love you?"

I wasn't sure if it was a laugh or a sob welling up in my throat, but I nodded. "Pretty much, yeah."

"We suck at timing, don't we?"

"We do."

And then David smiled. "Good thing we're so good at kissing."

He kissed me again then, and again, sitting on the edge of his bed, our arms twined around each other.

After a long while, David lifted his head, his fingers playing along the back of my neck. "Choose," he mused, and I shook my head, letting my hand rest on the back of his neck, too.

He sighed, his breath ruffling my hair, and I tightened my grip on him. "I choose you," I whispered. "I choose you, David. No matter what."

David wanted to argue. I knew him well enough to know

that, to understand that that was why his mouth quirked down, why his eyebrows drew together, why he said "Pres" one more time.

But then I kissed him, really kissed him this time, and there was no more arguing.

There were hardly any more words at all.

Chapter 30

"ALEXANDER WANTS to see us." I have to be honest, those were not exactly the words I wanted to hear from David after everything that had happened the night before, but when he came up and found me at lunch, that was what he blurted out.

I was eating in the library again, thinking that after a few more days like this I'd have to buy an all-black wardrobe and stop combing my hair, so when David suddenly appeared in the stacks, my cheeks flushed bright red, and I felt weirdly nervous.

As a result, it took a minute for what he was saying to sink in. When it did, I stood up, dusting my hands on my pants—I'd taken to wearing pants more often at school on the offhand chance that something Peirasmos related could happen—and crammed my half-empty water bottle back into my bag.

"Did he say what it was about?" I asked, and David gave me that look from underneath his brows. There were still little pin-pricks of light in his eyes, glowing brighter in the dim library, and I noticed he still had sunglasses hanging from the collar of his shirt.

"Pretty sure there's only one thing it could be about, Pres. He has to know about last night."

Again with the blushing. I knew David was referring to the vision at the golf course, but I remembered the way Alexander had looked at the two of us when he'd figured out what we were to each other. What if he wanted to talk about . . . the other thing that had happened yesterday?

The same idea had apparently occurred to David, because it was his turn to go pink, his eyes dropping to the floor. "I'll meet you by your car after school?" he asked, and I nodded.

I could barely concentrate on anything else for the rest of the day, and when Bee found me as I made my way out to the parking lot after the last bell, she had to call my name more than once.

It was another beautiful sunny day, and Bee looked just as beautiful and sunny herself as she jogged toward me in a lime-green shirt and white jeans. "Hey," she breathed when she caught up with me. "Are you okay?"

"Yeah," I said with a quick nod, even though I felt anything but. The weirdness between me and David, knowing that Alexander was waiting . . . It was a lot on my mind, almost too much for me to focus on the fact that things with me and Bee weren't exactly the best right now. But then she reached out, laying a hand on my shoulder, and looked down into my face.

"Are we okay?"

Taking a deep breath, I shook my head. "Probably not?" And then I smiled, a little shakily. "But we will be."

Now it was Bee's turn to take a deep breath, but she smiled back at me, squeezing my shoulder. "Good. That's . . . good."

I wanted to stay and talk to her longer, but I could already see David standing by my car, so with a little wave at Bee, I made my way toward him.

"How?" It was the first thing Alexander had said to us when we walked in the door, and he seemed determined to repeat it now. We were in his office, but for once, he wasn't sitting behind the desk. Instead, he was pacing, a hank of hair coming forward to fall over his forehead.

David and I stood on the rug like a couple of kids called to meet the principal, and I wondered why I felt so guilty. David could do whatever the heck he wanted with his visions, and while, yeah, it had gotten a little scary there for a second, it wasn't like anyone had been hurt. Besides, he'd proven exactly how powerful he was, and that seemed like something we should actually be pretty pumped about.

"Was it from one of the books your Mage kept?" Alexander asked, almost frantic. His tie was loose, one cuff of his shirt unbuttoned where it peeked out from underneath his jacket sleeve. "A . . . a ritual or something that you found and decided to experiment with."

"There wasn't a book," David told him, jamming his hands into his back pockets. "I just . . . I felt like if I tried, I could have a vision, and I did. It was cloudy and . . . I don't know, murky. Like they used to be before Blythe did the ritual."

Alexander stopped pacing, coming to stand in front of his desk with both hands braced on the edge. "But you *did* see something?"

David kept his hands in the pockets of his skinny jeans, his shoulders tight. After a moment, he nodded, and Alexander dropped his head with a deep sigh.

I'd never seen Alexander look anything besides 100 percent with-it and together, but now, he wiped a hand across his mouth, and I could swear he was shaking. There was also something about the way he was looking at David that I definitely did not like.

"It's impossible," he said. "Even with the ritual Blythe performed, there's no way you should . . . No one has ever overcome the removal spell I did on you. *Ever.*"

Next to me, David gave a familiar shrug. "Well, I did." He said it as a challenge, and as I watched, David pushed his shoulders back, meeting Alexander's gaze head-on.

"What was it you saw?" Alexander asked, and David flexed his fingers. I was waiting for that answer myself, but if David wouldn't tell me, I knew he wouldn't tell Alexander. And sure enough, after a pause, he shook his head.

Alexander stood there, his hair still messy, his gaze fixed on David's face, and while his expression didn't change, it was like I could see the gears whirring in his head. I sometimes felt that with David, too, that I could sense all that was going on beneath the surface, and it was weird to have the same feeling watching Alexander.

Then he straightened up abruptly, fixing his tie and tugging at the unbuttoned cuff with a sniff. "The Peirasmos is cancelled," he said in a tight voice, and I blinked, caught totally off guard.

"What?"

"There's no need for it anymore," Alexander continued, and when his eyes met mine, they were hard chips of pale green ice.

But I'd faced a lot of scarier things than one pissed-off snooty guy, so I met that cold gaze and asked, "Why? A few weeks ago, this was so important that if I didn't do it, I'd *die*, and now you're telling me, 'oh, no big, totes cancelled, everyone go on your merry way!'"

Alexander stood ramrod straight, his fingers still on the cuff of his shirt. "I do not know what 'totes' means in this context, but I assure you, no one is 'going on their merry way,' Miss Price."

With that, he crossed over to his desk, pulling open a drawer and yanking out an ancient-looking binder of some kind, the leather cracked and peeling. As he smacked it on top of his desk, he glanced up at the two of us.

"You may go now," he said, lifting one long-fingered hand to more or less shoo us away.

I stayed right where I was, hands on my hips. "Um, I will not be shooed. What is going on here?"

"What is going on," Alexander replied, bracing both hands on his desk to look up at me, "is that our Oracle is more powerful than I'd guessed, and now I have to rethink some things. Which I can do much better without you standing there yammering at me."

I was pretty sure I'd never been accused of "yammering" in

my life, and I was about to *show* Alexander what real yammering was, but David tugged my elbow, pulling me toward the door. "Let's get out of here, Pres."

I followed him through the house, and as we got close to the front door, a loose board tripped me, the tip of my shoe catching its lip. David paused, but I gave him a little wave, saying, "I'm fine, no worries." But as I looked back at the board, I noticed it wasn't the only one that was loose. There were a couple that were warped and not fitting flush against the floor anymore. That was weird. As was how . . . unshiny the hardwood looked. And when I glanced at the wall, I could see wallpaper peeling in the corners. Even the paintings seemed less glowy than before.

Maybe whatever magic Alexander had used to make this place was fading. Or maybe it looked worse in the afternoon sun. I had no idea, and at the moment, my brain was so full of thoughts, I couldn't stop to consider that.

We paused on the porch, David's hands thrust into his pockets, my own dangling limply at my side. I had no idea what I wanted him to say. We weren't fine. No matter what had happened last night, we weren't back together, and none of the issues between us had been solved. I knew that, and from the slump in his shoulders, I think he must have, too.

"Guess you don't have to do the pageant now," he finally said. The afternoon light was turning his hair a dark gold, almost the same color as Alexander's. I could hear the hum of insects, the soft whisper of the breeze through the tall grass, and all I wanted to do was step back into his arms like I had yesterday after the golf course.

But I stayed where I was on my side of the steps, watching David. "I guess I don't," I agreed, "but I might as well at this point. I think Sara Plumley might actually murder me if I dropped out."

That made him smile, but it didn't reach his eyes, and I felt a million unsaid words sitting between us.

"Pres, about last night—"

"If you say you're sorry," I interrupted, "I'll murder *you*. Not that I can, of course, but I could try."

This time, his smile was genuine, but there was something sad in it. "I wasn't going to. I was going to say . . . Look, it's not like I can say it didn't change things, exactly, but . . ."

My chest hurt, but it had nothing to do with any Paladin powers.

"But it's still easier when we're not together," I finished, and David sighed, his eyes searching the horizon.

"It's not easier," he said, and I heard the slight catch in his voice. "But it's still the best thing we can do."

He turned to look at me then, and I wasn't sure if it was the sun on his glasses or that glow that still wasn't going anywhere. "I meant everything I said last night. Every word. But—"

"We need to stay Paladin/Oracle and lose the whole boyfie/girlfie thing," I said, and David's lips twitched.

"Still the worst word."

I smiled at him even though nothing in me felt all that smiley. He was right, I knew that. But that didn't mean I had to like it.

And then he turned to me, taking my hands in his and searching my face. "Even if the Peirasmos is over, that doesn't suddenly make things right, you know? There could still be people want-ing to take me, you'd still have to deal with Bee and her Paladin powers, I could turn into . . . Pres, look into my eyes."

I knew he didn't mean that in a romantic way, and sure enough when I looked closer, I could see the dots of light there in his pupils.

"That's not going away," he told me. "And I have a feeling that every time I have a vision, they're going to get bigger and brighter. You keep saying you don't want me to go with Alexan-der because he'll turn me into a 'thing,' but . . . Harper, I think that's going to happen anyway."

"It's not," I said, shaking my head. "I know that if we—we work at it, and try to—"

"Harper." He squeezed my fingers tighter. "It's going to happen."

Stupid as it was, I heard myself blurt out, "You can't know that."

But of course he could. Of course he *did*.

I stepped back, letting my hands fall from his. "That's what you saw, isn't it? Last night at the golf course."

"Part of what I saw, yeah," David said, turning away and heading down the porch steps.

I stood where I was, and despite the warmth of the late spring afternoon, I suddenly felt very cold. "What was the rest?" I asked.

He didn't answer.

Chapter 31

THE NIGHT of the pageant was hot and muggy. Mom and Dad still didn't quite get why I even wanted to do it, but they came anyway. "I missed Cotillion," Mom had said as she'd carried my baton out to the car, my costume in a garment bag draped over one arm. "I won't miss this."

Without Ryan's powers, there was no way to keep my parents from coming, although, trust me, I'd been trying to find an excuse. Of course, now I guessed that didn't matter so much. Alexander had said that the Peirasmos were over, but you couldn't blame me for not trusting the guy. He'd looked plenty freaked out the last time I'd seen him, and I'd thought he'd sounded sincere. But then I remembered Cotillion and the Ephors' flair for the dramatic. It would be just like them to make me lower my guard, only to attack when I was unprepared.

That wasn't going to happen.

So by the time we got to the rec center, I was already pretty tense.

So was Sara Plumley. Granted, she wasn't worrying about the boy she loved possibly turning into a mystical being, but from the way she was running around shrieking, you would think something a lot more dire had happened than one girl running a little late.

"Harper!" she barked at me as soon as I walked backstage. "I thought you weren't coming!"

"It isn't that big of a deal," Bee said, walking in behind me. "She was—"

"What if she hadn't been here?" Sara near-shrieked. "One girl missing creates a hole in the choreography!"

With that, she stomped off, clipboard in hand, heels clacking, and as soon as she was gone, Bee and I burst into giggles.

"Maybe we should have told Sara about Cotillion," I said, hanging up my talent costume. "It might have put things in perspective."

I'd meant to make Bee laugh, but instead, she frowned. And when she reached out to take my hand, I realized she was shaking.

"Hey, are you all right?" I asked, stepping closer.

Bee smiled brightly, and something in my stomach twisted. I knew that smile. I'd made that smile before. That was the smile of a girl desperately trying to fake it.

"What—" I started, but then the lights blinked twice, signaling that it was almost time for the pageant to start.

"That's our cue!" Bee chirped, and then she was out of the dressing room, leaving me to trail in her wake, confused.

We gathered in a straight line toward the back of the stage, and as the curtain went up, music blared from the sound system. I was between Bee and Rebecca Shaw, which made me feel about three feet tall, but that was actually okay. The fewer people noticed me as we launched into our supremely cheesy dance routine (one that involved smiling too hard, thrusting our arms out, and the occasional pivot) the happier I was.

As I thrust out one hip, I shot a look at Bee out of the side of my eye. Honestly, the things I did to be a good friend.

The dance portion mercifully over, Sara emerged from the wings. Her dress wasn't quite as sparkly as the contestants' were, but she was still wearing her Miss Pine Grove sash and tiara from five years ago.

Pushing her dark glossy hair back off her shoulders, Sara smiled out at the audience. "Good evening, y'all!" she drawled, the words nearly echoing throughout the room. When there was no reply, she tilted her head a bit, that bright smile stretching even further.

"I said good evening!" she called again—and I guess once head cheerleader, always a head cheerleader, but I resolved right that second to never, ever be Sara Plumley. In fact, I might turn in my uniform first thing Monday morning.

After the audience gave her the response she wanted, Sara beamed harder, taking a sip from the water glass on the podium, leaving a bright red lip print on the rim. "All right, folks, we're going to go ahead and get started," she announced. "First we'll give y'all a chance to meet these lovely ladies before proceeding to the talent portion and then the evening gown competition. And before we leave tonight, one of these very lucky girls will be Miss Pine Grove."

There was a round of applause for that, and I bit back a sigh. The whole night seemed to stretch out in front of me, and I suddenly wondered what David was doing tonight. Was he sitting all alone in his room, listening to that whiny music I hated? Was he thinking about me?

Rebecca Shaw had completed her circuit of the stage and answered the judge's question—the ever-so-original "What would you do if you won the lottery?"—but I hadn't heard Rebecca's answer. I assumed it was something equally original, like "Give it all to charity." It wasn't until she slid back into place next to me that I remembered I was next.

I broke off from the rest of the line, walking to the front of the stage as Sara rattled off my name, age, and who my parents were. The lights nearly blinded me and my smile felt frozen on my face as I walked, but I tried to keep my head high and my shoulders back.

The Aunts and my mom and dad were sitting in the front row, and seeing them, my smile felt a little more natural. But then, in the row behind them, I could see David.

What was he doing here? My eyes met David's, and it might have been the lights, but I was sure that his eyes were glowing faintly behind his glasses. Not only that, but his whole body was drawn up tight in his seat.

Maybe he was weirded out from seeing me after the last time we'd talked, but I wasn't sure. What I was sure of was how my heart thudded painfully against my ribs when I saw him.

I was so distracted by worrying about that that I almost

walked right past the microphone. It was only when I heard Sara hiss, "Harper," that I stopped, disoriented. There was the squeal of feedback as I grabbed the mike stand with unsteady hands.

From behind the podium, Sara winced, but she kept that bright smile on her face as she chirped out, "Harper, your question from the judges tonight is: If there was one thing in your life you could change, what would it be?"

I swallowed, my eyes still on David's. In the audience, I could hear the rattle of programs and someone unwrapping a hard candy. The lights were still too bright, and I was suddenly afraid that I might actually be sweating.

But my voice was calm and sure as I answered, "Nothing."

When I didn't elaborate, Sara gave a nervous laugh. "Not a single thing?"

David was watching me, sitting up straighter in his seat. The auditorium was full of people, but in that moment, I felt like we were the only people there. "No. I wouldn't change anything. Not one bit of it. I mean, don't get me wrong, not everything in my life has been . . . easy. There's a lot that's been harder than I ever thought it would be, and there may have been times I've wished things were different. But that doesn't mean I'd ever want to change it. No matter what."

My words echoed through the room, but they were only for David, and when he smiled, I smiled back, feeling almost light-headed with relief. Until I'd said the words, I hadn't realized they were true, but now that I knew, now that I was sure, there was nothing I wanted more than to climb down off this stage and go find David and make things right between us.

But then Sara gave another one of those laughs and said, "Well, all right, then, Harper. Thank you for your answer."

Dismissed, I made my way back to the line of girls, taking my spot beside Bee. She glanced down at me, and something strange passed over her face for a minute. Pursing her lips slightly, she studied my face before turning to the front again.

The talent portion was next, and as the girls all raced off to the dressing room, I hung back in the wings. Could I just leave? Maybe I could tell Sara I'd gotten sick. The last thing she'd want was one of the girls puking all over her stage, so I was sure she'd let me go.

I wanted to go out in the audience and find David, grab him, and get the heck out of here.

But then Bee stopped beside me, taking my elbow. "Harper? Come on, we need to get changed."

"I'm actually thinking I might leave," I whispered, leaning in close as Rebecca dashed past me in a pink tutu. "I don't feel so great."

Frowning, Bee studied my face. "You can't leave in the middle of the pageant."

With a light laugh, I shrugged. "Why not? You can stay, obviously. To be honest, I'd much rather watch you win from the audience."

Bee reached out, her fingers closing around my elbow. "No," she said firmly. "You can't leave."

I stared up at her, surprised. "Bee, I know you wanted us to do this together, but it's not really my thing, and I need to talk to David—"

Her fingers squeezed tighter. "I thought y'all broke up."

Shaking off her hand, I stepped back. "We did. Kind of, but that's not—Bee, are you honestly mad at me because I don't want to finish the pageant?"

The lights backstage outlined her in soft blue light, her dress twinkling and shimmering in the gloom. And then I realized she was trembling.

"Bee?" I asked, and then it hit me.

Pop Rocks exploded in my stomach, racing through my veins, my whole chest tightening.

Gasping, I leaned forward, one arm banded around my waist. "I have to go," I said, panicked. "David—"

But Bee only grabbed my elbow again, and now she wasn't so much trembling as shaking. "No," she said, her voice wavering. "You have to *stay*."

I tried to shake out of her grip again, but she was holding on too tight, and my Paladin powers were no help against hers. "Something is wrong with David," I told her, reaching out to pry her hand from my arm. "That's a lot more important than a freaking pageant, Bee."

Looking up, our gazes met, and just like that, I understood. Bee wasn't holding me so that I wouldn't leave the pageant. That wasn't what this was about.

Tears pooled in her big dark eyes. "I'm sorry, Harper," she said. "But I can't let you go."

Chapter 32

I FROZE. If it had been anyone else, I wouldn't have hesitated. But this was Bee. I couldn't just start swinging fists.

But apparently Bee didn't have any reservations on that front. Placing her hands firmly on my shoulders, she shoved, hard.

It was enough to send me stumbling backward, and I heard a delighted gasp from behind me. "I told you what pageants were like," someone said, but I was already regaining my footing and taking off after Bee.

I stumbled over cables in the dim light, barely able to make out the blue sequins on her dress flashing as she dodged behind one of the curtains.

One of the stage managers gave a startled cry as she pushed past him, and he may have used a four-letter word when I did the same.

Bee was right against the back wall of the theater now, a giant fake oak tree blocking her path.

She turned to face me, wearing an expression I'd never seen before. One that, to be honest, I never would have thought Bee was even capable of. She was practically snarling.

"I trusted you." It was the only thing I could think to say, the only words that seemed to be pounding inside my head, and they hurt coming out of my mouth. They hurt maybe more than anything else I'd ever said. This couldn't be happening. I couldn't have been wrong. Not about Bee.

"Trust me now, Harper," she choked out in reply. "This is the only way."

I reached out and yanked a branch off the fake tree. The crack was probably loud enough to be heard in the audience, but I didn't care. "By letting the Ephors take David? That's what this is about, isn't it? You're working for Alexander."

Bee reached out and did the same with another branch, and we stood there facing each other, fake branches clutched in our hands, both of us breathing hard.

"I'm not working for them," Bee said, her fingers tight around that branch. "It isn't about Alexander or any of that, Harper, I swear, but you can't go to him. I can't let you."

"He's in danger," I cried, my chest seizing even as I said the words.

Nodding, Bee gripped her branch harder. "He might be, yeah. But I promised him I'd let him do this."

The words landed harder than her blows had. "What?"

"I promised David," she said, and I felt like my head was spinning. "He knew you'd never let him leave, knew you'd fight to keep him here. But this—" She clutched the branch harder, and I saw tears start to pool in her eyes. "This is what's actually best for him." Her voice had turned pleading now. "Please, Harper, don't make me do this."

Out onstage, I could hear Sara announcing the beginning of the talent portion of the pageant. The stereo system was blasting some kind of terrible smooth jazz, but even that couldn't drown out the rush of blood in my ears as I faced down Bee. I knew what she meant. We were both protecting David, albeit in different ways. My Paladin instincts weren't going to quit until the threat—Bee—was eliminated. Bee wouldn't stop until she'd fulfilled whatever vow it was she'd made to David.

"Nothing bad is going to happen to him," Bee said.

"That's a lie," I cried, "because I wouldn't feel like this if he were going to be fine."

Bee shook her head, hard enough that her blond hair began to spill out of her updo. "It's the only way."

With that, she swung the branch at me. I raised my own, blocking her blow. Whoever had made the fake tree had done a darn good job, because even though I could feel the reverberations all the way down my arms, the branch didn't break.

Throwing my weight behind it, I pivoted the branch in a wide circle, trying to disarm Bee, but she was prepared for that. She'd planted her feet, and while she grimaced, she kept her hold on the branch, and then, with a sharp stabbing motion, managed to drive me back.

"The only way for what?" I asked. "For him to run away and get caught by Alexander and the rest of the Ephors, who will kidnap him and turn him into their personal fortune-teller?"

I gritted my teeth, hands nearly numb with how tightly I was holding on to my weapon, and let myself be led backward. That had been one of Saylor's lessons: Let them think they have the upper hand. Bet on their overconfidence giving you a window of opportunity.

"No," she replied. "It's the only way for any of us to have a normal life again."

Bee pushed forward with her branch and I stepped back, my high heel catching on the velvet curtain a little.

And then suddenly I was blinded by bright lights and I heard a big intake of breath, like a bunch of people had gasped all at once. What the—

In front of me, Bee hesitated for a second, her head swinging to the left.

Oh. Crap.

We were onstage.

As I looked out into the audience, I saw my parents tilt their heads to the side, faces wrinkled in confusion. Next to them, Aunt Jewel raised one hand to cover her mouth.

Aunts May and Martha were still eating lemon drops, seemingly unconcerned that their niece had just torn down the curtain and appeared onstage with her best friend, both of us swinging giant fake branches.

The music was still playing, something from *Swan Lake,* and I remembered Rebecca in a tutu.

She was frozen at the corner of the stage now, staring at me and Bee, one arm still raised over her head, her feet in second position.

Then, with a grunt, Bee swung at me again, the branch connecting with my thigh. The pain helped me focus, and I turned back to her, parrying with a vengeance. My blow caught her on the ribs, and as she staggered back, she cried, "Just let it happen, Harper. I promise, it's for the best."

I gave one quick glance to the audience, my eyes searching for David. But his seat and the ones around it were empty, and my stomach was jumping, my chest still so tight I could hardly breathe.

With a snarl, I launched myself at Bee. "That's what Blythe said, too. That the ritual was for the best, and look what it did to you. Can you honestly"—I sucked in a breath as Bee's branch grazed my knuckles—"say it was for the best?"

I wished now I'd picked a looser dress. The tight sheath skirt made it hard to maneuver quickly, and Bee's dress was a lot more voluminous, giving her a freedom of movement I just did not have.

We stumbled across the stage, the music from *Swan Lake* still blasting through the auditorium, our arms a blur of thrusts and swings and blows. Bee's hair had completely fallen by now, and her long blond curls swung around her face as we fought. Her face was blotchy with tears and sweat, and I knew mine was, too.

"Let him go!" Bee yelled again, and this time, when her branch hit me square in the chest, I fell to my knees. Even over the music, I could hear a gasp from the audience.

Pressing one hand against the stage, I tried to catch my breath. My body ached from David being in danger, and I could feel every one of Bee's hits. I'd only ever fought another Paladin like this—seriously—once, the night I'd killed Dr. DuPont. I realized then that every cell inside me was crying out to kill Bee.

That she was the thing standing between me and David. But for once, my mind was overriding my instincts.

No matter what my duty, no matter that she had lied to me and led us to this, this was Bee, and I couldn't kill her. Not for David, not for Pine Grove. Not for anything.

She swung the branch down in an arc toward my head, probably hoping to knock me out.

I reached up with one hand and caught the wood in my palm. The shock of it jarred all the way down to my shoulder, but I used the branch to leverage myself back into a standing position. Gripping Bee's branch as hard as I could, I looked into her tear-streaked face.

"I'm sorry," I gritted out, and then I swung.

I pulled back at just the right moment, the branch glancing off her temple instead of crashing into her skull. But it was still enough to make her eyes roll back, and Bee slumped to a sequined heap on the floor.

At that exact moment, the music cut off, and for a long moment, all I could hear were my own ragged breaths and the thundering of my heart in my ears.

And then, from the auditorium, Aunt May said, "Ooh, performance art!" and started to clap.

Hers was the only applause, though, and as I looked out at the audience, I saw my parents sitting like they were frozen in their seats, their mouths open in identical Os of horror. It was a sea of pale, shocked faces as far as I could see.

Another pair of hands began clapping loudly. As I watched, Aunt Jewel rose from her seat, her tall form sparkling slightly from the sequins on her dress. "It's part of the show!" she said loudly, still clapping and giving me a nod. "Performance art!"

Her words slowly started to penetrate the rest of the crowd, and there was the slightest smattering of applause, but for the most part, everyone was still gaping at me, and I felt sick to my stomach.

The sick feeling increased when I looked down and saw Bee, slumped there on the stage, her temple already swelling, black and blue.

But I couldn't worry about that right now. Not when something was happening to David.

Nodding at Aunt Jewel in thanks, I dropped the branch and ran.

Chapter 33

My instincts were leading me outside, and as I ran backstage, I dodged the other girls, all of whom were blinking at me. "What was that?" Abi asked, her hand closing around my elbow, but I shook her off, making my way to the back door that led to the parking lot behind the rec center.

I pressed down hard on the bar, but the door wouldn't budge. The tightness in my chest was getting worse, my blood and heart racing, and I tried again, even harder this time.

But whoever had sealed this door had done a darn good job, and when I squinted at the bar, I saw crude runes scratched into the metal.

My whole body went cold.

Those were wards. A Mage had put those there.

"Harper," Ryan said, panting, and I turned to see him standing beside me. His tie was loose, his cheeks flushed, and he'd shed the jacket he'd been wearing earlier.

"Can you undo this?" I asked, gesturing to the door. "We've got to get—"

"To David, I know. But . . . Harper, let him go."

I'm pretty sure my mouth actually fell open. "You're in on this?"

He winced. "Don't say it like that. Like we're not on the same side."

My chest was so tight it was a wonder I could breathe, but I managed to say, "If you did these"—I pointed savagely at the wards—"then we are *not* on the same side, Ryan. Not even remotely."

Ryan's gaze swung to mine, his face pale. "We both want what's best for David, right? Harper, this is what's best."

Tears spilled down my cheeks all over again, and I wiped at them. "Then why is my chest on fire? Why do I know he's in danger, Ryan?"

When he didn't answer, I kept going. "Did Bee talk you into this? Did she tell you she was doing this to save David? Because that wasn't her call to make. Or yours." I hit my breastbone with my fist, but that was nothing compared to the pain there. "It was *mine*. You lied to me, both of you lied, and—"

Ryan crossed the space between us, one warm hand coming down on my forearm. "David didn't want to tell you. He knew you'd never let him go. That you *couldn't* if it was dangerous. So he . . . he asked us to help, and what were we supposed to say?"

I didn't know how to answer that. They were supposed to be loyal to me? Supposed to tell me what David had planned?

From the stage, I heard music start up again and I stood up fast enough to make me dizzy.

Looking back toward the stage, I couldn't see any sign of Bee and I ducked back down beside Ryan, hissing, "She's gone. Bee."

Ryan sighed, scrubbing a hand over his face. "You didn't hit her that hard," Ryan said. "And my magic fixed the rest."

I stared at him, confused. "Your magic doesn't work."

"After the vision at the golf course, it came back," Ryan answered, and I nearly squawked.

"And you didn't think this was worth telling me?" I hissed, but before Ryan could answer, there was a loud pop, followed by a hiss.

The lights overhead flickered once, twice, then went out altogether.

"That cannot be good," I whispered, and when the entire building began to shake, the screams of the audience filling my ears, Ryan muttered, "The hell?"

We crouched in the darkness, my skirt pooling around my legs, my heels wobbling slightly. I could hear Ryan breathing hard and could nearly feel the fear vibrating off him.

"Take the damn wards off the door!" I whispered. It was too dark to see him, but I could tell from the change in his breath that Ryan was looking at me. "I'm not supposed to," he answered, and honestly, I could have slugged him.

"Look," I said, leaning in closer to him. "I'll forgive you for this, and I'll even forgive you for stealing my best friend."

"I didn't—" he started, but I cut him off.

"I figure I owe you a couple of things after nearly getting you killed last year. And for . . . other stuff."

Ryan didn't say anything, and even though I knew this was not exactly the best time to get into this, I felt like it was now or never. "We should've broken up a long time before we did. I should've . . . I don't know, set you free or whatever. But we'd been together too long, and I didn't know how, and I nearly kissed David while I was dating you."

At that, Ryan gave a sharp intake of breath. Miserable, I continued. "I know, I know. I am a terrible person. But I promise nothing happened between us until after we broke up. I mean, it was like ten minutes after we broke up, which I still don't feel great about, but—"

"Harper." Ryan grabbed my elbow, his fingers digging into my skin. "First off, I think Bee and I might have made a mistake about letting David go. Secondly, we have no idea where David is right now, and seeing as how it is more or less our sacred duty to protect him, that's kind of an issue. And third, I kissed Mary Beth before we broke up."

For a moment, all I could hear both of us breathing and the rush of blood in my ears. "You what?" I was proud of how non-shrieky I managed to sound, considering how shrieky I felt.

"I kissed her. That night at the movies."

The same night I had almost kissed David. I had spent all these months feeling terrible about that, and the whole time, he had been making out with Mary Beth Riley? Seriously?

I jabbed my finger in the general direction of Ryan's face. "You are so lucky we are busy right now, because if we weren't, you and I would be having a major discussion about this."

Ryan snorted and swatted at my hand. "Why? Didn't you just say we should have broken up earlier?"

"Yes! That doesn't mean it was okay for you to cheat on me."

"You had been cheating on me way before that, Harper," he hissed, and I gave a squawk of outrage.

But then he raised up on his knees, whipping out a pocket knife and scratching at the marks. The door gave with a creak, spilling Ryan out into the parking lot. He glanced over his shoulder at me.

"Harper?"

Outside, the wind was blowing hard, reminding me of the night we got Bee back from Alexander's house. Just like then, there was this almost overpoweringly electric feeling in the air, racing along my nerves and making my hair stand on end.

The parking lot was full, and several car alarms were blaring. Underneath the sodium lights, Ryan's hair was orange, his skin pale.

"This is bad," he said, his gaze darting around.

Shooting him a glare, I bent down and grabbed my skirt in both hands, ripping the little slit in the side until the dress was open to my upper thigh. I wasn't going to let the skinny skirt get in my way again. "Yes, Ryan, that's been established."

Ryan shook his head. "No, Harper, I mean . . . this is not just run-of-the-mill bad. I can feel something. There is major magic happening out here. Scary magic. It's like . . ." Trailing off, he shook his head and looked at me. "We shouldn't have done this," he said, and it wasn't the cool spring air raising goose bumps on my arms.

"We have to find David."

Chapter 34

My PARENTS had driven me, so I turned to Ryan and said, "Car!"

He was still standing there in his white button-down and khakis, looking around with a pained expression. "It wasn't supposed to go like this," he muttered, and I grabbed his shirtfront, forcing him to look in my eyes.

"It *is* going like this, though," I said, "And we need to find David now. Before it gets worse."

I remembered the wards Alexander had had Ryan put up, wards that were meant to keep David in town. We'd never tried to break a ward before; I didn't even think that was possible, but if that was what David was doing now . . .

From somewhere in the distance, there was a loud boom, and both Ryan and I flinched.

"He can't leave town," I said to Ryan. "It's not that simple. Did he not bother to explain that to y'all?"

Dazed, Ryan shook his head. "He said he had to leave, that it would be better for everyone if he did."

Looking down at me, Ryan's eyes seemed to focus. "Harper, I

think whatever he saw that night at the golf course scared the hell out of him."

I remembered what I'd seen in the Fun House. If David had seen that, if Alexander was wrong about the Fun House only showing me my worst fears . . .

"We have to get to him," I told Ryan, dropping my hands from his shirt. "And . . ."

My words trailed off. Why did we have to get him? If the wards were going off, he was already gone, and this was point-less. But I could still feel that ache in my chest, telling me that he was in danger, that we at least had to *try*.

"We're wasting time," I told Ryan, scanning the parking lot. I could still hear people leaving the rec center, and I sent up a quick prayer that my parents wouldn't worry too much about me.

Ryan took my elbow, pulling me in the direction of his car. As I hopped into the passenger seat, he glanced at me from the corner of his eye. "Bee," he said, and I held up a hand.

"We can talk about her later, but for now—"

"No, I mean Bee is heading this way," Ryan said, nodding out my window.

I turned and sure enough, there she was, a knot on one side of her forehead, but other than that, totally fine.

"We can't take her," I said to Ryan, even as he clicked the but-ton to unlock the back doors. "She'll try to stop us, she'll—"

"No, I won't," Bee replied, sliding into the backseat. When she looked at me, her expression was pleading. "I had no choice, Harper, but now that he's gone—"

"We don't know that," I snapped back, even though she was

258

probably right. Whatever the three of them had planned, it had worked.

"Where do you want to go?" Ryan asked me, and I closed my eyes, taking a deep breath and trying to sense where David was. Just outside of town, I thought. Close, still. I could find him, I could talk to him, I could get him to see that this wasn't the solution.

"Head toward the city limits," I told Ryan. "He'll be going for the highway; we might be able to catch up."

Ryan started the ignition, pulling out of the parking lot.

"When?" I asked as we left the rec center. "When did y'all put this whole plan in motion?"

There was a pause, and I could see Ryan catching Bee's eye in the rearview mirror. "Four days ago," he said, and I racked my brain, trying to remember what had happened four days ago.

We'll think of something, David had said, and I guess he had. Too bad he'd never thought to let me in on this.

"So he comes to you, says he wants your help leaving town," I clarified, and Bee leaned forward, sticking her head between our shoulders.

"Yes. He chose the night of the pageant because he'd thought you'd be distracted, and he'd hoped that it wouldn't . . . I don't know, trigger your Paladin senses or whatever."

She looked at me, and I could see the whites of her eyes around her dark irises. "He didn't think it would be dangerous."

The car rounded the square just as Adolphus Bridgeforth exploded in a shower of sparks and stonework.

All three of us instinctively ducked, and when a large piece of marble bounced against the hood of Ryan's car, denting it, he gave a groan.

I wanted to remind him that this was all his fault, his and Bee's for deciding to handle this without me, but then I remembered how much Ryan loved his SUV, and decided that would be adding insult to injury.

"Well, clearly it is," I said through clenched teeth, and Ryan took his eyes off the road long enough to flash me a panicked glance.

"What's happening?"

"Those wards Alexander had you put up, genius. Either David did some kind of crazy spell himself to get rid of them, or this is what they do when they're broken." Either option seemed possible at this point, and then something occurred to me.

My hand flew to my mouth, stomach clenching. "You put the wards where we'd put the other ones." I looked at Ryan and saw the same realization dawning on his face.

"We put hundreds of wards on Magnolia House."

I turned my head east, in the direction of the huge mansion where we'd had Cotillion, and saw a faint orange glow in the sky.

Without a word, Ryan turned the car that way.

Magnolia House was on fire. Cotillion hadn't destroyed it—although it had come pretty freaking close—but this . . . this had finally done it.

We sat in the car for a while, watching flames lick out of the windows, racing along the white wood, wrapping the huge pillars out front in fire.

"How?" Bee asked, and the words almost stuck in my throat.

"Alexander put up different wards," I told her. "To keep David here. But they . . . they didn't work." One of the upstairs windows suddenly burst outward in a spray of glass. That was the bedroom where I had kissed David for the first time, finally understanding what had been between us for all those years.

"We need to get to him," I said, even though I hated to do this. "Alexander. Maybe he can stop David."

I didn't think that would actually work. I could actually feel David getting farther away from me, a steady pulse beating behind my ribs like a second heartbeat.

I'd failed.

The one job I'd had was to keep him safe, and I hadn't been able to do that. Saylor had told me that one day, I might have to protect David from himself, but I'd never thought it would be like this. I'd imagined him having too many prophecies, burning up his mind. Never running from town—from *me*—and leaving this kind of destruction in his wake.

Silently, we drove out of town and onto the dirt road where Alexander had set up headquarters.

I waited for the house to loom out of the darkness, its windows glowing, but the closer we got, the darker it seemed to get. Frowning, I sat forward in the seat, squinting into the inky blackness.

"Where is it?" I said, then glanced over at Ryan. His hands were so tight on the steering wheel, it looked like he could snap it right off, and from the back, I heard Bee take in a sudden sharp breath.

"Harper," she said softly. "Look."

Chapter 35

THERE WAS no house left.

It was like Ryan had described that first night, just a charred and broken chimney rising from tall grass, a few stray cinder blocks littering what appeared to be an empty field.

Alexander sat on one of those blocks, his head in his hands. His hair was a mess, his tie dangling limply from his fingers, and it looked like one sleeve of his jacket was singed.

"Holy crap," Ryan murmured as he stopped the car, and I laid a hand on his sleeve.

"Let me go by myself, okay?" I wasn't sure why, but this seemed like something that should be between me and Alexander.

I thought both Bee and Ryan would argue that, but neither said a word, and I opened the car door, stepping out on shaking legs.

I took a few steps forward, my high heels crunching on stones and broken glass. My dress snagged on a tall weed, but I kept walking. Overhead, there was no moon, but the sky was full of stars.

And smoke. Not much of it—we were still a few miles outside

of town—but I could see the bright glow in the distance and took in a deep breath at the thought of Magnolia House burning.

At the knowledge that my parents were probably frantic and looking for me.

Alexander only lifted his head when I was a foot or so away, and when he did, his face looked . . . broken. His eyes were bloodshot, circled in lines, and when he smiled at me, it was one of the scariest expressions I'd ever seen.

"Is this what you wanted, then?" he asked, his voice hoarse. My chest was still aching, telling me that wherever David was, he was in danger, so I shook my head. I had never wanted David to belong the Ephors, but I hadn't wanted him to leave, either. Especially not like this. If he had known . . .

Maybe this was what he'd seen that night at the golf course? Our town burning, me standing in a deserted field with Alexander? It was difficult to speculate about what David had known or not known.

"I didn't have anything to do with this, believe it or not," I told him, coming to stand in front of him. "This was David's doing. He . . . he didn't want to go with you, but he knew he couldn't stay here." The words stuck in my throat. I hated them. Hated that as I said them, I knew David had done the right thing. Or at least the best thing he could think of.

Not that I thought this would last very long, of course.

Staring down at Alexander, I said, "I'm guessing you'll report back to the rest of the Ephors and drag him back."

"There are no more Ephors," Alexander said, his voice dull. "Only me."

I'd never thought surprise could actually knock you on your butt, but I swear I rocked back on my heels. "What?"

Still looking at the ground, his tie wrapped around his hand, Alexander gave an entirely humorless huff of laughter.

"It's flattering to know I fooled you, Harper Price, it truly is." He looked up at me, his green eyes sharp despite the obvious devastation there. "What a Paladin you would have made."

"I am a Paladin," I answered without thinking, and he smiled again. This time, there was something like fondness in it, and to be honest, I think that freaked me out more than the whole sardonic-in-the-face-of-destruction thing he'd had going on.

But then he looked back at the tie in his hands, heaving a sigh. "We can't last without the Oracle, you see. Her—or in this case *his*—power feeds ours. We're all very, very old men, no matter how dapper we appear." He gestured to himself, and I thought it would probably be mean to point out that he wasn't exactly rocking it on the dapper front right now.

"Without the Oracle, we wither. We *die*. It's why we were so desperate to find him."

Bee and Ryan still stood by the car, watching, and I gave them a little wave to let them know that I was all right. Then, clutching my skirt in my hands, I sat down on a cinder block next to Alexander, watching him carefully.

"The Peirasmos?" I asked, and Alexander heaved a sigh, grinding the heels of his palms into his eyes.

"Had you completed them, the trials would have increased your powers enough for me to use you if I had to. Ephors gain most of our strength from the Oracle's magic, but the Paladin and the Mage help as well. Not enough, not *nearly* enough, but some."

I took a deep breath. "That's why you stripped Ryan's powers. It wasn't so that he couldn't help me. It's because you were draining his . . . his Mage energy or whatever."

With another one of those humorless laughs, Alexander nodded. "Indeed. All of this had been an elaborate ploy to keep myself alive, and"—sitting up, he placed his hands on his knees, the headlights from Ryan's car winking off the heavy gold ring on his pinky finger—"you see how well it has gone for me."

"So the house was an illusion?" I asked, and Alexander shook his head.

"It was real enough. Created by magic, yes, but real."

My head hurt. My *heart* hurt. And while I wasn't sure how it was possible, I was pretty sure my soul hurt.

"If you were dying or . . . fading, how did you get enough power to set all this up?"

Alexander looked down again. His normally shiny shoes were covered in dust, and he poked at a loose stone with the toe of one. "Blythe proved useful."

They were only three words, but they sent a finger of ice down my spine. I hadn't liked Blythe—I'd hated her for taking Bee—but the idea that Alexander had killed her to take her magic . . .

Shaking his head, Alexander chuckled. "God, what a mess this is. And to think, all we wanted was to have things back the way they should've been. The way they've been for millennia. A powerful Oracle at our side, a brave Paladin, a crafty Mage. Now we have nothing."

The night was warm, but I was nearly shivering now, wrapping my arms around myself. "Will you go after him?" I asked, and Alexander looked off into the distance. It was probably just my imagination, but I could swear his cheeks looked more hollow, the lines around his eyes deeper than they were when we started talking.

"There's no point," he said. "I won't last long enough to find him, and whatever he did to blow through my wards seems to have drained the last bit of magic from me."

He smiled that ghoulish smile. "So you see, Miss Price? I am just a sad old man now. You are just a pretty girl in a silly dress. Your friends are now simply your friends. Oh, you'll all retain some powers for a while, but they'll fade over time, and all will go back to the way it was."

His smile turned fierce, almost a grimace. "Isn't that what you wanted?"

It had been. I'd spent all this time trying to make my life resemble what it had been before, trying to convince myself that I could balance it all. Paladin and SGA president, Oracle and boyfriend, family and duty. Now I had what I wanted, but as my chest ached and I thought of David, speeding off into the darkness, the cost seemed so high.

Placing his palms flat on his thighs, Alexander heaved himself to his feet, and I heard the creak of his knees. "I suppose this is my cue," he said, and I stood up, too.

"Harper?" Bee called, and I held up a hand.

"So this is done?" I asked Alexander. "My powers will . . . go away, and Bee's and Ryan's will, too?"

"Oh, it's very done," he assured me. "For you, for your friends, for David, and most certainly for me."

And with that, he fell to the ground, his eyes open.

Unseeing.

Chapter 36

"Do you have David's jump drive?"

I glanced up from my desk to see Chie standing in front of me, a sheaf of papers clutched to her middle. I hadn't thought there was anyone in all of Pine Grove who looked as wretched as I did, but she was coming in at a close second. Her dark eyes were huge and bloodshot. Apparently she hadn't been sleeping either.

Shaking my head, I murmured, "I don't know what you're talking about," but then she nodded at the bag by my feet. David's bag. I'd found it in Saylor's house that last night. There hadn't been anything else of his, other than a couple of sweaters too not-ugly to bother taking, I guess.

Maybe I'd taken those, and maybe they were hanging in my closet right now. I wasn't admitting anything.

But I'd been using David's bag since he'd left, not caring what anyone thought. Ryan had done one of his Mage tricks, convincing everyone David had taken an early acceptance at some college up North, so no one questioned my whole grieving-girlfriend thing.

Chie was watching me with an unreadable expression as I

pulled the bag into my lap, and as I rifled through it, she said, "I miss him a lot."

Her voice was soft and quiet and it made me look up at her. There was no universe in which I'd thought Chie and I could ever be friends, but seeing my own loss reflected in her face felt . . . good. Or at least comforting.

I'd been keeping my stuff in the main part of David's satchel, but I hadn't looked through the little pockets. That's where I found the jump drive, there in one of the tiny pouches inside the front flap.

It was the same bright blue as The Doctor's TARDIS, and looking at it made my eyes well up. Still, I handed it over to Chie and watched her make her way over to one of the computers in the back.

It was bizarre how . . . normal everything felt. Ever since Homecoming, I'd been wishing for normalcy, trying to shove my anything-but-ordinary life back into the box where I'd lived my actual ordinary life. And now everything *was* normal again, and I hated it.

Opening my notebook, I did my best to outline a story I wanted to write for next week's edition of *The Grove News*. It was about the chemicals they use to keep the lawns so green, and I thought it would make Chie happy.

It would've made David happy, too, probably.

For two weeks now, I'd been waiting for some feeling, some idea of what was going on with him or where he might be. I had that same faint sense that I'd always had, a weird awareness of him, but all it told me was that he was far away from me.

And moving farther.

I was so involved in sketching out my idea for the story that I was almost startled when Chie suddenly appeared in front of me again, holding out the drive. "Thanks," she said, and when I took it back from her, she hesitated for a second. I glanced up and saw her chewing on her bottom lip, watching me cautiously.

"You should look at that," she told me, gesturing toward the bright blue stick still in my hand. "I didn't read it," she went on to add quickly, "but it seems like there's something on there for you."

I almost went to one of the computers in the back and plugged it in then and there, desperate to know what David had left for me. Was it an explanation? Or a clue to where he'd gone?

But I was afraid it might not be either of those things, and I couldn't stand the idea of bursting into tears in here, in front of these people who were trying to be nice to me, but weren't really my friends.

No, there was only one place I wanted to read this. And only one person I wanted with me.

"You're sure?" Bee asked, her hand on my shoulder.

We were sitting in David's house, at the computer in his bedroom. I still had a key to the place, although with Saylor dead and David gone, none of us had any idea what to do with it. But for now, it sat like it always had, most of David's things still in his room.

Including his computer.

Nodding, I plugged in the drive and clicked on "Open."

It took me a minute to find what I was looking for. I was scanning the various documents looking for my name, so the first time I saw it, my eyes actually drifted over the file meant for me. It was Bee who leaned forward and tapped the screen, saying, "I think it's this one."

Egregious Felicitations.

With a choked laugh, I shook my head, murmuring, "You idiot."

Bee gave my shoulder a quick squeeze, and then went to sit on David's bed, leaving me alone with the computer.

I opened the file. *Pres*, it started, and then the tears were on my cheeks, splashing onto the desk. *I know you're going to say this is dumb, and I know you won't understand. Which is why I asked Bee and Ryan for help. Don't get me wrong, I like fighting with you, but there are some things you just can't argue. This is one, and I hope you'll come to accept that.*

I have to leave Pine Grove. I have to leave Alabama, and I have to leave you. After tonight, that's all completely clear to me. This whole situation is so effed up (hope you appreciate my discretion there), and it's clear to me now that the only way to un-eff it up (do I get bonus points for that one?) is to take myself out of the equation. Without me, you, Bee, and Ryan can just be you, Bee, and Ryan. Not Paladins or Mages. People. With your own lives.

It's like you said at that time at Cotillion practice—you want to be a good woman who chooses the right thing for everybody. Well, so do I. (Minus the woman part, obviously.)

Have a good life, Pres. I love you. Always.

D

I read the note two more times before closing the document and turning away from the computer.

Bee sat on the edge of the bed, watching me, her long blond hair caught in a braid over one shoulder.

"Well?" she asked.

"You did the right thing," I said, even though the words hurt, hitting my heart like broken glass. "You were the Paladin I couldn't be, I guess."

At that, Bee stood up, her skirt swishing across her knees as she crossed the room to stand in front of me.

"No," she said, shaking her head vehemently. "I wasn't his girlfriend, so it was an easier choice to make."

When I didn't say anything, Bee sighed, folding her arms across her chest. "So what do we do now?" she asked me.

I got out of David's chair, picking up his bag, but leaving the jump drive in his computer. When I walked out into the hall, Bee followed me, and we stood there, looking back into David's room. There was a steady ache in my chest, and I had no idea if it was some residual Paladin thing—if David was in danger, but too far away for me to feel that normal crushing, burning sensation—or if it was just my heart breaking all over again.

I wrapped my fingers around the doorknob and turned back to Bee.

"We go back to normal," I said, letting the door click shut.

Bee gave a little snort at that, looking around at Saylor's house, still strewn with books about Oracles and magic and history, all these weird, incongruous things tucked alongside the china figurines and ugly paintings.

"Can we do that?" she asked, and I made myself walk down the stairs, my eyes on the front door.

Have a good life, Pres.

"We're going to try."

Acknowledgments

WRITING A BOOK involves a fair amount of mayhem, and I'm lucky enough to have a bunch of fabulous mischief-makers on my side.

Thank you to my amazing editor, Ari Lewin, who gets me and my books so very well, has been such a champion for me and Harper, and never minds when I send her pictures of People I Find Attractive. You are a rock star, and I love making books with you!

Thanks, too, to the amazing Katherine Perkins, who is so smart I'm a little afraid of her, and whose notes on this book were insightful and encouraging and sharper than Harper's favorite high heel.

This is the sixth book that I've been lucky enough to thank Holly Root for, and I could fill up six more books just explaining why I feel so fortunate to have her as my agent. Everyone should have a Ninja-Angel like Holly on her side.

Massive thanks to the people at Penguin who have done so much for me and my books and who make me so grateful to shout "TEAM FLIGHTLESS BIRD!" on the regular. Special thanks to Anna Jarzab and Elyse Marshall for being both amazing at their jobs and just amazing humans in general.

Thank you so much to all of my readers, especially the Rebel Belles on Tumblr who have embraced Harper, Bee, David, and Ryan and made such lovely things to go along with the books. Best Readers Ever!

For me, these books are about the power of ladies and the special bond that is Lady Friendship, and I am, as the kids say, #blessed to have so many wonderful ladies in my life. I have to single out one of those ladies in particular, Julia Brown, for all her encouragement when I was working on *Miss Mayhem*, and for the ridiculous amounts of Happy she's brought into my life. Lady Bros 4-Ever.

As always, all the love to my family. Y'all are the reason I get to make up things for a living, but you've made the world I live in an even better place than all the worlds in my head. I love you.